"Tonight, I ask, on behalf of Her Royal Highness, the Princess of Wales: will you do what no other young women are called to do, and place your lives and honor at the feet of your country?"

E valine Stoker and Mina Holmes never meant to get into the family business. But when you're the sister of Bram and the niece of Sherlock, vampire hunting and mystery solving are in your blood, so to speak. And when two young society girls disappear—one dead, one missing—there's no one more qualified to investigate. Now fierce Evaline and logical Mina must resolve their rivalry, navigate the advances of not just one but *three* mysterious gentlemen, and solve a murder with only one clue: a strange Egyptian scarab. The pressure is on and the stakes are high—if Stoker and Holmes don't figure out why London's finest sixteen-year-old women are in danger, they'll become the next victims.

"The mishmash of popular tropes (steampunk! vampires! Sherlock Holmes!) will bring readers in, but it's the friendship between the two girls that will keep them."

—*Kirkus Reviews*

"The geek meets the goth. The fun comes from two main characters' quick-witted sparring, slowly developing friendship, and grudging admiration."

—*The Horn Book Magazine*

"The author's writing exudes energy, romance, and humor, and she gives her heroines strong, vibrant personalities as they puzzle out the expansive mystery unfolding before them."

—*Publishers Weekly*

"A captivating, amusing crossover tale."

—*Library Media Connection*

"Charming, addicting, and oh-so-much-fun! I absolutely couldn't put it down!"

—**KRISTI COOK,** author of *Haven*

"Victorian-inspired girl-power at its finest. Daring young ladies born of famed literary legacies are beautifully written and artfully woven into a historical past with fascinating futuristic elements."

—**LEANNA RENEE HIEBER,** author of the Magic Most Foul series

"Colleen Gleason manages to twine together steampunk, Holmesian mystery, Egyptian mythology, and even time travel into a seamless and fun read."

—**LEAH CYPESS,** author of *Nightspell*

The Clockwork Scarab

A STOKER & HOLMES NOVEL

*T*HE
*C*LOCKWORK
*S*CARAB

COLLEEN GLEASON

CHRONICLE BOOKS
SAN FRANCISCO

To Mary Kay Foley, Madelyn Gostomski, *and* Helen Collins . . .
Three women who have touched my life very deeply.

First paperback edition published in 2014 by Chronicle Books LLC.
Originally published in hardcover in 2013 by Chronicle Books LLC.

ISBN 978-1-4521-2873-3

The Library of Congress has cataloged the original edition as follows:
Gleason, Colleen.

The clockwork scarab / Colleen Gleason.

p. cm. – (Stoker & Holmes ; 1)

Summary: In 1889 London young women are turning up dead, and Evaline Stoker, relative of Bram, and Mina Holmes, niece of Sherlock, are summoned to investigate the clue of the not-so-ancient Egyptian scarabs–but where does a time traveler fit in?

ISBN 978-1-4521-1070-7 (alk. paper)

1. Scarabs–Juvenile fiction. 2. Time travel–Juvenile fiction. 3. Secret societies–Juvenile fiction. 4. Detective and mystery stories. 5. London (England)–History–19th century–Juvenile fiction. [1. Scarabs–Fiction. 2. Time travel–Fiction. 3. Secret societies–Fiction. 4. London (England)–History–19th century–Fiction. 5. Great Britain–History–1837-1901–Fiction. 6. Mystery and detective stories.] I. Title.

PZ7.G481449Clo 2013

813.6–dc23

2012036578

Manufactured in China.

Design by Jennifer Tolo Pierce.
Cover photograph by Alex Farnum.
Beetle sculpture on cover by Mike Libby/Insect Lab.
Typeset in John Baskerville.

10 9 8 7 6 5 4 3 2

Chronicle Books LLC
680 Second Street
San Francisco, CA 94107

Chronicle Books–we see things differently. Become part of our community
at www.chroniclebooks.com/teen.

LONDON, 1889

Miss Holmes

A Summons at Midnight

*T*here are a limited number of excuses for a young, intelligent woman of seventeen to be traversing the fog-shrouded streets of London at midnight. A matter of protecting one's life or preventing another's death are two obvious ones.

But as far as I knew, I was neither in danger for my life, nor was I about to forestall the death of another.

Being a Holmes, I had my theories and suspicions as to who had summoned me and why.

The handwritten message had told me that its author was not only female, but a person of high intellect, excellent taste, and measurable wealth. Its content had been straightforward:

Your assistance is requested in a most pressing matter. If you are willing to follow in the footsteps of your family, please present yourself at the British Museum tonight at midnight. Further direction will be provided at that time.

As I looked at the letter, I saw so much more than those simple yet mysterious words.

Lack of name and address, no seal or watermark—*the anonymous sender hand delivered the message.*

Heavy créme paper, neat feminine handwriting lacking embellishment and free of ink blots and errors—*an intelligent, pragmatic woman of considerable wealth.*

Faint perfume scent—*expensive but in excellent taste; from the incomparable Mrs. Sofrit's on Upper Bond.*

Traces of rice powder and a smudge of silver glitter—*sender is involved with the theater, likely* La Théâtre du Monde *in Paris.*

Big Ben tolled as I walked along the middle level of New Oxford-street, the soft yellow glow of the streetlamp cutting into the ever-present fog. I heard a soft scuttling sound followed by a low, dull clank and slowed to listen, my hand covering the weapon at my waist as I peered into the dim light.

I had borrowed from Uncle Sherlock the Steam-Stream gun that hung in my unfeminine belt over loose gabardine trousers. One pull of the trigger would release a puff of searing air, a concentration of burning steam. Enough to incapacitate a grown man or slice through his skin, my uncle had assured me. The beauty of this steam-powered gadget was that it never needed to be reloaded.

Not only was I armed, but I was suitably attired—for bustles, crinolines, and tight sleeves are cumbersome and impractical for a pedestrian on shadowy streetwalks. Between the weight of the layers of my normal ensemble and its incessant rustling (not to mention the length of the dratted skirts), I would have been a walking target for anyone, from whoremongers looking to find a new girl, to the footpads who lurked in the shadows—or to any threats that existed for a tall, gawky, yet intelligent young woman who'd been cursed with the beaklike Holmes nose.

I felt confident I was prepared for whatever dangers I might encounter.

One of the self-propelled Night-Illuminators trundled below on its four wheels. I looked down from the raised walkway on which I stood and watched its welcome glow putter through the shadowy night. The cool air stirred, bringing with it the familiar scents of dampness, dry ether, burning coal, and sewage. Below, at the ground level, I heard other common sounds of night: the clip-clop of hooves, the rattle of various wheeled conveyances, shouts and laughter and, threaded through it all, the constant hiss of steam.

Steam: the lifeblood of London.

I paid two pence to take a street-lift to the middle level of the block, where it was ostensibly safer to walk alone. But at midnight in London, I wasn't certain that any street level was safe.

The entire day had been rainy and dark clouded. Trapped inside, I read three books from cover to cover (including the amusing, fanciful, American novel *A Connecticut Yankee in King Arthur's Court*), worked on two different projects in the lab, and managed to annoy Mrs. Raskill enough that she refused to cook me dinner before she retired for the evening. I hadn't meant to knock over the flask of silver polish, but my elbows and arms always seem to get in the way.

I didn't clean it up well enough for her (I confess, I found conducting my lab work a better use of time than getting on my knees and scrubbing), so instead of cooking, she mopped, then emptied the bucket of dirty water from Tufference's Super-Strength-Mop-Wringer. All the while, she complained. Why couldn't Mr. Tufference invent a way to make the device empty the mop water afterward as well? To punctuate her foul mood, Mrs. Raskill turned off the mechanized levers on the stove and fairly slammed a plate of cold meat and cheese onto the counter for my dinner.

It was a shame, for what she lacked in competence in the way of chaperonage, Mrs. Raskill more than made up for in the kitchen. I counted both as benefits. Her skill with the culinary arts was the reason those layers of crinolines over the torture chamber of my corset had become a tad more difficult to fasten around my waist as of late. Before Mother left, our meals hadn't been quite as fancy and overloaded with gravies, sauces, and butter because she'd been the one planning the menus.

I thrust away the pang of grief and emptiness. Mother had been gone for more than a year, and other than a few brief letters from Paris, I'd heard nothing from her. I'd taken to wandering into her empty bedchamber just to remind myself that she had, indeed, existed.

The Night-Illuminator had rumbled off as I walked over an arching fly-bridge to cross the air-canal half a block from Russell-street. Just a few steps away were the hallowed halls of the British Museum, one of the few buildings left in London that had grounds. Real grass and even trees surrounded it.

Above me, the buildings rose so tall they seemed to meet, blocking the sky. Great dark sky-anchors soared above the cornices of the tallest structures. They floated like eerie gray clouds chained to the roofs, keeping the uppermost parts of the buildings stable.

To the south were the spires of Westminster, barely visible in the drassy moonlight. Or perhaps I just inherently knew their location, as I did the steeple of St. Paul's Cathedral, Big Ben's glowing face, and the more recent landmark of the turrets at Oligary's. Uncle Sherlock boasted he knew every level of every block of every street, alley, and mews in all of London—and so did I.

At last I approached the stately columns of the museum, and for the first time since leaving my house, I paused. My palms were damp beneath my lacy, fingerless gloves. Was I to boldly climb the steps to the front entrance and present myself? Would the doors be open? Or—

"Pssst."

I turned to see a cloaked figure, one of the female race, beckoning to me from a clump of bushes along the west wing of the museum. After a moment of hesitation, I edged toward her, fingers curling over the hilt of my Steam-Stream gun.

As I approached, I noticed a patch of yellow glowing from beneath the wall of the museum. A door.

"I expect you've been summoned just as I have," said the figure. She peered at me from beneath a heavy hood, holding what appeared to be a wooden dagger. A remarkably incompetent weapon in comparison to my own more lethal one.

"Perhaps you'd be so kind to show me proof of that summons," I said, retrieving the folded note from my coat pocket as she did the same. In the dim light, I saw her message was identical to mine, and with that, I deduced her identity.

"Follow in the footsteps of your family"—*infamous relatives.*

Wooden stake—*vampire hunter.*

I suspected I was one of a small number of people who were aware of the existence of the legendary family of vampire hunters. "It's a pleasure to meet you, Miss Stoker. It appears you have the same dearth of information about this meeting as I. Have you any idea how or where we should gain entrance or find our hostess?"

She gave a soft surprised laugh, obviously startled by my quick deduction. "You recognize me? You have the advantage, then, Miss . . . ?"

"Holmes."

"Miss *Holmes?*" Dawning comprehension was present in her voice. "Right, then. . . . It appears we're to go through here," she said, gesturing to an unobtrusive door. "I arrived only a few moments ago and was given this by a street urchin.

Before I could question him, he ran off." She showed me a second piece of the same creamy paper.

There will be two of you. When the other has arrived, enter together at the door with the diamond cross.

"Very well, then," I said.

Miss Stoker found and slid a hidden lever, and the door opened, accompanied by the soft hiss of escaping steam and the grind of well-oiled gears.

I was aware of the increase in my pulse as I followed my companion across the threshold. Illumination from small gaslit sconces spilled into a passage, bathing me and my companion in a soft yellow light. The door closed behind us.

A low rattle, a soft *thunk*. Then: *click*.

We were locked inside the museum. My breath became shallow and quick as the possibilities assaulted me. What if we were trapped? In danger? What if this was some sort of scheme to discredit the Holmes and Stoker families?

Or . . . what if my most private, desperate hopes were correct?

I held my steam gun at the ready and noted that Miss Stoker had replaced her wooden stake with some slender weapon that gleamed. I recognized it as a traditional firearm.

"Please"—came a feminine voice from a door that opened at the end of the brief corridor—"come in. I am delighted that you've accepted my invitation. And I see that you've come prepared." She gestured to our weapons.

I crushed a wave of disappointment and annoyance with myself as I made my way toward the door. I hadn't *truly* thought it was my mother who'd summoned me so secretively . . . but the absurd possibility had crossed my mind.

Miss Stoker followed me into the small cluttered office. I observed the room's furnishings and contents, noting heavy walnut chairs with brocade upholstery, books in French, Latin, Greek, and Syrian, and papers organized with curious metal clamps. There were museum cabinets, a jumble of gears, a frayed rug, and the outline of a secret door or chamber behind a painting of Sir Anthony Panizzi, the man considered to be the father of the British Museum. The chamber smelled like age, roses, and Darjeeling tea.

In the center of the room was a circular table around which four chairs had been arranged. Bookshelves lined the walls, and a Deluxe Tome-Selector with gloved metal fingers leaned against the corner, one finger holding a spot in an aged book.

Off to the side there was a desk covered with more books, ivory pens, a lamp, pencils, and a mechanized quill sharpener that seemed to be able to handle three pens at a time instead of only one. A trio of narrow, floor-to-ceiling windows were shuttered against the night though a faint limner of moonbeams shone from between two slats.

Turning from my review of the chamber, I bestowed my full attention on our hostess. She was no longer half concealed by dim light and a door, which allowed me to recognize her from the portrait Uncle Sherlock had on his mantel. Until now, I'd never met the individual whom he called *the* woman.

Irene Adler.

"Please, sit," she said, gesturing with an elegant hand and a warm smile. "Miss Stoker, Miss Holmes. It is a pleasure to meet you at last."

I wasn't clear on the details, but there had been some scandal involving *the* woman and the King of Bohemia, in which the king had required my uncle's assistance. The case was resolved, but only after Miss Adler had outsmarted Uncle Sherlock by being one step ahead of him during the entire affair. As he was often heard to say, the people who'd outsmarted him in his life numbered fewer than the fingers on one hand. Three of them were men, and here, now in front of me, stood the fourth. In reluctant honor and admiration for his feminine opponent, my uncle's only request for compensation from the King of Bohemia had been a picture of her.

Approximately the age of thirty, Miss Adler looked at me from the head of the table, her fingers curled around a pair of spectacles. An air of competence and intelligence emanated from her, and though her dark eyes sparkled with wit, I suspected they could sharpen with thought and determination.

"The pleasure is mine, Miss Adler," I said, trying not to appear in awe of the woman who had outwitted my famed uncle.

She was a tall woman, slender, dark of hair, pale of complexion. One couldn't precisely call her beautiful, but I considered her appearance striking and her presence mesmerizing. Tonight she wore a sateen bodice the color of chocolate, striped with bronze and decorated with jet buttons marching down the curve of her substantial bosom. A faint sparkle dusted her cheekbones, hardly detectable unless one was looking for it. And beneath the musty, damp smell of this antiquities-ridden chamber I scented a hint of the perfume that had clung to her message.

"Perhaps you're wondering why I did not contact you openly," Miss Adler said, looking from one to the other of us. The faint hint of her American heritage colored her voice.

"Indeed not," I replied as I selected the seat nearest her, for I had already deduced the reasons for her secrecy. "When one considers your previous encounter with my uncle, it would be out of the question that you would make an open attempt to contact me."

"But of course," Miss Adler said, a smile twitching the corners of her mouth.

"Apparently the two of you are acquainted," said Miss Stoker pointedly. She'd declined to take a seat, and now she pushed back the hood of her cloak.

Her hair was thick and ink-black. I knew that one branch of the Stokers was a family named Gardella from Italy, which explained the faint olive tone of her skin. Her eyes were dark, and her face very pretty in an arresting way. The sort of girl young men would find attractive. The sort of girl who danced at parties and shopped and laughed with her friends, and who knew just what to say when she met an interesting young man.

The sort of girl who *had* friends.

I pushed away the wistful thought and concentrated on examining my companion.

Miss Stoker was petite, while I was tall for a woman, and she boasted a much more feminine figure than my own gawky, angular one. Now that she had thrown back her dashing cloak, exposing a simple skirt and bodice without bustles or crinolines, I observed several accoutrements tucked into the waistband. Mostly wooden stakes, as well as a sheathed dagger and a slender wooden device I couldn't readily identify. Relatively primitive weapons.

"Please forgive me, Miss Stoker," said our hostess. "I hope you'll accept my apologies for the manner by which I contacted you and Miss Holmes. If you'll make yourselves comfortable and allow me to explain, your concerns will be allayed. If not, I assure you, you are free to go at any time."

She settled into the chair at the head of the table. "First, I'd like to introduce myself. I am Irene Adler." She pronounced her name the American way, as *eye-REEN*. "I'm here in London and in the employment of the British Museum at the direction of none other than Her Royal Highness."

Miss Adler withdrew a small metallic object from her voluminous skirts and offered it to Miss Stoker. Even from my position across the table, I recognized it as a Royal Medallion, a token that is bestowed upon someone who has found favor with a member of the royal family. My father was in the possession of several of the peach-pit-sized spheres, each engraved with the seal of the individual who'd given it. If one pushed on it a certain way and released its hidden lever, the contraption snapped open to display the name of the bearer and a full seal and signature of the royal.

In this case, it was clear who had given the token, for *Her Royal Highness* could only refer to the Princess of Wales, the wife of Prince Edward, Her Majesty the Queen's daughter-in-law. Princess Alexandra had requested Miss Adler's assistance.

Miss Adler looked at us with a sober expression. "Miss Holmes. Miss Stoker. There are many young men your age who are called into the service of their country. Who risk life and limb for their queen, their countrymen, and the Empire. Tonight, I ask, on behalf of Her Royal Highness, the Princess of Wales: will you do what no other young women are called to do, and place your lives and honor at the feet of your country?"

Miss Holmes

In Which Our Heroines Accept an Intriguing Invitation

"Yes." I should have thought about it more carefully—the risks, the dangers, the commitment. But I was feeling impetuous, spurred by my infatuation with Irene Adler and my desire to *do* something other than rattle about my empty house or sit in my mother's vacant chambers, and read book after book and study experiment after experiment in the laboratory. I wanted to put my knowledge and deductive abilities to the test in something *real*.

"Yes, I am willing," I said again.

Miss Adler was offering me a way to prove that, despite my gender, I was a Holmes in more than mere name and the size of my nose.

At the same moment as my response, Miss Stoker said, "Certainly I will. The Stokers have long been in service to the Crown."

A light of relief and determination came snapping into Miss Adler's dark eyes. "Thank you. Her Royal Highness shall be more than pleased. But I must warn you that your service to the princess—and by extension to His Royal Highness Prince Edward—must be a secret from the very start." Miss Adler looked at us both. "Are you willing to keep this arrangement a secret, even to your death?"

I nodded regally and peeked at my companion for her reaction. Miss Stoker nodded as well. I resisted the urge to roll my eyes. She didn't look like the sort of girl who could keep a secret.

"Very well. Perhaps you are wondering how I came to be employed by the British Museum as keeper of the antiquities." Miss Adler's eyes twinkled with humor as she met my gaze. "You may be aware of my reputation as a singer throughout Europe. But what you cannot know is that I used my travels as an entertainer to obscure my other work for both the American and British governments.

"After some recent events, including my brief marriage to Mr. Godfrey Norton, I've chosen to retire from the stage. Since then, I have been engaged by the director of this great institution"—here she indicated the walls around us—"to catalogue and study the large number of antiquities that were acquired from Egypt in the fifties and sixties. But in reality, I am here at the request of the princess and am serving her in a variety of ways. The two of you are well suited to one of the problems currently of concern to Her Royal Highness.

"But before I tell you any more, perhaps I should further acquaint you with one another, for you shall be working together very closely."

I detected a faint sniff from Miss Stoker, but resisted the urge to look over. Miss Adler nodded to my companion. "Miss Evaline Stoker, granddaughter of the famous Yancy Gardella Stoker, great-grandniece of Victoria Gardella—both vampire hunters of excellent repute."

I was familiar with Miss Stoker's family, whose legacy of vampire hunters from Italy had been written about in an old, rare book called *The Venators*. Mr. Starcasset's book detailed the story of her ancestors and how they were given the responsibility and skills to keep the world safe from the blood-feeding demons. Her elder brother, Bram, happened to be an acquaintance of my uncle's, and I understood Mr. Stoker was writing a novel about a vampire named Count Dracula.

"Vampires are nearly extinct," Miss Stoker noted. "My great-great-aunt Victoria and her husband killed off most of them more than sixty-five years ago, in the twenties. That has left me and other chosen members of my family with little to do in recent years."

"You will find plenty to do in service to the princess, even if it doesn't involve slaying vampires," said our hostess. "Now, you've already met Miss Alvermina Holmes. Niece of the famous Sherlock and daughter of the indispensable Sir Mycroft Holmes."

"I'm familiar with your uncle, of course," said Miss Stoker. "But I know nothing of your father."

"Uncle Sherlock claims Mycroft is even more brilliant than he and would be his greatest competitor should my father ever bestir himself to action. But he refuses to go out in public or to social events. He is never found anywhere but at his office or his club, even sometimes neglecting to come home to sleep."

That was in part the reason my mother had left us. The other reasons were best ignored, even by someone as practical as myself.

"Mina is just as brilliant at observation and deduction as her uncle and father," said Miss Adler. I was relieved she'd used the shorter version of my name, for, in the tradition of the Holmes family, my given one is ridiculous. Even Mother couldn't convince my father to give me an unassuming name like Jane or Charity, and instead I was encumbered with the hideous appellation Alvermina.

Miss Adler continued, "I am certain you understand why the princess and I chose the two of you for this . . . well, shall we call it a secret society? But let me be clear—your invitation is not only due to your families' loyalty and service to the Crown. It's also because of who you are, and the talents and skills you have."

"Of course," I said. "As young members of 'the weaker sex,' we would be dismissed as flighty and unintelligent. Never mind that males our age go to war and fight for our country.

Women haven't even the right to vote. Our brains are hardly acknowledged—let alone our brawn."

I glanced at Miss Stoker. According to *The Venators,* the vampire hunters of her family were endowed with superior physical strength and unnatural speed. I wondered if it was true. She certainly didn't appear dangerous. "Thus we two would be considered incapable of doing anything important, of being any sort of threat. In addition, I am an excellent candidate for secretive undertakings because I am fairly independent and"—I hesitated, then forged on—"somewhat reclusive."

I saw wariness in Miss Stoker's expression and a twinkle of humor in Miss Adler's, so I finished my thoughts. "In other words, we're both relatively solitary individuals who haven't many other obligations of family or friends who might ask questions or be potential recipients of our secrets. We're eccentric wallflowers."

"It might be true for you, Miss Holmes," Miss Stoker said, "that your social obligations are few and far between, but that's not the case for me. I have a stack of notecards and invitations overflowing the platter in the front hall of Grantworth House."

My chest felt tight, for I had just enumerated my shortcomings and pointed out my shameful lack of social invitations, and Miss Stoker had done just the opposite. It was difficult to make me feel inadequate, but her pointed comment bruised my feelings more than I cared to admit. Things might have been different if Mother were here to usher me through the intricacies of Society, but she was not.

Despite my discomfiture, I continued, "The number of invitations and obligations aside, Miss Stoker, I suspect you'd rather be doing something *other* than attending parties or dances. You might have obligations, but perhaps you would prefer not to have to accept them."

She closed her mouth rather sharply, and I recognized her tacit agreement. It was obvious through her demeanor and tones that she had an underlying need to prove herself worthy of her family legacy.

Perhaps we had more in common than I realized.

"You are quite correct, Mina," Miss Adler said. "Now, shall we move on? Are either of you acquainted with Miss Lilly Corteville?"

The name, though familiar, did not produce the image of a face or personality. In many ways, London Society was a foreign environment to me. The thought of dressing up and lining the walls at a party waiting to be asked to dance by some eligible young man terrified me. I knew I'd be standing against the wall alone all night, watching everyone else spin about the dance floor. And even if I was asked to dance, I'd either smash the poor man's foot or trip and fall on my face. Which was why I preferred not to waste my time with such nonsense as balls and the theater and shopping.

"I've met Miss Corteville," said my companion. "She's Viscount Fauntley's daughter, and she's engaged to Sir Rodney Greebles."

"Indeed," Miss Adler said. "She's gone missing since the twenty-fifth of April, three weeks ago."

"Could she have eloped? Run away? Been abducted?" Miss Stoker's eyes glinted with the same interest that bubbled inside me, although my fascination was tempered by concern. I wasn't convinced one could say the same for the other young woman. "We must conduct a search for her!"

"Of course the search has been ongoing." Miss Adler smiled, and Miss Stoker settled back into her chair looking disappointed. "The facts are Miss Corteville left no note or other message. It appears she absconded in the middle of the night, and there was no evidence of struggle."

"Perhaps she didn't wish to marry Sir Rodney and eloped with someone else. He's not at all attractive, and he's more than twice her age," suggested Miss Stoker.

"It's possible. Yet, according to her maid, Miss Corteville didn't appear to have packed any personal items to take with her as she'd do if she were going away permanently—eloping, for example."

"Unless she didn't plan to be gone for more than a brief time," I interjected.

"Indeed. However, there was one other thing. We found this slipped down behind her dressing table and the wall." Our hostess laid an object on the table for both of us to see.

"An Egyptian scarab," I said. There were countless examples of the beetle-shaped medallions here in the British Museum. Miss Adler handed the item to me for closer perusal.

"No . . . something modern that's made to *look* like one. This amulet isn't thousands of years old."

The object was made from soft metal, unlike an original Egyptian artifact (which would have been crafted of stone), and it was in the shape of a very large beetle that would fit comfortably in the center of my palm. Twice as large as a coin, and a bit heavier.

"Scarabs were like talismans," I mused, turning it over in my fingers, noting the coolness of the metal, its smooth edges, and the intricate embossing on it. "They were put in Egyptian tombs or used as jewelry or even a token of affection."

"They could also be employed as a sort of identification," Miss Adler said, "among a connected society."

The scarab's bottom was flat, and the top rounded like an insect with two wings folded tightly over its dome-like body. It was made of verdigris metal, and the ridged carvings were filled in with black and green paint. I pressed on the wings, the head, and even the edges to see if it might open like the Royal Medallions. When I squeezed the tiny pincers at the head, at last something clicked and whirred, bringing the scarab to mechanized life. I watched in fascination as the shiny wings opened to reveal clock-like inner workings of tiny cogs and gears.

I turned it over. On the reverse were carvings, and I identified the image of a half beast, half man. "A cartouche? Of a lion-headed pharaoh? No . . . it's not a pharaoh. It's a god." I frowned at Miss Adler. "A goddess. It's Sekhmet."

She nodded as Miss Stoker spoke up, her voice peremptory: "If you don't mind."

I handed her the object, seizing the opportunity to educate her as she examined it. "Sekhmet is the Egyptian goddess of war and destruction. She has the head of a lion because she's known as a great warrior and ferocious fighter. She's also been known as the Lady of Flame and the Lady of Slaughter."

"Legend has it that her breath was so hot and powerful it created the desert," Miss Adler said. "She is also the goddess of immortality and the underworld."

"You believe this has something to do with Miss Corteville's disappearance?" Miss Stoker smoothed her finger over the round top of the beetle.

"We wouldn't have thought so if there hadn't been another, similar object among the belongings of Miss Allison Martindale."

My new partner's face sobered. "Miss Martindale? Didn't she hang herself?"

"Yes. It was a most tragic and horrifying discovery. She was found dangling from a tree in Hyde Park. The family tried to hush it up, but news does travel."

"Do you mean to say Miss Martindale had a scarab as well?" I asked.

"It was found among her personal effects. It could be a coincidence, but I don't believe so. Two young women of the same age, within the same month. One took her own life, and the other disappeared."

"There must be a connection. Uncle Sherlock doesn't believe in coincidences."

"Why is Princess Alexandra taking such an interest in something like this?" asked Miss Stoker. A crease had appeared between her brows.

"Because—" Miss Adler hesitated and looked down at the scarab that had just been handed back to her. "Because she is very fond of Lady Fauntley, one of her ladies-in-waiting, and wishes to help find her daughter."

"Is there anything more?" I prompted.

"If these two events are connected, the only clues we have are the scarabs. The two girls were acquainted, but they weren't particular friends. Neither was known to have a deep interest in Egyptology, although they both visited the museum at least once."

Just then, I heard a sound in the distance beyond the door inside a vast museum that should have been empty. The rumbling of a heavy door closing.

Miss Adler stood abruptly as Miss Stoker bolted to her feet. I did likewise. "Hurry," our hostess said, moving toward a door through which we hadn't entered.

The soft hiss of steam and a quiet squeak heralded an opening into a small square alcove. Our hostess hurried us through a silent, shadowy corridor that smelled of lemon wood polish. Mahogany floors shone unevenly in the moonlight, filtering through glass cases and over the paneled walls and mechanized cabinets that rotated slowly, even here at night.

I strained, listening for sounds of an intruder as we rushed through a back room of shelves, tables, and crates of antiquities.

"This way," Miss Adler said.

We followed her through a little transept approaching the long, narrow Egyptian gallery where the famous Rosetta Stone was displayed. We all stopped beneath the ornate arch. I caught my breath at the sight before us.

A young man knelt in the center of the gallery, bathed in the moonlight. A large knife glinted in his hand, and he was looking down at a lump that even an untrained observer would recognize as the dead body of a woman.

MISS HOLMES

Of Mudless Shoes and Murder

"Don't move." Miss Adler was the first to speak, and she took charge instantly. I'm certain her bravery was helped in no small part by the gun that shone in her hand.

"Step away," she said. "Place the knife on the floor, then raise your hands." She stood so the man had no opportunity to slip behind a sarcophagus or the statue of Ramesses II that loomed to his left.

"I didn't—I was trying to help," said the man caught in shadow. "I think she's dead." I couldn't place his accent.

"Evaline," Miss Adler said without taking her eyes from him. "On the wall next to the fist of Ptah. Find the lever. We need light." As she spoke, she moved away from the body on the ground, all the while keeping the gun trained on the man, edging him away from the center of the chamber.

Moments later, a glow illuminated the space. The looming seven-ton statue of Ramesses II and massive pieces of frescoes and hieroglyphs were no longer casting long, dark shadows that hampered my observations. The gaslights now shone on the intruder. He was hardly any older than I and wore a style of clothing I'd never seen before.

"Is she dead?" asked Miss Adler, glancing at Miss Stoker, who had refrained from approaching the body. The question was clearly meant to spur my counterpart into action.

"Er . . ." Miss Stoker began. She moved forward with reluctant, robotic movements. She looked ill.

Impatient, I went to the unmoving figure and crouched next to the rumpled mass of skirts and limbs. I'd never come across a body, or a fresh crime scene like this before. I had certainly seen corpses, even studied them under my uncle's tutelage. But not like this. Not so . . . *raw*.

I forced myself to actually look at her, then to touch the pulse point on the girl's throat. Even before I did that, I knew she was dead. But her chill skin and lack of pulse confirmed it. "There's no hope for her."

"I'll ring for the authorities. They must be notified. Evaline, if you please." Miss Adler gestured for my companion to take her place with the pistol.

I returned my attention to the victim. The poor thing could have been no older than seventeen or eighteen, a peer of my very own age. The fact that a short time earlier we had been talking about the disappearances and death of other young women was not lost on me. Could Miss Adler have anticipated such an event might happen here, tonight? Had she meant for us to prevent it?

I drew in a deep breath, smelled the sharp iron of blood and other bodily excretions, and pushed away my uncertainties. Only minutes ago, I had pledged my loyalty and self to the Crown. The moment of truth had come sooner than we could have realized.

Who was she? How had she come here? Why would someone do this to her and how? I forced myself to observe. Coldly. Objectively.

She lay on her side, curled up, eyes open—*fallen or dumped here.*

Her hair still pinned in place—*she hadn't struggled.*

Not enough blood on the floor—*she hadn't been killed here.*

Which meant . . . I looked at the intruder, who, still under the control of Miss Stoker, had nevertheless edged closer to the sarcophagus at the side of the gallery.

No bloodstains on his odd clothing—*he had not moved the body. He wasn't the murderer.*

Grateful for an excuse to edge away from the girl, I approached the young man. "Did you touch her or change her position?"

"No, I didn't move her." His accent sounded American, but not like any other American accent I'd ever heard. "I was checking to see if she was alive when you showed up. I just touched her . . . for a pulse." His voice was tense, and his eyes darted from me to Miss Stoker and back again.

I believe even the most objective of persons would agree he was a handsome man, with his golden-tan complexion and startling blue eyes. His jaw was square, and his chin firm. He looked as if he were not even twenty, and as he stood there, his hands raised in surrender, I admired his mussed, too-long dark blond hair plastered around the ears and neck.

He wore a red shirt with no opening down the front. Its material made it cling to his chest as if it were wet, even though it wasn't. Strangely, there were large letters painted or sewn on the front of it. I could see enough to make out AEROPOSTA—a French word, which added to my suspicions that he was a foreigner. If there were more letters, they were hidden by an unbuttoned plaid shirt. I'd never seen a man wear a shirt like that, open and unbuttoned. I found it scandalous.

Over the unbuttoned shirt, the intruder wore a jacket of black leather that was much shorter than any other coat I'd seen, ending just at his waist instead of halfway to the knees. The hem of the plaid shirt hung below it. His trousers were just as unfamiliar—made of dark blue denim, like the Levi Strauss pants worn by American laborers. They were frayed a little at the hems and worn in the knees.

And his shoes! I wanted to crouch and examine them, for I couldn't identify the material from which they were made. They laced up the front like a woman's shoe, but without the tiny little buttons that took forever to hook. (My mechanized Shoe-Fastener had broken three weeks ago.) Gray with age, yet decorated with an odd swoop-like design on the sides, they looked as if they were made of *rubber*.

Despite being worn, his footwear was not blood- or mud-splattered, which was curious because it had been raining today—as was usual for London. It would have been impossible to avoid the muck outside, even on the upper streetwalk levels.

He'd not been outside today.

Curious.

Had he been hiding in the museum since before it had begun to rain at dawn? My eyes narrowed in thought and I exchanged glances with Miss Stoker. I didn't expect her to have followed my train of thought—after all, one must be a trained observer, my uncle always said—but nevertheless, I saw intelligent question in her gaze.

"You claim you didn't move her, that you were trying to help her. But what are you doing here in the museum, in the middle of the night?" I asked.

"I'm—uh—I'm part of the custodial staff," he said. "We were going to wax the floors." His smile was forced, yet I couldn't help but appreciate the attempt at an explanation, regardless of how implausible it was.

"That's absurd," said Miss Stoker. The gun wavered in her hand.

"What? The waxing? Hey, it needs to be done—" He must have noticed my severe expression, for he changed his tack. "Look, I swear I didn't touch her. I just found her lying here. I know I shouldn't be here at night, but it wasn't exactly my fault. Circumstances beyond my control. Really freaking *odd* circumstances."

"You can explain all of these—erm—odd circumstances to the authorities when they arrive," I said. "But you needn't worry about being arrested for murder. I can attest to the fact that you're innocent of that, at least."

"Well, thank goodness you figured that out," he said, his voice dripping with insincerity.

With a little sniff, I returned to the victim, leaving Miss Stoker to deal with the intruder. It was imperative that I finish my examination before the authorities arrived and disturbed everything.

Face, jaw, and fingers beginning to stiffen—*rigor mortis in early stages; dead at least three hours, possibly four or five.*

Steeling myself for my first good look at her, I turned the girl onto her back. I couldn't hold back a little shudder. Her sightless eyes stared up into the high ceiling of the gallery. With a catch of breath, I closed them with two fingers, hoping she'd found peace without too much pain first.

Blood stained the front of her shirtwaist and her left sleeve, but only a bit on her right. Slender burn-like marks around her arms, as if a thin cord or wire had been wrapped around them. And a terrible slash along her left wrist. I sniffed her hair. *Opium.* Faint but unmistakable.

Too little blood on the left sleeve—*no splashes of blood on the arm that made the cut? Impossible to be self-inflicted.*

"Miss Stoker. Do you recognize this young woman?"

Before she could respond, I heard the sound of approaching footsteps. More than one pair, so it would seem Miss Adler had not only rung for the authorities, but fetched them as well. "Hurry," I said as Miss Stoker moved toward me, still holding the gun pointed at our intruder.

She swallowed audibly. "Yes, I believe that's one of the Ho—"

Whatever she was about to say was cut off by a loud, strange sound. It was perhaps a sort of music, but it was like nothing I'd ever heard before. I spun on my haunches and saw a small silver object sliding across the floor. A colorful light shone from its flat top and the sound—loud, screeching, vibrating—seemed to be coming from it. Miss Stoker jumped out of the way just as one of the large stone statues at the edge of the gallery teetered and began to fall.

"Look out!" I shouted as the bristly-haired stone satyr crashed to the floor.

"Stop there!" ordered a commanding voice as two men and Miss Adler came rushing around the corner from the Roman Gallery.

"He's gone!" hissed Miss Stoker, who still held Miss Adler's gun and was now next to me. She was pointing to where the young man had been moments ago.

Ignoring the shouts from the new arrivals, we dashed over to where the intruder had been standing. Having either taken advantage of or manufactured the distraction, he had slipped into the dark shadows.

"I'll go after him," said Miss Stoker, starting off, but a voice ordered, "You! Miss! Stop there!"

"Drat," I muttered, snatching up the silver object that had presumably belonged to the intruder. Clever to use it as a distraction for us, and convenient that he'd left it behind.

The smooth, flat device had gone silent and dark by now. I shoved it in my trouser pocket to examine later, hoping it wouldn't start screeching again. I turned at last to greet Miss Adler and the two gentlemen: Scotland Yard inspectors. They were out of breath from running along the gallery.

"Ladies, this is Inspector Luckworth." Miss Adler gestured to the older of the two men.

About forty, Luckworth was a man of average height and a spare amount of hair, except for the neat beard and mustache that hid his lips. I gave him a brief examination.

Misbuttoned jacket, shirt half untucked, mismatched boots—*dressed hurriedly in dark, likely to keep from waking wife.*

Tarnished wedding ring, tight but removable—*married at least three years; enjoying wife's home cooking.*

Small fingerprints just above the knee and a swipe of dried milk on the front of his trousers—*toddler in the household.*

The faint shift of gears and quiet rumble—*mechanized left leg, overdue for oiling.*

"Miss Adler." Luckworth's voice was less friendly than hers had been. "Who are these girls? And what are they doing here at this time of night? What are *you* doing here at this hour? And how did *that* happen?" He gestured to the rubble that had once been the stone satyr.

Miss Stoker and I exchanged glances at his remark, which made it sound as if we were schoolchildren.

"I've been engaged by the museum to catalog its unorganized antiquities acquired over the last three decades, Inspector," Miss Adler replied. "I'm certain you are aware of that."

"Yes, and I still find it inconceivable that the director selected you to do so."

"Unfortunately, that opinion is not relevant to our current tragedy," Miss Adler pointed out with a cool smile.

The younger inspector, who couldn't have been more than a few years older than I, rose from his examination of the girl's body. "Right. Regardless, madam, that doesn't explain your presence here at"—he paused to flip open an elaborate pocket watch that had four small folding doors and, once open, rose into a complicated three-dimensional timepiece arrayed with buttons—"twelve forty-three in the morning." He pushed a button and the clock folded back into place with soft, pleasant clicks.

Miss Adler's smile turned gentle. "But of course it does. There is no limitation on my work schedule. Sir Franks has given me access to the museum at any and all hours of the day. You of all people, Inspector . . . ?"

"Grayling," the young man replied. "Ambrose Grayling."

"Inspector Grayling, you and your colleague should well understand that there are certain occupations which are not regimented. One works whenever one must. Even in the dead of night." She made a smooth gesture with her hand. "Perhaps we could quibble about my employment restrictions later. I rang Scotland Yard because we have a crime to investigate, and I'm certain the two of you would like to get to work before more time has passed."

"*We* have a crime to investigate?" said Luckworth. He laughed. "Miss Adler, there is no 'we' about it. You and your companions will give your statements and leave the investigation to us."

"But I beg to differ, Inspector—with all due respect," Miss Adler added in a sugar-coated voice, "we have already begun the investigation."

I took this as my cue to step forward. "I have already begun a preliminary examination of the body. If you wish, I shall enlighten you with my conclusion—"

"Pardon me," said Inspector Grayling in a flat voice that carried a bit of the Scottish. It was no surprise, for it matched the dark copper color of his thick, curling hair.

I turned my full attention on him, aware that he was a rather attractive young man. He had a freckled complexion over tanned skin; however, the freckles did nothing to make him look boyish or innocent. Instead they gave a pleasantly ruddy cast to his square jaw and prominent nose.

Unevenly stubbled chin and tiny cut near left ear—*needs to sharpen his razor and is impatient in character.*

Cuts and scrapes as well as a large blister adorned his left, pencil-holding digit—*doesn't wear gloves, works hard but not without haste and clumsiness.*

No wedding ring and one button dangling from jacket cuff—*unmarried and lives in a household without females.*

Jacket cuffs frayed, short for his elegant wrists, two years out of style—*handed down clothing, not of upper class.*

Ornate, complicated pocket watch but wears used clothing—*an utter cognoggin; more concerned with his gadgets and devices than personal appearance.*

Grayling was saying, "This is no concern for a civilian. Now, if you—"

"Inspector Luckworth and Inspector Grayling," interrupted Miss Adler, "may I introduce Miss Mina Holmes?"

Both of the gentlemen turned to me, and if I weren't so shocked at being back in the spotlight, I might have found their expressions comical. Luckworth looked as if he'd swallowed a biscuit whole, and Grayling lifted his Scottish nose as if he smelled haggis gone bad. (Incidentally, I am of the opinion that haggis is always bad.)

"I daresay—" Luckworth began, but his younger colleague interrupted, "*Holmes?* You don't expect us to believe—"

"I am the niece of Sherlock and the daughter of Sir Mycroft. Ponderous appellations and high powers of deductive reasoning run as rampant in my family as the pox does in Haymarket." I wasn't certain from where I dredged up such confidence, but the words tripped from my tongue.

"I can't imagine how a young lady such as yourself would be familiar with the curse of Haymarket." Grayling cast me a cool gray-green look that threatened to bring a warm flush to my cheeks. "But regardless of your *name*, Miss Holmes, which I will accept as proof of your relation to the esteemed Misters Holmes, your assistance is unnecessary. Inspector Luckworth and I are well trained and able to do our jobs without interference by a fe—civilian."

"Very well," I said, lifting my nose. "Carry on." At that moment, I wished I had a skirt hem to snatch up for a bit of feminine emphasis in my vexation. His expression made me prickle: supercilious yet polite.

But my new mentor wasn't about to be cowed. "We won't be leaving until we've completed our own investigation." Miss Adler gave me an affirming nod that meant I should continue with my work. I sidled away from the cluster of people.

"Your investigation?" Luckworth choked as I knelt next to the dead girl. "This is not tea time, Miss Adler. Nor is it a woman's salon nor even a ruddy—'scuse me—suffragette meeting. This is the scene of a crime, and only the investigators will remain."

Swallowing hard, I searched through the pockets in the victim's voluminous skirts as Miss Adler responded to the inspector in her low, even tones. It wasn't that I expected to find something as obvious as a Sekhmet scarab, but anything could be a clue. She wore no jewelry except for a comb of topazes in her dark hair, and her gloves were missing.

"Her Royal Highness has authorized *you* to—" Luckworth bit off his own words as if to keep from saying something regretful.

As the discussion (I use that term loosely) raged between the inspector and Miss Adler, I used my hand-cranked Flip-Illuminator to examine the wound on the girl's arm. When he noticed, Grayling made a sharp sound and stalked over to me. This placed his shoes in my field of vision—right next to my legs, where I crouched in voluminous trousers, and I noticed that his footwear gleamed in the mellow light except near the soles where they were speckled with mud. That reminded me of the foreigner and his mud-free shoes. Was he still in the museum?

"Miss Holmes, this is the scene of a crime," Grayling said in a tone that indicated clear displeasure.

"I'm aware of that. I'm making my observations and deductions. Shall we compare notes?"

He looked down at me, and the light from my small illuminator shone in his eyes. They were still spots of exasperation, spoiling an otherwise pleasing countenance. "If you feel it necessary to share your information with us, I cannot stop you, Miss Holmes. But my partner and I are able to draw our own conclusions." He crouched next to me.

I could smell the clean, lemony scent of his skin and see the freckles on his large, square, capable hands. All at once I felt uncomfortable in my dusty men's trousers and ill-fitting coat, and wished that I wasn't dressed like a street urchin. Perhaps if I wasn't, he would take me seriously.

Inspector Luckworth and Miss Adler approached. "Well, whatta you found, Brose?" asked Luckworth. He sounded disgruntled but resigned.

"A variety of things," Grayling replied. "Death occurred four hours ago—"

"Closer to three," I interjected, "based on the morbidity of the fingers."

He turned those grayish eyes on me. They were close enough that I could see amber flecks in them. "A temperature reading I took from this device," he said, producing a slender silver implement from some pocket of his vest, "indicates that the body began to lose heat at least four hours ago."

Drat. I closed my mouth and nodded in agreement, trying not to look at the instrument with too much fascination. I'd never seen one so sleek and efficient. And even though mine was more primitive, I would never leave my thermometer home again. It was a much better measure of time of death than estimating rigor mortis.

"As I was saying," Grayling continued in a smooth voice touched with Scottish brogue, "death occurred at approximately nine o'clock this evening from an apparent self-inflicted wound on the left wrist."

"Suicide?" Luckworth said, his face going sharp and serious.

"It wasn't suicide," I said, just as Grayling interjected, "I said *apparent*."

We looked at each other. His lips tightened, and he said, "Pray go on, Miss Holmes."

My heart was pounding as I lifted the woman's right arm, the unwounded limb. "It would be impossible not to get blood on this sleeve if she used this hand to cut her wrist," I said. "It's much too clean; only a few tiny drops. And—"

"Aside from that," Grayling interrupted, "she wouldn't have cut herself on that hand because—"

"She was left-handed," we both said in unison.

"Indeed," said Miss Adler, her eyes going back and forth between us.

"We'll need to identify her," said Luckworth, speaking to his partner.

"That won't be difficult," I said.

"No, it won't," Grayling said. "Based on her clothing, which is well-made of good fabric and from a seamstress, she comes from a well-to-do family. We can observe her shoes—"

"Or Miss Stoker can tell us her name," I said, perhaps a trifle too loudly. I looked at the young woman in question, who'd been peering into the shadows as if looking for something. Or someone.

Grayling shot me a disgruntled look as Luckworth turned to my companion. "Well?" he said grumpily.

"I believe this is one of the Hodgeworth sisters. Lecia or Mayellen. Of St. James Park."

Luckworth grumbled under his breath and wrote down the name as I took the opportunity to move toward the knife, which had heretofore been left unexamined. It still lay on the floor where the young man had dropped it at Miss Adler's command. The blood had long dried on the blade and handle. I resisted the urge to pick it up to examine it.

"Look at this," I said, forgetting Grayling and I were at odds. "Do you see this?" I crouched once again and lifted Miss Hodgeworth's wounded arm to show him the incision. "Now look at the blade."

Grayling knelt to get a closer look. The museum's light glinted over his hair, highlighting occasional strands of copper and blond in the midst of dark mahogany waves. "That blade couldn't have made this incision. The cut is too smooth, and—"

"The blade is dull and too thick," I interrupted. "It would have made the skin jagged."

"Precisely," he murmured, still looking down at the wound. Grayling fished in another vest pocket and withdrew a gear-riddled metal object hardly larger than a pince-nez. It clinked as he settled it over one eye, fitting an ocular lens into place. Leather straps held the device over his temples and around the crown of his head; it looked like the inner workings of a clock with a pale blue glass piece through which one eye could see.

I'd never seen an Ocular-Magnifyer of that type before; this particular device seemed not only to magnify the objects, but to measure them as well. Grayling lifted his large, elegant fingers to his temple and turned a small wheel attached to the gears. I heard soft clicking sounds as it measured the wound on Miss Hodgeworth's wrist.

Uncle Sherlock often complained about the lack of care taken at crime scenes by the authorities. They trampled over grounds and moved objects and, in his words, "wouldn't notice a weapon unless it was pointed straight at them." But even he would have found little to fault in Grayling's handling of this crime scene, except, perhaps, for the use of such fancy gadgetry. My uncle was a medievalist when it came to such devices.

"What's that there?" said Luckworth as he approached, noticing his partner's task for the first time. "Wastin' yer time with the numbers again, Brose? Why aren't you questioning the witnesses here? They found the girl. Witnesses and people, not mathematics, is going to solve this case—and all of the others on your desk. I'm tired, and I want to get back to m'bed."

Grayling stood, and his face appeared ruddier than usual. He didn't look at me, but spoke to his partner in a stiff voice, one greenish-gray eye still magnified behind its lens. "Bertillon's process has already proven useful in three cases—"

"In *Paris*," Luckworth said. "Not here in London. Waste of blooming time—pardon me, Miss Holmes," he added. "Hasn't helped us to find Jack the Ripper, now, has it? Or the bloke who done away with the Martindale girl."

"I thought the Martindale girl hanged herself." I stood abruptly. "Are you saying she was murdered too?"

Grayling's teeth ground together, and he shot Luckworth a glare as he yanked the magnifyer off. Then he looked at me for a moment. "There was no step," he growled at last, as if in challenge. His Scottish burr had gone thick.

"Do you mean to say, there was nothing that she'd stood on to—ah—affix the rope to the tree branch, then knocked away?" I swallowed hard.

Grayling didn't reply; therefore, I took that as an affirmative response.

If there was no step for her to stand on, Miss Martindale *couldn't have hanged herself*. Someone else had to be involved.

We had two cases of young women dying in apparent suicide, that were not really suicides. And a third young woman who'd disappeared. Two of the women were connected by the Sekhmet scarab.

Would Miss Hodgeworth be as well?

Like my uncle, I didn't believe in coincidences.

Miss Stoker

In Which Miss Stoker Is Fanned by a Glocky Sprite

I watched Mina Holmes climb into the horseless cab that had stopped in front of the building. The marble of the museum's front colonnade entrance was cool to the touch as I slipped away. A wide stripe of moonlight filtered over the top of the vehicle and illuminated the glistening road. The gas lamps that normally lit the grounds were dark. Someone had been busy, making certain to keep the area in shadows.

Another carriage trundled by, this one pulled by a clip-clopping horse, but otherwise, the lowest street level was deserted. The only movement was a slinking cat and the something small and dark that was its prey.

I still couldn't dismiss the rumble of shame at the way my insides had earlier pitched and churned at the scene of the dead girl. All that *blood* . . .

But the sight of poor Miss Hodgeworth had been nothing compared to my memory of Mr. O'Gallegh, his neck and torso torn open, his innards spilling out . . . and the red-eyed vampire that looked up at me, its fangs dripping with blood.

It had smiled at me.

I closed my eyes even now, curling my fingers tight. I fought away the horrific images, the memory of fear and terror that rushed over me as I stumbled toward the vampire, stake in hand. I'd never forget the smell. Blood.

Death.

Evil.

I remembered washing my hands over and over, trying to scrub the blood away even as I tried to recall exactly how it got there. I had no clear memory of what had happened: whether I'd killed the vampire as I'd meant to do . . . or remained paralyzed by the sight of Mr. O'Gallegh's blood spilling everywhere.

Had my mentor, Siri, intervened? Or had the vampire escaped?

That uncertainty and the knowledge of my failure haunted me.

Now, a year after my only encounter with a vampire, I still shuddered over the memory of that night . . . and from the horror I'd witnessed in the museum.

Mina Holmes had approached that awful scene so readily. She'd seemed so fascinated with it, I half expected her to crouch and sniff at the blood with that long, slender nose of hers.

Shame rushed through me, landing like a stone in the pit of my belly. I was the Chosen One of my family, *born* to hunt vampires, endowed with superhuman strength and speed. And yet at the sight of blood and carnage, my insides curdled, my stomach heaved . . . and I became paralyzed.

I often wondered why Bram hadn't been the one called. He had a morbid interest in all things UnDead and considered himself an expert. And yet he had no comprehension of what it was like learning how to fight them. How to wield a stake and where to slam it into the vampire's chest for the fatal blow. Preparing to take the life of a creature, damned or not.

But I was the one who'd been chosen, the one who'd been called to this life. And I was determined to follow in the footsteps of my ancestor Victoria, the most famous female vampire hunter to ever have lived.

Naturally, Mina Holmes and her steel-cased stomach lacked the physical attributes that enabled me to protect myself from dangers on the dark streets. Miss Holmes might have a brilliant mind, but I was faster, stronger, and possessed the ability to sense the presence of a vampire by the unpleasant chill over the back of my neck. That, at least, was small consolation.

As Miss Holmes's cab trundled off on damp cobblestones, leaving me alone with the night, I closed my eyes and listened to the familiar sounds of sleeping London. There was the faint *shhhhhh* and the accompanying rumble of a Night-Illuminator meandering its way down the street. On the next block, one of the heavy gates to a street-lift clanged. The air smelled of damp grass and coal smoke, along with the ever-present twinge of sewage—stale, putrid, dank.

"Waitin' for something?" said a male voice. Very close behind me.

My eyes popped open, and I barely managed to swallow a gasp of surprise. "I was simply waiting for you to show yourself," I replied without turning around. Though my heart was ramming in my chest, my voice came out smooth and steady. I eased a hand toward the pistol weighing down my skirt pocket.

His low, rumbling laugh sent a prickle of awareness over the back of my neck. It was almost . . . pleasant. Not like the eerie warning that an UnDead was near.

"Cop to it, luv," he said, a heavy dose of Cockney in his tone. "Ye didn't granny me till I spoke."

I turned, searching the shadows. I spied him in a dark nook of the wall, tucked behind a slender bush. I could just make out his form next to the sharp line of the bricks, but no details other than the angle of his hat.

"Right," I replied. "Neither your presence nor your absence matters to me." My pulse had spiked, and anticipation barreled through my veins. At last, something interesting was happening.

Something dangerous.

He chuckled again and shifted a little. A splinter of moonlight slashed down from the hat brim to his face, jolting over a shoulder covered in a long, flowing coat. I had the fleeting impression of a dark brow and the quirk of a smile.

The man eased out of the shadows. He was taller than me and had broad shoulders. I caught the glimpse of a square, clean-shaven chin. Although I hadn't seen more than an impression of his countenance, from his voice and demeanor, I guessed he wasn't much older than I. "Pr'aps you were waiting for someone else to appear? Some 'andsome gent t'woo ye in the moonligh'?"

The cool metal of the firearm felt comforting in my pocket, but I saw no need to pull it free. I was more curious than anything. And even with my unfinished training, I could easily defend myself against a mortal man.

"I was merely taking in the night air," I replied. Why was I still standing there talking to him? Unless . . . "What are you doing, lurking about at this time of night? You must be up to no good."

Again he smiled. This time, I caught a glimpse of white teeth and a dimple in his right cheek. "I'm allus up to no good, Miss Stoker," he said in a voice that dipped low and dark and velvety.

A little surprised flutter went through my belly—*only* because he knew my name. Not at all because of the way his voice seemed to wrap around me and tug, deep inside. "You seem to have the advantage of me, boy."

But my juvenile insult didn't have any effect on the young man, who was years past being a boy.

He gave another of those low, rumbling laughs. "'Aving the advantage o'er a vampire rozzer is quite the accomplishment, then, aye?"

This time, the prickle that squirreled up my spine wasn't as pleasant. Not only did he know my name, but he knew my secret identity as well? My fingers tightened around the cool butt of the pistol.

"What do you want?" I asked again. I'd definitely lost my advantage, if I'd ever even had one.

He seemed to sense the change in my demeanor, for his own easy personality became more intense. "I don't know all that 'appened inside there tonight, but when the Jacks get called in, even a glocky like me knows 'tain't for the good. Someone buy it? The Ripper at it again?"

I raised my eyebrows, even though I'm sure he couldn't see them in the dim light. "A glocky like you?" I understood his Cockney slang and the false modesty he was attributing to himself. Even from the few moments in his presence, I knew this man was not the least bit half-witted or, in his term, "glocky."

"Nothin' wrong with a bit o' modesty, luv, now, is there?"

Just then I caught the faintest shadow of movement from above. He noticed it too, for we both looked up at the same moment. It was an odd airship, cruising much lower to the ground than usual.

My companion muttered something, and the next thing I knew, I was propelled back into the deepest niche of the building's exterior. The force of his body, strong and quick, shoved me into the dark V of two brick walls as if he intended for us to melt into them.

Surrounded by the damp, tobacco-scented wool of his coat, I found my chin pressed into his shoulder as a strong arm curved around my waist. Nevertheless, I kept looking up and watched as the strange airship slid past us. Low enough to enter an air-canal, it slid between the buildings. It was so close, a person could step from the upper streetwalks onto the vessel.

This was unlike any airship I'd ever seen. It was a slender, elliptical shape, smaller and more elegant than the ones I was familiar with, and it boasted wicked-looking fan-like wings and a swallowtail.

This one . . . it moved like a dark cloud. Eerie and forbidding. Breathless. Ghost-like.

"Bloody hell," my companion murmured.

I realized with a shock that I was still plastered up between his formidable chest and the damp brick wall. And that his Cockney accent was all but gone. "What was that?"

"'Tis jus' as well ye don't know. 'S a battle ye'd be best out of." He looked down. His face was close, his eyes focused steadily on me. The bridge of his nose was a slightly lighter shade than the shadows around him. I realized my breathing had gone shallow.

"I'm certain they didn't see us." I had to say something. Then I started to push him away, but he didn't move. And although I could have shoved him to the ground with ease, I held back. I didn't want to expose the full extent of my strength . . . even though he knew my identity.

It was only then that I remembered to uncurl my fingers from the lapel of his coat.

"What's the 'urry, luv?" he asked in a low, rumbling voice. "Ye' afraid I'm gonna fan ye 'ere?"

The accent was back, thicker than ever. He was definitely faking it. "You won't find anything of value in my skirts," I replied, and tried not to think about where his hands had been . . . or could go . . . if indeed he tried to feel around my clothing in search of valuables. My cheeks heated there in the dark.

"Not even this?" he asked, and suddenly there was my dratted pistol, right there between us, in his hand. The moon glinted off the engraved barrel as if magneted to it, being the only light in a dark corner. "A nice piece o' iron, luv. Though I would've expected somethin' a bit more fancy from the likes of a fang rozzer."

Blast! I hadn't even felt his hand moving about. "Who are you?" I needed to at least know the name of this man, who smelled like wood smoke and something else that was fresh and spicy.

Our pivot into the corner had resulted in his soft cap being jolted to the back of his head, and I caught a full look at his face. I saw sharp eyes and a few waves of hair curling about his temples, but couldn't tell its color. He had a slender, elegant nose and dark slashing brows, and looked about twenty years old.

He turned away, as if realizing I could see him clearly. "I'm called Pix," he replied, adjusting his cap low. To my surprise, he handed back my pistol.

"Picks?" I repeated, slipping the pistol back into my pocket. There was no sense in letting him think I felt threatened and in need of a weapon. "As in . . . what you do to pockets? How appropriate."

"Nay, luv. Just Pix. Like the dangerous little sprites of legend that canna be caught." His grin came again, but a bit lopsided this time.

I smothered a snort. He was about as far from being like a little pixie fairy as I was from being a properly demure lady-in-waiting to Princess Alexandra. Although . . . I might have agreed with him on the dangerous part.

"If ye ever get into trouble in the stews, ye just say you know Pix." His voice had dropped to that low rumble again, and he captured my hand in his. Before I could pull it away, he lifted it between us, watching me . . . and then as my breath caught and my insides fluttered, he pressed his lips to the back of my hand.

They were warm and soft, and left just the faintest bit of damp when he lifted his face.

I couldn't believe his boldness, and I yanked my hand away, giving him a good, solid shove in the process. The back of my hand felt as if it were alive, burning from some searing mark, and my pulse pounded as if horses galloped through my veins. "Why would I need to invoke anyone's name for help?" I told him haughtily, resisting the urge to rub the imprint of his lips from my skin. "I am a Stoker, after all."

"Aye, ye are . . . every bit o' you," Pix replied, his voice low and smooth. He began to ease back, into the shadows cast by a row of hedge. "Which is why I'll leave ye to your own devices wit' nary a twinge o' my conscience."

"Wait," I said, remembering what he'd said earlier about seeing someone near the musuem. I stepped toward him, but he slid into darkness. The moon had gone behind a heavy cloud, and the lights that should have dotted the perimeter of the museum were dark. The bushes shifted.

He didn't stop, but his voice floated in the night air, "If you need me, Miss Stoker, ye can find me through Old Cap Mago."

"Why would I need you?"

"To tell ye what I saw tonight." Now his voice was even farther away. "Before the razzers arrived. Big crate, bein' moved out. Guilty-lookin' flimpers, four o' 'em."

"A crate? How big?"

He'd stopped, and although I had only an impression of where he was, I stared into the darkness. Why couldn't I see him? I had excellent night vision.

"Bigger'n me. 'Eavy, from the looks o' it," Pix called from the shadows. "Put it in th'back o' a wagon. One of 'em 'ad another thin' too—long and slender. Like a cane. Went off southwise."

"When? When did you see this? And what were you doing here?"

Silence. Drat. "Pix?"

There was no response from the darkness but a faint chuckle and the rustle of leaves.

In the distance, St. Paul's tolled four, and I gave in to the urge to rub his kiss from my skin.

I hoped he was watching from the bushes.

ℳiss Holmes

Miss Holmes Has an Unexpected Visitor

I was exhausted when I climbed into the horseless cab outside the museum. Miss Stoker had somehow excused herself from being escorted home and disappeared on foot into the shadow of the colonnaded building. I had given my official statement to Luckworth, leaving out the minor detail of the museum intruder. I felt certain I'd see the foreigner again soon.

The cab had traveled a mere block from the museum when my suspicions were proved right.

A black shape across from me in the vehicle shifted and became a face, followed by two hands shining pale in the gray light of near dawn.

I froze, realizing that what I'd assumed was a pile of cushions and blankets—granted, not the usual accoutrements of a hackney cab in London—had been the foreign intruder, hiding in the darkest corner of the carriage. I'd been too tired and distracted to look closely.

I fumbled the Steam-Stream gun out and into my grip. It took me longer than it should have, yet the intruder held up his hands and said, "Don't worry, I'm not going to hurt you."

"Of course you aren't," I said, juggling the gun into position, pointing at him from my seat. My fingers were a trifle shaky, but in the dark, he wouldn't be able to tell. "Who are you, and what are you doing here?" It occurred to me that I could have screamed and drawn the cabbie's attention, but I'm by nature a curious person, and after all, I was the one who was armed.

"My name is Dylan Eckhert. And I . . . uh . . . I wanted to talk to you."

"Aren't you supposed to be waxing the museum floors?" I asked.

"I didn't really expect you to believe me." He gave a little laugh. "Um . . . could I put my hands down now? I promise I'm not going to do anything but talk to you."

"Very well. I want to talk to you too. But any movements on your part, and I pull the trigger and you'll be blasted with steam."

His first question surprised me. "Are you really Sherlock Holmes's niece?"

"Of course I am." I realized he must have been hovering about listening to the conversations with Grayling and Luckworth.

"But I thought Sherlock Holmes was a fictitious character," Mr. Eckhert said. His expression was bewildered and perhaps a little frightened. "Am I in London? What year is this?"

Clearly, the stranger was suffering from a case of amnesia. Or he was utterly mad. And here I was, closed up in a carriage with him. I gripped the Steam-Stream gun more tightly. "My uncle is as real as you and I. And yes, you're in London. The year is 1889. Who are you and where are you from? I want some answers."

"I'd like some too, to be honest," he said. "Actually, what I really want is my—that thing back. You picked it up off the floor."

I pulled the device from my pocket. It looked like a small, dark mirror, but its window or face was black and shiny and reflected a bit of light and no clear image. About as big as my hand, it was slender and elegant, made of glass and encased in silver metal. I turned it over and noticed the faint image of an apple with a bite out of it. "This? I thought you'd given it to us. After all, you threw it across the room."

"Yeah, right. You're too smart to believe that."

I couldn't disagree, so I changed tactics. "What is it?"

"It's . . . a . . . phone. A telephone," he said hesitantly. "A special kind of telephone."

It didn't look like any sort of telephone I'd ever seen. There was nowhere to listen, and nowhere to speak. And it had no wires. I smoothed my fingers over the device, amazed at how light and sleek it was. I must have activated it somehow, because all at once, it lit up and there were multicolored little pictures on its face. At least it didn't start screeching. "I might give it back to you if you answer my questions."

"What do you want to know? And by the way, why didn't you tell those detectives about me?"

As I wasn't certain of the answer to that myself, I declined to reply. There was something about this young man that I found compelling. I sensed there was more to him than met the eye. Instead of answering his question, I asked one of my own. "Did you see or hear anyone before you saw the girl's body?"

"I might have heard a door opening and closing, but I'm not familiar with all the sounds in the museum, so I can't be sure. Probably. Then I heard a scuffle, like someone's shoe on the floor. I was . . . um . . . walking through the museum, trying to find my way . . . out, and I almost tripped over her. I only got there a few seconds before you."

From Miss Adler's office, we'd heard the rumbling sound of a steam-powered door, but it had taken us a minute or two to get to where we'd found Miss Hodgeworth and Mr. Eckhert.

"Where was the knife when you got there? Was she holding it?"

"No. It was on the floor next to her. I think . . . I think I might have interrupted someone. It looked as if the knife was lying next to her, as if it had been dropped."

"Why are you living in the museum?" I asked, changing the subject.

"I'm not living in the museum. I just got there tonight. A few hours before I saw you."

"That's impossible. Your shoes are clean." I shifted the gun in warning. "How about the truth, now, Mr. Eckhert?"

"It's complicated. But I guess if there's any chance of me getting home, I'm going to have to trust someone." He looked out the window and a gaslight streetlamp cast a brief golden glow over his sober face and the tousled hair that brushed his neck and covered his ears and forehead. I felt my chest tighten and looked away. He was one of the most handsome young men I'd ever seen.

At last he turned and looked at me once more. "So . . . I'm . . . uh . . . from a long way away. And I'm not sure how I got here, and I'm *really* not sure how I'm going to get back home. It was freaky. I was in the museum, back in a far corner all alone. It was dark and empty, and it was—well, okay, I'll be honest. On a dare, I sneaked into one of the back rooms in the basement, and I found this door in the middle of nowhere. It was, like, locked, but the lock was old and rusty, and I got it to open. Inside, I found an old Egyptian statue, totally covered with dust. I don't think anyone had touched it for years. It was a person with the head of a lion. I looked it up. I think it was—"

"Sekhmet." I spoke the name in a whisper. A chill washed over me. *There are no coincidences.*

"Right. Sekhmet." He seemed to relax a little bit. "I noticed a sort of emblem, like a button, set into the stone base. It was so tall that I could crouch down and fit my head between its knees. It was glowing. I touched it, and then all of a sudden I felt this really odd vibration, this strange *buzzing*. It was in my head, my ears, all through my body, just crazy. I felt the emblem sort of move, like it sank in a little more, and the vibration got stronger. And then I felt as if I was falling and falling and falling . . . and then all of a sudden, I realized I was lying on the floor." His expression was one of misery and shock. "I don't know how long I was out of it, but when I opened my eyes, I was in the same room, but there were different things there. The statue of Sekhmet was gone. It was like I'd . . ."

I realized my jaw was hanging open, and I snapped it closed. He was telling the truth; I could see it in his eyes. At least, the truth as he understood it. He'd somehow *traveled* here by touching the emblem on a Sekhmet statue?

My mind was awhirl with questions and theories, but I managed to pluck one topic from the storm. "An emblem? What did it look like? You say it was glowing?"

"It was about this big," he said, drawing a circle on his palm. "And it was a really bright blue color—I think they call it lapis?"

"Lapis lazuli?"

He nodded. "And it had a picture of a beetle on it."

I felt as if a basketful of clockwork gears had just tumbled into my lap and I didn't have any way of knowing how they fit together.

"It looked a little like the one, the scarab—that was by the girl."

"There was a scarab by the victim?" I said sharply. How could I have missed that? "There was no scarab there."

"Yeah, there was. It was on the ground next to her." He shifted in his seat, and I lifted the gun. He stilled. "I took it."

Ahh. "May I see it, please?"

"How about a trade? I give you the beetle, and you give me back my phone." He flashed me a charming smile.

"You're in no position to be bargaining," I said, and held out my hand for what I was certain would be a clockwork scarab decorated with a Sekhmet cartouche. After a long moment, he sighed and complied, digging into the pocket of his denim trousers.

The item produced was similar in size and design to the scarab Miss Adler had shown us earlier. As I peered down at it in the dim light, unable to hold my illuminator *and* the gun, a thought struck me. I looked up at Mr. Eckhert. "Do you recall how long it was between the time you opened your eyes and found yourself in the room with the Sekhmet statue missing and when you found Miss Hodgeworth's body?"

"Like, three hours, maybe four. I was confused because the room had either changed, or I had . . . moved." His voice cracked with emotion.

Three hours, maybe four.

Miss Hodgeworth had been dead for about that amount of time.

Another coincidence?

As Inspector Luckworth might say, not blooming likely.

The sun was just coloring the rooftops when I stumbled into my chamber. I tore off my trousers, shirtwaist, and coat, thankful that I didn't need to struggle out of a corset tonight. The Milford Gentlelady's Easy-Unlacer, whose slender, metal fingers made a nuisance of a clacking sound as it went about its business, not only took too long to loosen the ties of one's corset, but was loud enough to wake Mrs. Raskill.

The house was dark and silent, except for the distant rumble of the aforementioned lady's slumberous breathing, and although I had stopped near my father's chamber, the sounds of his own snoring were not evident. His boots were not in their place, and his walking stick was still missing, thus leading me to conclude he had chosen to once again sleep at his club.

My mother's chamber adjoined his, and, as was my habit, I cracked open the door to look inside. Everything was as pristine as it had been the day she left, but now, a year later, I could no longer smell the soft lily of the valley scent that had always permeated the space. I closed the door tightly.

When I had realized Mr. Eckhert had no place to sleep, I invited him to stay at our house. As it turned out, my father's empty bedchamber was a blessing in disguise, and Mr. Eckhert had eagerly flopped onto the made-up bed.

One might wonder why I would do something so outside the bounds of propriety and invite a single young man—and one who'd come into my life so unusually—to stay in my home, unchaperoned, but it had become obvious he was out of sorts and had no funds. I sensed he meant me no harm and that he needed some sort of help. Besides, he was clearly linked to whatever was happening relative to Sekhmet and her scarabs. It was best I keep Dylan Eckhert under close watch.

Despite my physical exhaustion, the events of the night made me feel energetic and invigorated. I was confident I wouldn't sleep much at all, but once in bed, I forced myself to close my eyes and relax. I would need a clear mind and rested body for later, when our secret society reconvened.

But just as I slipped into the lulling embrace of Morpheus, a pair of sharp green-gray eyes popped into my memory and ruined it all.

I sincerely hoped I wouldn't encounter Inspector Grayling any time in the near future.

When I awoke much later that morning, Mr. Eckhert was gone.

Not only did he not leave a note, but he'd also sneaked into my chamber whilst I slumbered and pilfered the sleek, silver device he claimed was a telephone.

ℳISS STOKER

In Which Miss Stoker Is Twice Surprised

Neither Miss Adler nor Miss Holmes had indicated if or when we should meet again, so after the events at the museum, I was in no hurry to return to Grantworth House to sleep. Probably the two had plans for the next day—likely exciting tasks such as visiting the Hodgeworth family home, getting to know each other better, and searching for beetles. Miss Holmes could search for clues by interviewing every young woman in London if she wanted to. I had more important things to do, like saving unsuspecting mortals from the fangs of demonic vampires.

Barring that, at least I might be able to interfere in a mugging or other criminal assault between two mortals. I had to find something to do with myself.

After Pix melted into the shadows and left me wiping all trace of his soft, arrogant lips from the back of my hand, I took my time walking home. Unfortunately, nothing dangerous or exciting presented itself. By five o'clock, I gave up and returned to the house I shared with Bram and his family.

Though it wasn't necessary that I climb the oak tree growing outside my balcony, I did so simply because I could. It seemed only right that a vampire hunter should be sneaking in and out of the house, rather than walking through the front door. My brother Bram knew how I spent my nights, but his wife, Florence, did not. Even though she was like a mother to me, Bram and I chose to keep her in the dark about my vocation.

I'd been living in London since I was ten. Born to an elderly mother and father, I'd been raised by a variety of young relatives, most recently Bram and Florence. My brother was twenty-five years my senior and more of a father to me than my blood parents, and I'd come to love Florence as a mother as well. She was sweet and practical, though she was more interested in marrying me off than I was in finding a husband. Our family life was simple and uneventful until a little more than a year ago. I'd had a series of terrifying dreams in which I was being chased by a vampire, and that was when I learned not only of our family legacy, but of my calling to be a vampire hunter. When I told Bram about the dreams, at first he seemed surprised and then a little disgruntled. But apparently he knew what to do and arranged for my introduction to Siri.

The woman who became my mentor had trained other vampire hunters. Siri taught me that the UnDead tend to collect in populous areas, where their victims were less likely to be found or missed. She also arranged for our household to move into the spacious Grantworth House, which had been in the Stoker family since before my great-great-aunt Victoria. Not only did it give me space to practice, but it was almost like an inheritance I gained after learning I was the next vampire hunter. The move to the mansion had coincided with my debut into Society and gave me access to the upper crust of London. Florence couldn't have been happier with this turn of events, and she and I spent far too many hours shopping for clothing to wear to balls, dinner parties, the theater, and even summer picnics in Hyde Park.

My real parents still lived in Ireland, unaware of the secret legacy of vampire hunting by select members of our family. I wasn't certain how Bram even knew, and he never bothered to tell me. Although it was nice having someone I could talk to about my vocation, I also felt awkward. He believed it should have been he who'd had the calling.

But Bram had a wife and child. He couldn't put himself in the way of evil and danger. Who would take care of them if something happened to him?

I didn't have anyone to worry about. Just me.

Bram might love me as a sister and even as a daughter, but he was so enamored with our family legacy and the unnatural skills that came with it that he seemed more interested in encouraging me than protecting me. Sometimes I wondered if he was *too* certain of my abilities and assumed I was infallible. And since Siri had disappeared shortly after my encounter with a vampire, there really wasn't anyone else to worry about me.

I had dark moments when I couldn't help but wonder if she'd given up on me. Or had there been a mistake? Maybe I really wasn't a vampire hunter after all, and she'd moved on to train someone more worthy.

My mouth turned down, and I brushed away the unpleasant thought. I *was* a Venator.

I'd prove myself worthy. Somehow.

I slept well and woke when the sun raged through the window of my bedchamber. It was hours past noon, as well as being an unusually sunny day in our dreary London. Bram would be at the Lyceum Theatre, where he was the manager, and Florence would be shopping or making social calls. I considered myself fortunate that my sister-in-law hadn't awakened me to join her. My nephew, Noel, would be at school, and my maidservant, Pepper, was likely off with the cook, Mrs. Bullensham, on their daily errands.

I anticipated a quiet afternoon wherein I could sharpen some extra stakes and perhaps practice some of my fighting skills in the music room. Even though I wasn't a cognoggin by any means, I was looking forward to using a new device Bram had found for me. It was designed for gentlemen who liked to spar in a boxing ring and wanted a way to practice at home. Mr. Jackson's Mechanized-Mentor was a life-size machine sporting two "arms" and self-propelling wheels, along with the ability to squat or duck from side to side. With a small adjustment, it also could be used to practice the waltz, which was the excuse Bram had given Florence for acquiring the contraption. Her delight had likely been due to visions of me dancing flawlessly with some eligible duke or viscount.

When I came downstairs, our housekeeper, Mrs. Gernum, gave me a thick, white folded notecard. Another invitation to a ball or dance or picnic that I had no interest in attending. I would have tucked it away so Florence wouldn't see it, but I noticed the seal of the British Museum.

> *It is necessary to our recent appointment for you and I to attend a fête at the home of Lord and Lady Cosgrove-Pitt this evening. I presume you have a carriage at your disposal. I shall be dressed and prepared for you to call for me at eight o'clock this evening, at which time I will give you further details. Please respond soonest.*
>
> *—M. Holmes*

My response ranged from vexation at the tone of her letter to exasperation that I'd have to subject myself to the fawning attentions of anemic, boring young men who had no idea how easily I could outdo them . . . and ended with me rolling my eyes. What possible reason could there be for us to attend a party at the home of Lord Cosgrove-Pitt, the leader of Parliament?

. . . at which time I will give you further details.

And was it just my imagination, or was that phrase laden with smugness? Mina Holmes seemed like an insufferable know-it-all who ordered people about and rolled over anyone who disagreed with her . . . like one of the Refuse-Agitators that moved along the sewage canals and flattened everything into muck.

Right, then, Miss Holmes. I glanced down at the masculine writing, taking a page from her book and examining it. I sneered. One would have expected Mina Holmes to write with precise, neat characters instead of such a scrawl.

Then a prickle of guilt trickled over me, and my irritation evaporated like a puff of steam. Had I not promised my services to Princess Alexandra only hours ago? And here I was, grumbling about the next task set before me simply because it was not to my liking.

Maybe I wasn't the right sort of person for this assignment. Maybe I didn't quite fit in Miss Adler's society. After all, I couldn't even look at a dead body without turning into a jellied mass of paralysis.

I sat up straight and glared down at the letter as if it were Miss Holmes herself. *No.* I was just as able as she. Probably more so.

I wasn't going to let that gawky brain-beak show me up.

As I dashed off a quick response to Miss Holmes, I couldn't help but smile. I might prefer to be doing something other than having Pepper attend to my hair and then making conversation with a roomful of people I hardly cared to

know, but Mina Holmes was bound to be even less enthusiastic about the idea. From our conversation last night, it was
obvious she didn't know anyone in Society, nor did she seem
comfortable with the idea of interacting within it.

My smile turned into a smirk. At least *I* had something
suitable to wear.

When Miss Holmes climbed into my carriage at eight o'clock,
I goggled at her, and my snide thoughts about the contents
of her closet evaporated. Her gown was one of the most gor-
geous pieces of up-to-the-date, cognoggin-influenced fashion
I'd ever seen.

Made of velvet and silk, the fitted bodice and voluminous skirt were panels of rich chocolate brown alternating with
a golden rust color. The sleeves were large and puffy near the
shoulders, tapering into long fingerless gloves that ended in
a point at her middle finger. From the elbow to wrist, brown
and rust lace had been appliquéd onto the fabric, and buttons,
flowers, and little clockwork gears decorated the backs of the
glove-sleeves.

Her brown corset was short and leather, and she wore it
over the bodice in a new style that was just coming into fashion. But did she have another corset underneath? Four dangling watch chains and their matching clocks decorated one
side of the corset and on the other were two slender pockets.
And pinned to the front of her bodice was the most remarkable dragonfly pin, complete with rotating wings that made

a soft, pleasant buzzing sound and little whirring gears that made up its body.

Not only was she dressed at the height of Street Fashion, but the gangly, long-nosed girl had done something with her hair that made her look even taller . . . but in a willowy way. And even her blade-like nose seemed balanced by the pile of chestnut-colored hair that had been braided, woven with ribbons, and decorated with clockwork gears in a neat but intricate coiffure.

Not that my own gown was anything to sniff at. At the height of accepted Victorian fashion, my frock consisted of a narrow skirt of frothier, lighter fabric than Miss Holmes's, with many layers of ice-colored pink caught up by darker rosettes and gathered into a neat bustle at the lower part of my spine. But the most important aspect of the dress was its concealed split skirts. That was Pepper's inspiration, and practical for someone of my vocation.

"Is something wrong, Miss Stoker?" Miss Holmes asked, patting her head as if to make certain her hair wasn't about to fall.

We were sitting in the carriage, and Middy, the driver, was waiting for directions from me. "No," I replied, noticing the set of keys dangling from the edge of Miss Holmes's corset-vest. Surely they were for decoration rather than practical use, but nevertheless, even a traditionalist handmaker like me found them cunning. I blinked and stuck my head out the small window to give Middy the address and then settled back in my seat.

"Are you quite certain?" My companion glanced down at herself, smoothing her full skirts. Even in the drassy light, I could see a stiff, black lace crinoline peeping from beneath the rustling material and the hint of elegant copper-toed shoes. "Do you think my—I wasn't certain what to wear." She lifted her nose and managed to look down at me despite the fact that we were both seated.

Miss Mina Holmes was *nervous*. That was an eye-opening revelation and eased my . . . whatever it was that made me feel prickly and uncomfortable around her.

"Not at all," I told her candidly. "Your gown is stunning. I'm certain the gentlemen will be most taken with you."

"Well, that might be the case, but it's neither here nor there. We have business afoot tonight." Despite her brisk words, her fingers, which had been toying with a group of buttons on her glove-sleeve, relaxed in her lap.

"Yes, of course. You could bring me up to date on what you and Miss Adler discovered today." I kept my voice neutral but felt compelled to add, "My apologies for not joining you at the museum. I was out late patrolling for UnDead and overslept this morning." I didn't mention the fact that neither of the ladies had contacted me about a time or place to meet, so Miss Holmes must have taken it upon herself to visit Miss Adler first thing in the morning.

"Oh," she said, looking surprised. "It must be a rather difficult proposition, being out late and then being required to awaken shortly after dawn. I didn't think the UnDead were quite a threat any longer."

I gritted my teeth. No, they weren't, but she didn't need to remind me of it . . . and the fact that I'd failed the single time I'd faced one. "The reason they aren't a threat is because of people like me who ensure that they aren't."

"Right."

I quickly changed the subject. "I had a beast of a time of it, leaving tonight without my guardians. Did you have difficulty obtaining permission to attend the ball?"

"Permission?" Miss Holmes gave a short laugh. "My father rarely darkens the door of our house, and even if he does happen to find his bed for the night, he'd hardly notice whether I was present or not. Of course, it's because he's quite busy helping the government at the Home Office and spends long hours at his office or club."

"And your mother didn't object?" I'd had to lie and tell Florence I was attending a small musicale at the Tylingtons'. If she got wind that I was attending the Cosgrove-Pitt ball, the event of the season, nothing would have kept her home . . . which was why I'd hidden my invitation when it came two weeks ago.

"My mother is gone."

The tone of Miss Holmes's voice snapped my thoughts from dear, practical Florence. "Gone? Do you mean *dead* . . . or . . . ?" My voice trailed off.

"She left my father and me a year ago," she said in a voice that tried too hard to sound nonchalant. "Obviously, she cares even less than he does what I do and where I go." She shifted, her skirts rustling, and sat up ramrod straight. "Which is precisely why Miss Adler chose me to be part of this society, knowing I wouldn't be hampered by such authority figures as parents."

I couldn't imagine what it would be like not to have any adults about, meddling in my daily life. The thought made me uncomfortable rather than envious.

Miss Holmes changed the subject, her voice brusque. "Miss Adler and I determined it was of importance for us to attend the party tonight at the Cosgrove-Pitts' because of what we learned today at the Hodgeworth home. It was Miss Mayellen who was last night's victim, and her sister and mother were gracious enough to allow us to search her bedchamber."

"Did you find another beetle?"

"Aside from a scarab that was left on the floor next to her body, Miss Adler and I found this." She produced a creamy notecard from some hidden pocket. "Observe."

The engraved invitation to the party at Cosgrove Terrace this evening was familiar to me. I had the same one tucked in my small reticule. It was identical except for the faint mark in the bottom corner, hardly noticeable unless one were looking for something. "A beetle," I said.

"Look more closely," she said impatiently. "Do you not notice anything else of importance?"

"Perhaps if I had a bit of *light*," I retorted, then snapped my jaw closed when she produced a little device that flared into some bright illumination. Blasted cognog. But even though I stared at the invitation, with its formal script and detail of the party, I could see nothing else out of the ordinary.

Lord Belmont & Lady Isabella Cosgrove-Pitt
extend a cordial invitation to
The King & Queen of the Roses Ball
Wednesday, the 15th of May, 1889
at eight o'clock in the evening
Beneath the Stars
Cosgrove Terrace
St. James Park

I read the words thrice, turned the card to the reverse, and found nothing remarkable but for the small beetle drawing. At last admitting defeat, I looked up at my companion.

"That is precisely the problem with most people," she muttered. "Uncle Sherlock is right. People look, but do not *observe*. They examine, but they do not *see*. Behold," she said, pointing her light at the invitation. "Beneath the nine, do you not discern the tiny dot? And also beneath the word *Stars*?"

I frowned and peered down. She was correct . . . now that it was pointed out to me, I saw the small dots. "But that means nothing," I protested. "A drip of ink from a careless scribe."

"Miss Stoker, please observe. Those dots were made purposely. See how perfectly uniform and round they are? A drip would have an oblong shape. And aside from that, notice that the text is engraved upon the card, while those markings are not. Finally, although you likely cannot see it in our faulty light, the shade of ink used to draw the beetle is precisely the same shade of indigo ink as the two dots. From Mr. Inkwell's specialty shop on Badgley, I'd wager."

"So what's the purpose of these markings? Some sort of message?"

"That would be the logical assumption," she said crisply. "But what, I'm not yet certain. We'll both have to be vigilant this evening to determine what it could mean. I suspect that the nine might refer to a time, thus at nine o'clock, I shall be quite attentive to anything related to stars."

"What else?" I asked as she clicked her light closed and tucked it away. I could see her face only during the brief flashes of illumination from the streetlamps as we trundled along.

"We found no envelope or seal. So we have no way of knowing who made the marks or when—whether it was before it left the Cosgrove-Pitt residence, or afterward; whether Miss Hodgeworth did it herself for some reason or whether it was given to her that way by someone else who received the invitation or someone involved in the sending of the invitation."

"And so the rest of the plan for tonight is to . . . what? Look for more beetles?" I asked, trying not to sound bored. I was going to be subjected to simpering young men and gossiping ladies simply so Miss Holmes could look for beetles? The most dangerous and exciting part of the night would be to avoid getting my feet trod upon or a lemonade spilled upon my gown.

"Of course. We must look for more beetles or Sekhmet scarabs and attempt to direct conversations whenever possible to the topic of Sekhmet. Even superficially," she added as the carriage pulled up to the drive at Cosgrove Terrace. "If anyone should show interest in Sekhmet, that could be a lead. As well, I should like to gain access to Lady Cosgrove-Pitt's study to see if we can find the list of invitees."

"Do you mean break into her study?"

Miss Holmes once again managed to look down at me from her seated position. "I prefer to think of it as accidentally stumbling upon the chamber. Regardless of how it occurs, once we ascertain whether Miss Hodgeworth is on the original invitation list, we will then have narrowed down the identity of the person who made the marks."

"How?"

Miss Holmes sighed. "If Miss Hodgeworth *isn't* on the original list, then we can assume someone else marked up an invitation—presumably his or her own—and sent it to her. Narrowing down who the invitation was originally meant for, or who marked it up, will assist us in identifying the messenger, and hopefully provide us a connection between Miss Hodgeworth and Miss Martindale."

I blinked at her convoluted explanation. Yet it made sense. "But her mother or sister would have known whether Mayellen received an invitation to one of the most talked-about parties of the year." The carriage lurched forward, then stopped. I peeked out the window to see a long line of people disembarking from other vehicles. "The Roses Ball is the event of the season, and only the crème de la crème would be invited."

"Of course," my companion replied with a hint of aggravation. "That was my first question to the Hodgeworths. Neither Mrs. Hodgeworth nor her other daughter were aware of an invitation from Lord and Lady Cosgrove-Pitt."

I nodded and handed back the notecard, which she might need to gain entrance. I had my own, of course. "Very well, then." Sneaking into Lady Cosgrove-Pitt's study would at least bring some intrigue into what was sure to be a boring evening.

"I think it might be prudent," said Miss Holmes, "for your invitation to be marked up as well. One must be prepared for any eventuality."

"One must," I said, keeping my sarcasm to a minimum, "but I'm sorry to say that I don't happen to have in my possession any specialty indigo ink from Mr. Inkwell's—" I stopped when I saw the look on her face. "Right. Of course."

She produced a writing instrument that was, presumably, already loaded with the special indigo ink. I handed over my invitation without another word, and to my relief, she didn't make any further comment or show any sign of smugness.

The carriage jolted forward again, then stopped. Miss Holmes used the little fan-like wings of her dragonfly pin to dry the ink and then handed me my invitation. We lapsed into silence until our door was opened and a white-gloved coachman helped each of us down. The sun had set and any natural illumination was only a glimpse of moon from behind wispy gray clouds and a faulty swath of stars arcing over the dark sky.

The mansion, which was one of the few in the city that boasted large, gated grounds, loomed above us. A flight of steps led up to a well-lit entrance on a side of the building rather than the door facing the drive. A smooth mechanical ramp ascended so ladies in their cumbersome skirts and high-heeled shoes wouldn't wear themselves out from the climb. Some fashionable skirts were so narrow, with their high bustle over the rear, that the wearer could only take small, mincing steps. At least Mina had had the wherewithal to don a gown with petticoats that allowed for some movement, despite their weight and layers.

Medievaler that I am, I disdained the ramp in favor of the stairs and found myself waiting for Miss Holmes as she rode up the mechanized trolley.

A series of panels and doors had been removed from the building, leaving an entire wall of the foyer open to the night air, with no boundary between terrace and interior. The dull roar of people talking and laughing mingled with the music from a small orchestra, spilling into the outdoors. Even from where I stood, I could see glittering gold streamers and bunting, and hundreds of bloodred roses in vases, clustered on trellises and attached to potted trees. Someone had cut many large leafless branches, painted them dark red, and arranged them like trees. A number of self-propelled, copper-winged lanterns flitted about like hand-size fireflies.

"It's beautiful," Miss Holmes murmured. "Like a gilded English rose garden."

I couldn't disagree, but how often did they have to replace the gears in those silly flying lights anyway? "They'll want to announce us," I said. She grimaced, but stepped up with me to hand our calling cards to the butler.

"She pronounces her name Evah-*line*, not Evah-leen," Miss Holmes informed the butler as she pointed to my card. I rolled my eyes. I didn't care.

"Miss Evaline Stoker and Miss Mina Holmes," the butler intoned.

The place was an absolute crush, with people hardly able to move about the room. Lord and Lady Cosgrove-Pitt stood just inside the entrance to greet each guest, and we dutifully approached.

Lord Cosgrove-Pitt, who was older and grayer than his pretty dark-haired wife, was stately and a bit portly. He took my hand and bowed, but it was my companion who attracted his attention. "Sir Mycroft's daughter?" he boomed over the noise. "Mr. Holmes's niece? How can it be that we've never met? Bella, surely you've invited Miss Holmes to our parties, haven't you? Important young lady, you know."

"Why, Miss Holmes," said his wife, taking my companion's hand in her gloved ones. "I am so pleased to meet you, and I apologize for never having done so in the past. Mr. Holmes's niece, you say?"

My companion's nose had gone dull red, but she curtseyed and thanked Lord Cosgrove-Pitt for his kindness, then responded to his wife. "Yes, indeed, Lady Cosgrove-Pitt. Sherlock Holmes is my uncle."

"He is quite a clever man." She looked up at her husband. "He assisted me with a little problem some years ago— you do remember, don't you, dear?"

"Something to do with the upstairs maid filching the silver?" He rubbed his chin.

Lady Isabella patted his arm. "It was the downstairs maid, and Mr. Holmes proved she was *innocent*, as it turned out, of breaking one of the glass cases in the gallery." She turned back to us. "I do hope you enjoy yourselves tonight. Please make certain you take a stroll through the art gallery while you are here."

As we thanked her, turning to make our way into the throngs of people, I felt a sudden awareness sing down my spine. Someone was watching me.

I glanced around the party. Since we were still standing on the terrace, which connected the outside with the ballroom, we were several steps above the main floor. Through the dancing and visiting below, I could see quite well.

A huge cluster of potted topiaries festooned with rich red roses mingled with some of the painted trees. My attention focused there on a trio of manservants, standing at the ready with trays and white towels over their arms. Even as they watched the partygoers, they talked and laughed together. They wore gold jackets with a rose on each lapel.

As I stared at them, one in particular caught my eye. There was something familiar about him.

That tingle up my spine grew cold.

He reminded me an awful lot of Pix.

MISS HOLMES

Of Firefly Lanterns, Copper Heels, and Convenient Waltzes

I felt Miss Stoker go rigid next to me. I turned to follow her gaze, but even my sharp observation skills revealed nothing that seemed out of place.

"Impossible," she muttered, staring down into the crowded room. "Not a bloody chance."

I'd been around my uncle and his friend Dr. Watson enough not to mind curse words, but I was taken aback that Miss Stoker employed them as handily as the men did. Just as I was about to ask her for an explanation, an unfamiliar roar from outside caught my ears. I turned to see a sleek steamcycle shoot up the steps and onto the far edge of the terrace. Bent over the handlebars, the rider wore goggles, a tight aviator cap with earflaps, and a long coat that whipped out behind him. He manipulated the cycle neatly into a spot far beyond the partygoers.

The vehicle, which looked utterly dangerous—and possibly illegal—gleamed like the sun with its copper and bronze machinery and sported a bit of brass detail around the bottom. A bell-shaped metal skirt hid whatever mechanism kept the cycle gliding along more than a foot above the ground, and there was a trio of copper pipes at the rear from which the steam could escape. The rider turned off the engine and the vehicle gave a soft hiss, then sank to the stone terrace as if lowering itself on invisible legs.

Like dismounting from a horse, the steamcycle's rider climbed off and raised his goggles, giving an abrupt wave to the grooms who'd noticed his arrival. If their gawking was any indication, those young men would be easily convinced to give up their livelihood of managing horses in favor of this tempting new mode of transportation.

But it wasn't until the rider yanked off his hat by an earflap and revealed a head of ginger-colored hair that I recognized him.

Inspector Grayling.

What on earth would *he* be doing at an event like this? A simple Scotland Yard investigator? At a Society party? Surely he wasn't here as a guest. Which meant he must be here in some official capacity. That conclusion caused me to relax only slightly. Could he be investigating something related to Miss Hodgeworth's horrible death—just as we were?

I was not about to let him interfere with my investigation.

Grayling hadn't yet noticed me. As I watched, he pulled off his long duster and slung it carelessly over the back of the cycle, giving some direction to the nearest groom. He was dressed in evening wear and not the more informal garb of his occupation.

My eyes narrowed in consideration, and I turned to speak to Miss Stoker, but she was gone. I perused the room from a high vantage point, but saw no sign of my companion's dark head.

It was to my advantage *not* to be seen by Inspector Grayling when and if he should enter the festivities, so I lifted my skirts and made my way as expediently as possible down the steps into the shallow, circular ballroom.

I reminded myself of the reason for my presence at this crush of a party. But looking over the number of people crowding the room, spilling onto the terrace and into other interior chambers of the mansion, I despaired that I would find anything related to Sekhmet, an Egyptian scarab, or the meaning of the number nine and stars.

I lifted my chin in determination. I was a Holmes. Observation, deduction, and duty to the Crown were my life. I would brave even a Society event to fulfill my destiny, though I hoped I'd remain beneath the notice of the eligible young men who were in attendance. I had no interest in attempting to converse with any of them.

Or—worse—to realize that none of them had the least bit of interest in conversing with me.

Chin still firmly in the air, I made my way along the perimeter of the room, skirting past topiaries and innumerable roses. I considered the situation as I brushed past an urn containing man-size red branches. The beetle marking on the invitation could be a form of identification or perhaps a call to action, such as to a meeting, which would confirm my suspicion that the nine had to do with some event at nine o'clock. An event that had to do with stars. And one thing had become clear: several young women were connected by Sekhmet's scarab, which implied some sort of association—or at least a communication system.

If they didn't know each other, the scarab must identify another member of the group. If they *did* know each other, then that would make it all the more difficult for me to masquerade as the recipient of a scarab message. The fact that I had the invitation with the beetle symbol on it was definitely a point in favor of attempting the risky proposition.

Something Lady Cosgrove-Pitt had said echoed in my mind. *Please make certain you take a stroll through the art gallery while you are here.*

An art gallery could include many forms of art and possible topics of conversation. Including that of Egyptology and Egyptian antiquities. Aside from that, looking for the gallery might also help me with the other part of my plan: to find the guest list for this event in Lady Cosgrove-Pitt's study.

Exhilarated by these possibilities, I turned to the interior of the house. My skirt caught on my tall, skinny copper heel, and I felt the fabric of my crinoline tear beneath it. Even worse, in my haste, I bumped into one of the pots holding a tree-branch arrangement.

The urn wobbled, tipped, and then the whole cluster began to fall. I lurched at the branches and tried to catch them, my skirt still caught on my heel, and somehow managed to rescue the whole pot before it crashed to the floor.

Well, almost all of it.

One of the branches escaped my grip and fell into another set of false trees, throwing them off balance in their own vase. I grabbed them before they tipped over and spent the next few moments breathing heavily, rearranging the blasted things, and hoping no one had noticed my near disaster.

But when I turned away from them, ready to make my escape and to continue on my mission, I found myself face-to-face with Inspector Grayling.

"Are you quite finished, Miss Holmes?"

I wasn't certain whether to be mortified that he had witnessed my mishap or vexed that he'd stood by and watched me struggle without bothering to offer assistance. My face, which was hot and damp, was probably crimson—a fact which I tried not to think about, but couldn't dismiss, causing my cheeks to grow even hotter.

Since I had no good response to his query, I responded with one of my own. "What are you doing here?" I lifted my nose and tried not to be annoyed by how tall he was.

"I'm here in an official capacity," he said, lifting *his* nose.

"As am I," was my rejoinder. I was trying to inconspicuously extricate my slender copper heel from where it was still embedded in the lace trim of my underskirt.

"Is everything quite all right, Miss Holmes?" he asked, looking in bemusement at my skirts, which were moving due to my foot's contortions. I wished earnestly for one of the flying firefly lanterns to crash into his arrogant, too-tall head.

But before I could reply, a sunny voice from behind interrupted us. "Why, Miss Holmes! I see you've met our dear Ambrose."

I turned to see Lady Cosgrove-Pitt bearing down on us. Her pale gray eyes lit with enthusiasm, and she looked from Grayling to me and back again. Perhaps she read our tension, for she said, "Brose, darling, this is Mr. *Sherlock* Holmes's *niece*. It would be nice for you to get to know her a bit, since you might cross paths with him in your line of work. Miss Mina Holmes, please meet my husband's cousin's nephew by marriage, Inspector Ambrose Grayling. Perhaps the two of you would like to get better acquainted during this waltz?"

"Oh, no, I don't think—"

"Miss Holmes, would you do me the honor?" he interrupted, and offered his arm. His cheeks had gone a bit dusky beneath their freckles.

My face was hotter than ever. It was approaching nine o'clock, and I had other things to do. I didn't even *want* to dance with him, and I certainly didn't want to dance with a man who was forced into partnering me.

But words failed me, and before I knew it, I'd placed my fingers on his arm. It was warm and steady, and very sturdy. I took one step before I discovered my heel was still caught up in my crinoline.

I managed a muffled *"Drat!"* before the underskirt pulled my shoe off rhythm and I lost my balance. I released Grayling's arm, but not before I jolted into him.

He'd stopped after that one step and looked down at me. "Miss Holmes, is everything quite all right?" The bemusement was gone, and now he wore an expression of wariness.

That was when I noticed the dark mark on his square chin. A small cut from shaving. How could I have missed it? And then it occurred to me with a cold shock that I'd been standing next to him for several minutes and had *forgotten* to be observant.

"Erm," I managed to say. My head was pounding from the heat on my face and my thoughts had scattered. "Yes, I just . . . I tripped and—"

"Yes, I can see that," he said. "Although I'm not certain on *what* you tripped," he muttered, looking around on the ground, which happened to be devoid of anything trippable.

Once again, I had the strong desire to see one of the lamps veer down and slam into his forehead.

He was still looking down around the hem of my skirts, as if to discover what nonexistent item I'd tripped over. "Oh," he said. "Have you caught a shoe on your skirt? May I?" He made a move as if to bend and assist me in extricating the recalcitrant heel, then paused and straightened, as if realizing how improper that would be, fumbling around at the hem of my skirts and possibly seeing my ankles. Or worse—*my legs.*

Now *his* face was flushed.

"I'm perfectly capable of doing it myself," I said with sharpness meant to cover my mortification. I bent down to free my heel, taking care not to show anything more than a flash of ankle in that endeavor.

My shoe thus liberated, a section of my delicate crinoline in tatters and dragging on the floor, I once again curved my fingers around the wool sleeve of his forearm.

I'd never had occasion to dance with a young man before. Practicing the waltz with a Sure-Step Debonair Dance-Tutor and its creaking, mechanical pacing was hardly the same as waltzing with a tall, arrogant, ginger-haired, freckled Scot.

My palms were damp beneath my fingerless gloves, and my bare digits had turned to ice. My stomach fluttered as Grayling maneuvered us out onto the dance floor and turned me to face him. His movements were careful and deliberate, almost as if he wasn't any more sure of himself than I was. Or, more likely, as if he were expecting me to somehow trip again.

He put his right hand lightly on my waist and collected my fingers in the left. His hand, despite its white glove, was warm around mine. This proximity affirmed that not only was he nearly a head taller than I, but that his shoulders were so broad I could hardly see around them. He was so solid. I drew in a deep breath, trying to steady my pulse. He smelled pleasant, like German cedar, lemon, and Mediterranean sandalwood, with an underlying scent of—mechanical grease? Of course. From the steamcycle.

My other hand had settled on his shoulder, my fingertips sensing the soft bristle of wool and the movement of shoulder muscle beneath them. My skirts swayed, rustling between us as he stepped into the rhythm of the waltz. It was more of a hitch than a confident step, and the second one was just as jerky and abrupt.

"Miss Holmes," he murmured, his mouth just above my temple, "if you would allow me to lead, we might perhaps find ourselves waltzing a bit more gracefully."

"Oh, yes, of course." I forced myself to relax and allow him to dictate our movements.

Soon, to my astonishment, we were gliding about the dance floor in a sedate but smooth rhythm. If it weren't for the full layers of my skirts, our legs might have *brushed against each other*. He was so close to me I could feel the warmth of his body, and I found myself having to gaze fixedly over his arm to keep from staring up at the smooth skin of his clean-shaven neck and chin. The sandalwood and lemon scents were likely from his shaving lotion. And we must have been moving more energetically than I realized, for I found it hard to catch my breath.

"I must apologize for putting you in such an awkward situation," I blurted out.

Grayling pulled back a bit to look down at me and made a slight misstep that told me he wasn't quite as accomplished a dancer as he seemed. I wasn't sure why I felt a surge of gratification at that realization.

"I don't know what you mean."

I didn't know what I meant either, and I felt ridiculous. My thoughts simply seemed to disintegrate when I tried to make conversation with a member of the opposite gender. I hoped I wouldn't be required to interrogate many of them as part of my work for Her Royal Highness. Although I seemed to have no problem interrogating and conversing with Mr. Eckhert.

"I had no intention of dancing tonight," I replied. "I have other reasons for being here."

"As do I." His voice took on that Scottish burr and its proximity sent little prickles over my temple. "But taking a turn around the dance floor is a convenient way to observe the room and get my bearings."

"Indeed." So it wasn't that he had the desire to dance with me. He merely wanted an excuse to look around the room. My cheeks were hot again, and I felt the weight of my hair shifting as if one of my clockwork gears was coming loose. "I'm delighted I was able to be of assistance," I added crisply.

"Miss Holmes, I—"

"You need say no more, Inspector Grayling. I presume you've observed enough that you might release me to my own devices? Do you perhaps know where I might find some cool refreshments?"

I felt him swallow hard, then he seemed to release a pent-up breath. "My apologies, Miss Holmes. I meant no insult. Perhaps—*oow-mph*." He stifled a cry of surprise as my pointed copper heel landed on one of his toes.

The misstep was an accident, but I cannot say I regretted it.

Grayling looked down at me, his expression of exasperation mingled with apprehension and perhaps a bit of chagrin. "Very well, then," he said. "You've made your—ah—point. Perhaps you'd prefer to get some lemonade on the Star Terrace instead of finishing this dance? I'm quite certain my toes, at least, will appreciate it," he added not quite under his breath.

The *Star* Terrace?

My aggravation evaporated. "What time is it?"

"It's ten of nine. Did you not hear the clock chime the quarter hour?"

"I must go." I pulled away. "To—ah—attend to something."

He frowned but didn't release my hand. "Miss Holmes, I do hope you aren't about to get involved in something you shouldn't be."

"I'm quite certain," I said, pulling free of his fingers, "that you haven't any idea with what I should and shouldn't get involved. Good evening, Inspector Grayling."

With one well-placed query to a handsome young waiter, I learned that the Star Terrace was on the same level as the ballroom, but on the east side of the building.

Just as the clock struck nine, I broached the terrace in question. It was aptly named, for natural stars glittered above in a wide swath, and there were few lights to distract from those celestial bodies. Small sparkling lights hung around the edges of the space, but the area was darker than the main terrace, where Evaline and I had made our arrival.

Miss Stoker had disappeared into the crush of people shortly after our conversation with Lord and Lady Cosgrove-Pitt. I didn't have time to search for her, and even if I had, I would have done so only cursorily. She might have been pressed into service just as I had, but she was also more comfortable in these social gatherings than I. Aside from that, I preferred to work alone and saw no need to constantly point out information and data to someone who couldn't see it herself.

I turned my attention from thoughts of Miss Stoker—who was probably chattering happily with some other young ladies, her dance card (unlike mine) filled with the names of partners for the evening—and observed the area. There was, as Grayling had suggested, a long table filled with libations at one end of the terrace. People stood nearby, talking, laughing, and drinking their lemonade-strawberry punch. Others strolled around the terrace. There seemed to be nothing out of the ordinary, nothing to draw my attention.

Then I noticed a movement near the dark line of arborvitae and thick dwarf pines separating the stone terrace from
the rest of the grounds. A well-hidden someone was standing
there. As I watched, a young woman approached. She walked
up to the figure, handed over something white and flat, then
progressed past and into the shadows.

My heart began to pound, and excitement made my
mouth go dry as I made my decision. I had the fake invitation. I was going to use it.

I pulled it from my reticule and made my way quickly
across the stones. When I approached, I saw the figure was
cloaked and hooded in dark fabric so as to obscure gender
and any other identifying factors. I felt certain the individual
wouldn't be able to discern my features due to its enveloping
cloak and the drassy light.

He or she held out a white-gloved hand, and I saw that
the image of a scarab beetle had been inked on the palm.

I handed over my invitation and was gestured toward a
narrow pass between two tall arborvitae. Drawing in a deep
breath, I stepped through.

Miss Stoker

Wherein Our Heroines Encounter an Overabundance of Perfumes

By the time I made my way through the crowded party to find the familiar-looking waiter, he'd disappeared.

Surely it wasn't Pix. It was impossible for a streetwise Cockney pickpocket to be hired for the event of the season. I put the thought of him out of my mind and in doing so, let down my guard. This was a mistake, for I was promptly caught up in conversation with one of those anemic young men I preferred to avoid. But though I had to listen to him compare my lips to rose petals and my hair to spirals of ink, I also learned that the Cosgrove-Pitt home boasted a Star Terrace.

Miss Mina Holmes wasn't the only person who could make a deduction.

Moments later, as I stepped onto the Star Terrace, I saw a young woman making her way quickly toward the dark end of the patio. Miss Holmes.

Here I was, only a moment in deduction behind Miss Observation herself, and she hadn't even searched for me before continuing on her way. Satisfaction with my discovery faded into aggravation. A flimsy brain-beak like Mina Holmes had no bloody business walking into dark shadows alone. Blooming idiot.

I followed her across the terrace, grudgingly grateful that she'd had the foresight to mark up my invitation to match hers. Careful not to accidentally pull out my stake, I dug the crumpled card out of a hidden pocket in my skirt and handed it to the cloaked figure who reached out a silent, gloved hand. He gestured for me to move forward.

A rush of energy pumped through my veins as I walked between two tall bushes. Finally, things were getting interesting.

On the other side of the bushes and trees, I found a mechanized vehicle. It was in a secluded area of the grounds of Cosgrove Terrace. A tall wall ran along behind it and ended in an open gate. A lamp burned in the street beyond and in the distance, the spiky, oblong shapes of London proper loomed.

Several cloaked figures stood there, mixing with the shadows. Someone handed me a wad of black fabric, and I found the head and armholes of an enveloping cloak. As I finished pulling my hood up and over, a black-garbed figure stumbled into me as it contorted beneath its cloak. Snickering, I helped Miss Holmes find her way out from beneath the fabric. When her head appeared, I shifted my hood so she would recognize me.

To my disappointment, she didn't seem surprised. "So you figured it out. Excellent."

"Of course I did," I replied, noticing that the other figures were climbing into the vehicle. A soft rumble accompanied by the familiar hiss of steam indicated that the trolley-like carriage had been started.

"Yes, of course," she said dismissively as we edged along with the cluster of figures. "Once discovered, the message had to be exceedingly simple to interpret."

I was proud of myself for *not* planting my foot on the hems of her full skirts. Instead, I fingered the stake deep in my pocket and bit my tongue.

We climbed into the automated vehicle amid other cloaked figures who spoke briefly and in hushed voices. I'd never encountered a group of females who could be this quiet for so long. There'd hardly been a titter or giggle since I arrived.

I disliked the new carriages, propelled by a steam engine and with no visible driver or engineer. They ran on some sort of magnetic tracking system. Ever since the Moseley-Haft Steam-Promotion Act had been passed by Lord Cosgrove-Pitt and his Parliament, everyone in London had been keen on them and anything else that could be mechanized and automated. The current favorites were the sleek trolleys that were narrow enough to pass along even the uppermost streetwalk levels, the vehicles just wide enough for two people to sit side by side.

The trolley's doors closed. Miss Holmes tensed as I swallowed a thrill of excitement. The only thing I had cause to fear was a vampire . . . and as I didn't sense any UnDead in the vicinity, I settled in for an adventure.

There were no more than a dozen of us. From the amount of *eau de toilette* clogging my nose, it smelled as if each one of those present had spilled an entire bottle of perfume over her bodice. In the close quarters, my eyes began to water, and I had to pinch my nose to keep from sneezing.

My partner murmured street names, landmarks, and observations as we drove along at ground level. I had to reluctantly appreciate her comments. Unlike Miss Holmes, I didn't know the name of every single alleyway, bypass, or mews, let alone the different combinations of street levels and how the addresses worked. I'd always been awestruck by the height of the buildings and how close they swayed toward one another. And I wasn't convinced that the helium-filled sky-anchors attached to the tops of the tall structures did anything to keep their tops from bumping into each other.

More than once, I'd been resigned to walking at ground level because I'd forgotten to bring coins with me. You needed them to insert in the street-lifts to take a ride to the less smelly, cleaner, brighter level of fly-bridge. But I was very familiar with the smell of saltwater, algae, and fish that lingered near the docks, and when those aromas drowned out the perfumes from my companions, I realized we'd reached the East End and shipping yards on the Thames.

"Wapping," Miss Holmes muttered, and I looked out onto the street to see the gaslit sign for that underground railway station. The area was deserted, for trains didn't run this late at night.

When the trolley turned, maneuvering into the narrow passage between the station and its adjoining building, the interior became darker. The car stopped, and I felt my companion's attention sharpen.

A nervous giggle broke the silence, then a loud mechanical hiss startled the girl across from me. The door slid open to reveal a slender female figure holding a lantern. Her features were shadowed in part by a tall hat with a low-riding brim.

"Please disembark, ladies," said the woman, and gestured with a gloved hand.

We exited the trolley car and followed our hostess's mellow golden light down the alley at ground level. I managed to avoid stepping in anything that was soft and smelled disgusting, but Miss Holmes wasn't as agile.

"Drat," she muttered, pausing to scrape her shoe on a stone. "We're going toward the river."

Were they taking us to a boat? I groped in a pocket for my knife. I'd never had cause to use it, and I hoped tonight wouldn't change that. But before we reached the river, our guide gestured to the entrance of an octagonal structure built into the side of Wapping Station. "This way, ladies," she said as we walked through the door into a high-ceilinged, eight-sided chamber.

Although we still wore our cloaks, my companion and I held back. Until now, we'd been protected by our anonymity. But now there was the chance we might be recognized in the brighter light as uninvited guests.

I looked at as many of the hooded faces as I could see, and recognized several. All young women. All my age. Most from upper-class families, some from wealthier trade families. Each one of them vibrated with excitement. No one seemed to notice or care that we had joined them.

The windowed chamber was empty except for a grand staircase that led down into darkness. Dirty gold paint peeled from ornate molding around a high octagonal ceiling. There were other signs of neglect: a ragged chandelier and a few dusty, broken benches.

"The Thames Tunnel," Miss Holmes informed me as we began to shuffle with the rest of the group toward the stairs. "The first underwater tunnel ever constructed. The engineer, Marc Brunel, first proposed his excavation plan to Czar Nicolas of Russia—"

"It goes beneath the river?" I interrupted as the lantern began to descend in the hand of its carrier, leaving the room to darken by degrees.

She nodded. By now, the other young women were following the lantern down the staircase, but my companion seemed more interested in giving me a history lecture. She held back.

"It's part of the Underground now," she told me, speaking rapidly near my ear. "But in the fifties, it was open to the public. People could walk through to the other side of the river, and there were vendors and shops down there and entertainers—"

"Let's go," I said, but her fingers curled around my arm, holding me back.

"I don't think I can. I don't like . . . close, dark places. Deep places."

"Brilliant," I said, peeling her fingers away. "You stay here and keep watch. I'm going down there to see what's happening."

Without a backward glance, I moved toward the grand staircase. I justified abandoning her because she hadn't waited for me at Cosgrove Terrace. Miss Holmes would have left without me if I hadn't shown up. Besides, I was used to working alone. I didn't want anyone hampering me. And it was prudent to have someone keeping watch in case the worst happened.

Not that I thought she'd be all that much help if it did.

I pushed away my gnawing conscience as I hurried down the steps. Some people were meant for adventure, and others—as she'd pointed out to me—were meant to merely *observe*. Miss Holmes could observe all she wanted.

I was going to do something.

My pulse picked up. There could be vampires lurking below, living underground safe from the sunlight. This could be my chance!

The rest of the group had reached a spacious landing, and the glowing yellow lantern led the way down another set of stairs. We were probably a hundred feet below the ground (I was sure Miss Holmes would know exactly how deep the Thames Tunnel was) and for the first time, the handmaker in me wondered why there wasn't a lift or some other mechanized way to descend. The walls yawned around us, and I pushed away a niggle of guilt for leaving her alone. Bloody beans, I wasn't the girl's governess!

Just as I began to start down the second flight, I glanced up and saw a clear white light, very small, bobbing ever so slowly down the stairs.

It had to be Miss Holmes. Blast. Closing my eyes briefly, I let my conscience take over. I waited . . . for a minute. But she was moving so slowly I lost my patience and started back up the steps to meet her.

"Hurry." I tugged on her arm.

She gave a whimper, and then I saw her eyes were closed. I wanted to laugh. Wasn't it darker behind closed eyelids than in here with her light?

"Come on," I said, towing her down the stairs. I think she kept her eyes closed all the way to the bottom. But she kept going, even though her fingers felt like they were digging through my skin and muscle clear to bone. My impatience ebbed when I remembered the way she'd stepped in and helped me last night. She never said a word about my reaction to Miss Hodgeworth's body.

At the bottom of the steps, we found ourselves inside the train station. However, we were on the rear side of the two parallel rows of tracks. Each track disappeared into its own dark tunnel, and I could see light glowing down one of them. A single lantern hung on the far side of the space, casting a weak circle.

"Miss Holmes. You can open your eyes now. It's not dark. Let's go," I said, starting off down the tunnel to the right, where I could see illumination in the distance as well as the lamps glowing at intervals along the tunnel.

As we hurried along the walkway beside the train track, I noticed large, dark archways connecting the two tunnels. Each time we approached one, I peered into the darkness to see if danger lurked. I also carried my knife.

"When the Thames Tunnel was open to the public, the vendors set up shops inside those arches," Miss Holmes informed me. "It was a very busy shopping district for some time. There were a variety of shops, most of which carried imported items and all of which were expensive."

She droned on, and I noticed that the moving lantern ahead of us had disappeared. Our quarry had made a turn, and I had no idea where.

"Hurry," I said.

We had taken a few more steps when two dark shapes emerged from the shadows and stood blocking our way. One of them held something that gleamed silver in the light of his accomplice's lantern.

"An' wha' 'ave we 'ere now, Billy," said the one with the lantern. Grinning, he lifted it high to examine us. And, mackerel's eyes, I could see the bloody sot needed at least three teeth pulled. "Looks'a like we got a coupla nice, prime peaches 'ere."

"A pritty pair, they is," agreed a voice.

From behind us.

I kept the knife hidden in the folds of my skirt. Though my heart was pounding, I made my movements slow and easy as I turned to see what mischief had sneaked up on us. Meanwhile, Miss Holmes dug frantically among her skirts. What good is being armed if you can't get the blasted weapon out when you need it?

Behind us were two more men. One had a wooden truncheon, and the other was flexing his hands. No red eyes, no uncomfortable, prickly chill over my neck . . . these were mortal men. I relaxed. This would be amusing.

"I assume," I muttered, "you don't have that bloody Steam-Stream gun in your skirts."

"No," she murmured back from the side of her mouth. "But I have—"

"Never mind." I turned back just as the man with the knife swiped a hand toward me.

I dodged and then, to his surprise, lunged toward him. My cloak flapping, I caught him in the midriff with my head, sending him tumbling to the ground. Before he even hit the dirt, however, I spun toward the lantern man, whipping my cloak off and into his face as I did so. Kicking out with a well-placed foot, I felt a rush of satisfaction when my shoe connected with a soft area on his person. He squealed like a dry wheel cog and dropped the lantern as he collapsed.

Exhilarated, I turned to meet the man with the truncheon as he rushed up behind me. His club whistled through the air, and with a cry of delight, I ducked beneath it, then leapt behind him as the force of his would-be blow sent him pivoting around to face me.

I glanced over as I surged upright and saw Miss Holmes staring at me, her eyes wide. She held something in her hand, and a dark figure was crumpled on the ground at her feet.

My assailant must also have noticed his companions had been disabled, for he began to back away into the shadows. "Don' mean n'arm t'ye, loydies. Jus' tryin' t'be fren'ly."

I stepped toward him, brandishing my knife, showing him a tight, feral grin. He stumbled backward, then spun and dashed into the darkness.

Knowing my job wasn't done, I turned back to the first two. One of them had dragged himself off, and the other was still a sobbing bundle of skin and bones. He was hardly worth the effort, but I walked over to him and placed my foot on the hem of his coat anyway. "I took it easy on you tonight."

I gave him a good look at my knife. "Next time we meet, I won't be so friendly."

His eyes goggled, and he managed to nod.

"Get out of here," I said, and watched with satisfaction as he crawled off into the darkness. When I turned back to Miss Holmes, she was looking at me as if I'd grown another head. I gestured to the last attacker, who still lay unmoving on the ground. "What did you do to him?"

She handed me a slender metal object and explained, "It sends a little shock of steam. Unfortunately, it only works once, and only at close range."

We vampire hunters had been fighting with stakes and swords and knives for centuries. We didn't need cognoggin gadgets like that. Still . . . I felt a pang of fascination and maybe a bit of envy. "It's brilliant."

"*You* were brilliant. I—you moved so fast! And you're strong. Really strong."

I was a little stunned by her words and admiration, and it took me a moment to respond as I patted my hair back into place and picked up my cloak. "I'm a Venator. It's what I'm called to do. To be."

"And your gown! It's all beyond cleverness to have split skirts—you have such freedom of movement. I shall have to have some of my own made if these sorts of events are going to occur regularly."

"Thank you," I said, choosing not to point out that she could hardly expect to be as accomplished a fighter as I was.

"What I find difficult to comprehend is how you can inflict such pain and violence so easily and yet become ill at the very sight of blood."

My smile faded. "Right. Well, it's quite simple. Vampires don't bleed."

Or so I'd heard.

MISS HOLMES

An Introduction to a Secret Society

F illed with admiration for the way Miss Stoker had flown into action so competently and gracefully, I confess I was a bit distracted as we hurried along the tunnel after our quarry.

That doesn't mean I neglected to take note of the environment: the remnants of old shops in the alcoves, the evidence of human presence and of the nonhuman creatures that existed below the streets. Because of my dislike of dark, deep places, I'd never ventured into the infamous London sewers, where the tosher men lived and dredged up anything of value from the sludgy waste.

We'd lost our group by sight, but we were able to hear them and use the sound as guidance. It led us to a bright tunnel perpendicular to the railroad tracks, and off that tunnel was a room. Its door was open.

Miss Stoker and I approached the chamber, but seemed to draw no attention, for the rest of the young women were standing about talking in small groups.

The place could have been a parlor inside any well-appointed home during an afternoon tea party or musicale. It was lit by numerous electric lights, which gave off a cleaner, whiter light than gas lamps, but had been made illegal by the Moseley-Haft Act. The room was comfortable in temperature without the lingering dampness that pervades underground spaces, and was furnished with rows of upholstered chairs. Rich, heavy fabrics had been draped on the walls, and a small table of refreshments held lemonade, tea, and a generous assortment of biscuits. An odd scent lingered in the air, and I sniffed. Sweet and pungent, with an underlying note of muskiness.

At the front of the chamber stood an imposing statue of Sekhmet. The representation of the half-lion, half-woman stood a head taller than a man. Her regal body was shiny gold, and her leonine snout was rounded and feminine, yet fierce. Despite the fact that Sekhmet was a goddess, she was shown with a male lion's long, smooth mane. As was common in the depiction of any immortal, she had a disk atop her head. This represented her deism in relation to Ra, the sun god. A cobra in mid-lunge curled out from the circle.

Sekhmet's dark eyes captured my attention. Despite the fact they were carved from whatever medium the statue was cast (I couldn't tell for certain if it was gold or merely painted to look that way), those orbs were clear, shiny, and seemed alive.

I suspected this was the same Sekhmet statue that had somehow caused Mr. Dylan Ekhert's mysterious journey.

I turned to the group of young women. Their hoods had become slack, and I could see the faces of many of them. Counting fifteen in the room, I recognized some as familiar, but I knew none of their names. I judged them all to be between sixteen and eighteen years. Each was well dressed, with fancy coiffures and jewelry, and I glimpsed fine fabrics beneath the cloaks, confirming my deduction that they were all attendees of the Cosgrove-Pitt ball. They talked and laughed among themselves, and energy and excitement filled the air. My sharp eyes found no sign of the shadowy figure who'd carried the lantern and led us all to this place.

A delicate chime sounded from near the front of the chamber, and the occupants appeared to take that as a signal to find a seat. Just as Miss Stoker and I slipped into chairs in the last row, a door hidden by one of the wall hangings near the statue opened and the room fell silent. The only sound was from a young woman in front of me. If the noisy masticating coming from the vicinity of her jaw was any indication, she was enjoying a very crunchy biscuit.

In walked two women carrying torches, garbed in long, shimmering golden tunics. Around their necks, covering their shoulders and upper torsos, were the large, circular Egyptian usekh—the iconic gold collars worn by pharaohs. Both women wore heavy black eyeliner that extended beyond the outside corner of each eye and ended in a little circular flourish, as well as blue-shaded coloring on their eyelids. Their dark red lips, pale cheeks, and black hair pulled back into sleek chignons made them appear identical—although observation confirmed that they were not.

The pair walked toward the statue of Sekhmet, each placing a fiery torch in a sconce on either side of it. It was an odd sight: the ancient statuary from Egypt flanked by primitive flaming torches in a modern chamber illuminated by artificial light.

"Welcome to the Society of Sekhmet," said one of the women as they turned to face the group.

"The Ankh is pleased that you have accepted its special invitation," said the other.

Mirror images of each other, they continued to speak in turn, using low, modulated voices. They weren't automatons, but they gave off the impression of being two halves of one whole. I suspected one of them had been the lantern carrier and the second woman had been the owner of the white glove that collected our invitations.

"Now, it is our honor to welcome . . ."

". . . the Most Reverent Ankh."

A hushed rumble filtered over the group. Then it became still and silent, holding its collective breath.

When the two women deemed the small crowd to be properly reverent, they walked back to where they'd entered. One held the fabric covering aside, and the other opened the door. Anticipation crackled through the chamber as a tall, slender figure stepped into view.

At first I thought it was a man, for the individual was dressed in the masculine attire of a black stovepipe hat made popular by the American president Lincoln, along with a well-tailored black frock coat, trousers, and gleaming black shoes. Beneath the coat was a crimson shirtwaist and a waistcoat of black and red paisley. Black gloves, a black neckcloth, and a black walking stick topped by an ornate gold head completed the ensemble.

But as the Ankh walked toward Sekhmet, I became uncertain of his or her gender. The movements were easy and graceful, the facial features and hair were obscured by the hat brim's shadow. From my distant seat, I made out smooth, fair skin, a well-defined jaw, and a long, slender nose. The mouth was full, and the cheeks high, and I revised my opinion toward that of the feminine race. As I scrutinized the individual, I had a niggling feeling I was missing something important.

"Good evening." The Ankh's voice gave no further confirmation or denial of gender. It was smooth, hardly above a whisper, and somewhere in the range of a tenor. Despite its low volume, every syllable reached all corners of the chamber. "I am pleased to be with you at last, dear ladies of the Society of Sekhmet."

Another rustle filtered through the room. It has been my experience that young ladies can never sit still for long, particularly while dressed in corsets and heavy, clinging skirts.

"In the past, some of you attended our salon meetings dedicated to the study of Sekhmet and other fascinating aspects of Egyptology. And some of you have accepted the invitation to join us for the first time this evening. Please accept my apology that tonight's discussion will not be about the meaning of the uraeus, as you might have anticipated. Shall we save that for a more conventional meeting during the daylight hours?"

A few titters indicated that the Ankh had made some sort of joke.

"Indeed," the Ankh said with a dusky laugh, "I am gratified so many of you chose to leave the—what are they calling it? The event of the season?—to join us here in our humble meeting. After all . . . what can one expect from such a production as the Roses Ball when one is a young and single female? Or should I be more precise and call those Society events what they truly are? Competitions. Shows. Horseflesh fairs. *Slave auctions.*"

I leaned forward, intrigued by the Ankh's speech while listening intently for any inflection or accent that might help with identifying the individual.

"I refer to *you* as being the horseflesh—and the slaves— of course, my dearest young ladies. For that is what you are in the eyes of those wealthy, handsome young bachelors—and the not-so-attractive or rich ones as well. The ones whom you'd prefer to ignore when your mamas and papas introduce them to you."

An appreciative reaction—nods, exchanging of glances— from the audience was recognizable as affirmation of the Ankh's words.

"And why is it, I wonder, that *you* are the ones to be paraded about under the watchful eyes of your chaperones whilst waiting for—nay, *pining* for—a glance from the young man you favor? Why is it that *you* are kept pristine, confined in your corsets and your restrictive parlors? Why, I ask of you young ladies, is it the *female* race who must sit still and take pains to be slender and pretty, all the while taking care to have nary a relevant thought in their heads? Why can you not have opinions and adventures, and do interesting and exciting things . . . and why must you be under constant guard by a mother, a maid, or some controlling male? A father, a brother, an uncle . . . a *husband.*"

The Ankh's words were nothing I hadn't thought before, nothing that hadn't settled in my mind as, day after day, I observed the restrictions imposed on others of my gender— particularly of the upper class. I was an unusual case because I existed with little chaperonage and adult interference, but I still experienced the societal restrictions and expectations. And although the suffragettes preached of gaining the right to vote, tonight the Ankh was speaking of concepts beyond politics. Listening to her, I became incensed anew at the plight of my feminine race.

Apparently, I was not alone, for someone clapped and then, all at once, the chamber was filled with the roar of applause. I joined them and noticed Miss Stoker had done so as well. She seemed just as fixated on our speaker as I had been.

The Ankh gave a cool smile to the room and then she (I use the feminine pronoun for simplicity's sake) walked over to the statue. It seemed as if she were consulting with Sekhmet. A fanciful concept to be sure, and I'm certain the Ankh was merely attempting to lead the more gullible and impressionable women in the room to believe it to be the case.

Then the Ankh faced us once more.

"Why can't young ladies choose where they go and what they do? Why do you not have the same *freedom* that your male counterparts do?"

A low rumble swept the room as if the occupants were asking themselves the same passionate questions.

"Ah," the Ankh said, once again employing that cool smile, "but you do. You *have done so*. By accepting the invitation for tonight, you have taken the first step in making a change. In freeing yourselves from restrictions and repressions. Of freeing yourself from being locked away like some bird in a gilded cage—until you are shunted away to a different cage with a husband whom you only *might* love. A husband who will make every little decision for you. A husband who will control whatever you want and need. A husband who will *own* you. He will quite literally *own* you. Yes, my lovelies . . . like a slave.

"No, dear ladies . . . you have all taken the first step on a path of independence and excitement by coming here tonight. By enrolling in the Society of Sekhmet."

I frowned, both fascinated and stymied by the Ankh's speech. Was this a suffragette group, gathering together for women's rights?

And was someone hunting down the members and killing them, making it appear that they had taken their own lives?

Why? Who?

Although strange, the group seemed harmless enough. In fact, the element of adventure and clandestine activity was attractive even to myself. I could only imagine how a young woman such as Lady Hodgeworth, whose most exciting moment of the day was likely determining which frock to wear to afternoon tea, would be roused by this titillating speech. I peeked at Miss Stoker. Surely, being a vampire hunter, she felt much as I did.

The Ankh's voice dropped. "I know what it is you truly want, ladies. You yearn for adventure and excitement. But most of all, you want . . . *him*. Whoever he might be, you want *him*. Is that not the case? Whether you be beautiful or homely, slender or plump . . . whether you have straight white teeth and a demure laugh or protruding ones and a spotted face. Whether you are a rich heiress or one whose family has nothing but a powerful name, you want *him*. You want him to notice you, to want you, to *love* you. And, my dears, I will help you. I, along with the Power of Sekhmet, will help you gain control of your lives in a manner such that women have never done."

She was more animated and passionate than she had been so far. "Despite the fact that we are ruled by a queen, the laws and governance of this country—and this world—are controlled by men. That must change. It *will* change. I will have the power to do so, and those faithful of you shall join me in this change. The day is nigh."

Again, a single clap launched a roar of applause, and it was several moments before it died down again.

The Ankh looked as if she meant to speak further, but all at once, Miss Stoker threw back the hood of her cloak and rose.

I hissed as everyone in the chamber hushed and turned to look back at her. *Sit down!* I shouted in my head. *You brash fool! This wasn't part of the plan!*

"You," said the Ankh, her eyes steady from beneath the brim of her hat. They shifted from Miss Stoker to me and back again. The weight and heat of her stare was shocking, but it seemed to have no effect on my companion.

Then Miss Stoker's voice rang out. "What did you do to Mayellen Hodgeworth?"

MISS STOKER

Miss Stoker's Grudging Regret

The moment I interrupted the speaker, I realized I could have been a little more subtle. Perhaps I should have had some sort of plan. Yet, as pandemonium broke loose, once again I felt energized and in control. Miss Holmes was screeching at me, the other attendees were babbling in shock, and the Ankh was shouting orders.

"Seize them! Hathor! Osiris!" The Ankh cried, then swiveled to point to the twin female hostesses. "Bastet! Amunet!"

Two large men appeared from behind the silken wall-hangings, and the identical women sprang into action. Grinning with exhilaration, I leapt over a row of chairs with ease, putting a cluster of young women and tumbling chairs between me the Ankh's minions.

I wanted to get closer to the Ankh, to see if I could pull off the stovepipe hat that obscured his or her face. But the guards were quick, and even amid the chaos, I was aware of Miss Holmes. I could fight my own way out, but she couldn't.

Time to make our exit. I looked up, judged the distance to the chandelier that hung there, and vaulted up off a chair.

I clocked either Amunet or Bastet on the chin as I swung halfway across the chamber, thanks to the length of the chandelier's chain. I landed exactly where I planned—next to Miss Holmes—and grabbed her by the arm.

Hathor and Osiris, the two large guards, converged on us as the Ankh and her guests watched the chaos unfold. But thanks to my excellent reflexes, speed, and exceptional strength, I created a riotous barrier of chairs and the refreshments table at the door. My partner and I escaped the chamber with nothing more than a ripped hem (Miss Holmes's), a sagging hairdo (Miss Holmes's), and a broken copper-heeled shoe (also Miss Holmes's).

Because I could run and she couldn't, I fairly carried my companion down the long, dark tunnel to escape. By that time, she no longer seemed to appreciate my fighting skills.

Once we were back outside in the fresh night air, I saw that the clouds had rolled in. The moon and stars were obscured. Despite the fact that I had done all the work, Miss Holmes was panting in between demanding to know *what* I was thinking, what had I *done*, did I *realize* what danger I might have put us in, and other variations on that theme.

I ignored her and led the way to the nearest busy thoroughfare and flagged down a hansom cab. A few streets away, behind the new Oligary Building and its belching steam, Big Ben's gears ground rhythmically. A glimpse of his illuminated face through an air-canal told me it was approaching midnight.

Almost three hours since we'd left the party.

"Are you aside of *mad*? I can't show myself in this condition," Miss Holmes snapped when I directed the driver to take us back to Cosgrove Terrace. She was trying to rearrange her hair on the top of her head and having a hard time of it. Her voice was tight. Fury and accusation rolled off her like angry waves.

I felt a little pang of . . . well, it certainly wasn't guilt. It was . . . regret. Maybe.

"Let me help you," I said grudgingly, and slid over to her side of the carriage. I stuck a few pins in place, rearranged the cunning little clockwork hair clips, and adjusted some tendrils of hair over one shoulder.

When I was done, she settled back in the corner. Her nose remained in the air during the entire ride back to the party. My hair was in even worse condition, but did she offer to assist me? She did not. Thus, using a hint of reflection from the carriage windows, I put myself to rights before the cab arrived at the Cosgrove-Pitt home.

"I don't expect to stay very long," Miss Holmes said from between stiff lips as she climbed down from the carriage without waiting for assistance. "Just long enough to go inside and say good evening to our host and hostess. You needn't bother to make your carriage available to take me home, Miss Stoker."

Her spine ramrod straight, she stalked off toward the ascending glider that would take her back into the ball. Her heavy skirts dragged because one of her delicate heels had snapped off during our escape and she had taken off her shoes.

I stifled a smile. Good riddance. And if she was leaving, this would give me the opportunity to find Lady Isabella's study and locate the invitation list after all. It would be a welcome challenge to avoid the scores of young bachelors looking for a rich and pretty heiress to marry. I happen to fall under both categories.

At the party, I eluded Sir Buford Grandine, who had breath that rivaled the stench from the sewers, and Lord Peregrine Perry-Stokes, who, although quite wealthy, had clammy hands and the tendency to pick his nose when he thought no one was looking. Unfortunately, the habit tended to stain the fingertips of his gloves.

I avoided even Mr. Richard Dancy, who was the least offensive of the lot. He was handsome and had a very comfortable income. Unlike most of his peers, he actually asked *me* questions and listened to my answers when we conversed, instead of rambling on about horses or hounds or the newly signed Hartford Act.

But even if a young man *did* show interest in what I might think, I still couldn't allow any of the bachelors into my affections. What young man, even in our modern London of

1889, would understand the duty and role of a female vampire hunter, let alone want to be married to one? What young man would understand or accept a wife who was not only compelled to spend her nights patrolling the streets, but also who was stronger and faster than he?

I wound my way through the ballroom and down the nearest hallway. I'd been to Cosgrove Terrace once before and remembered the basic layout. The deserted corridor lined with closed doors, gilded mirrors, and a few interesting statues led to Lady Isabella's parlor. It was logical that her study was nearby.

The noise of the party faded. I heard only the soft hum of whirring gears and the ever-present *shish* of steam. I tried several doors before I heard someone approaching. I ducked into the next chamber to wait for them to pass.

"Miss Stoker?"

I froze. The door opened, and Mr. Richard Dancy poked his head in.

"Ah, Miss Stoker," he said, "I thought I'd seen you slip away from the festivities. Is everything all right? Whatever are you doing here in the dark?"

Bloody *hell.*

"I needed to attend to . . . a private matter," I replied.

He stepped into the chamber and somehow found the light switch. A soft, mellow glow filtered over the room from the wall sconces, and I realized I had found Lady Isabella's study after all. Now if I could just get rid of my unwanted companion.

"I've been attempting to find you all night, Miss Stoker," he said, closing the door behind him.

He was a handsome young man with light brown hair that curled, falling in thick waves over his forehead. His dark eyes focused steadily on me. It wasn't surprising I had no problem dismissing the impropriety of being alone in a chamber with him.

"And now you have found me," I said. My heart was pounding, but not from fear.

Mr. Dancy remained at a proper distance, leaning against the door. His warm smile made my insides flutter a bit, and I drew myself up sharply. *Focus, Evaline. You've got work to do.*

"I've been looking for you everywhere," he said, and stepped away from the door. "And you seemed to have disappeared. I cannot tell you how many parties and fetes and balls and picnics I've attended this Season, hoping to see you and further our acquaintance. Since your presence is so rare, when I heard your name announced, I thought I'd at last have an opportunity to lead you out for a waltz. And perhaps a stroll on the moonlit terrace?"

"Mr. Dancy . . ." I began, hoping fervently Florence would never learn of his apparent interest in me. She'd have us betrothed in a trice.

"I do wish you would call me Richard, but I suppose it won't be proper until we've come to know each other better. And until we're better acquainted, I don't believe it would be prudent for us to be found in such an inappropriate situation," he added, his smile turning almost shy as he gestured to the room. "I wouldn't want to besmirch your reputation. Perhaps you'd consent to a dance, in full and proper view of an array of chaperones?"

"I'm in complete agreement that we shouldn't be here," I said. Hadn't he been the one to follow me, putting us in this compromising position? "And—" I caught sight of a movement out of the corner of my eye. My heart stopped, then surged back into rhythm.

From where Mr. Dancy was standing, he couldn't see the figure who slipped out from behind a decorative Oriental screen. I wasn't certain if I should call an alarm or deal with the intruder myself. But then I realized *I* was the intruder.

The shadowy figure flashed me a cocky smile, and I jolted with recognition. I'd know that insouciant pose anywhere. *Bloody blasted drat!* And then Pix had the effrontery to raise a finger to his lips. To tell *me* to hush!

Somehow I managed to keep my expression blank when I turned to Mr. Dancy. "And"—I finished the sentence, which had dwindled off for a moment—"I would be honored to have a waltz with you."

He smiled and for the first time, moved toward me. I changed my angle so he wouldn't see Pix in the shadows and accepted Mr. Dancy's offered arm. My mind raced as he led me out of the study. Actually, I was fairly towing him away. How was I going to extricate myself from the dance I'd promised? And from my companion?

Pix's plan was obvious: he intended to rob the place and had somehow gotten himself hired as part of the staff. I had to return to Lady Isabella's study and apprehend him before he filled his pockets.

"Oh, dear," I said, pretending to trip. I bumped into a young woman who was holding a cup of lemonade. It sloshed all over the front of my gown, and the cup landed on the floor with a crash. I danced aside as it shattered. "Oh, my goodness, I'm so terribly sorry," I said, just as she echoed my words.

"What a mess," said the girl. "And your gown!"

"Oh, fiddlesticks," I said, looking up at Mr. Dancy. His expression was a mask of regret, and I felt a twinge of guilt. "I must see to this stain before it sets. And perhaps you could see to getting Miss . . . ?"

"Miss Laurel Bednicoe," said the girl, looking up at my companion with hopeful eyes.

"Miss Bednicoe a new drink while I attend to this?" I asked, gesturing to my damp, lemonade-scented bodice. Drat. The gown was completely ruined.

"Of course," replied Mr. Dancy. He looked down at me with warm eyes and a matching smile. "But please don't take too long. I understand the orchestra stops playing at half past one."

Thus excused, I rushed back to Lady Isabella's study, then paused for a moment before easing the door open. The room was dark once again. I slipped inside and closed the door behind me. And waited, listening and watching.

After a long moment, I judged the chamber to be empty. Drat and bloody blast. Pix had gotten away, likely with sagging pockets filled with . . . well, what would be of value in the study? Surely Lady Isabella didn't keep money here, and most definitely not jewels.

Right. At least I could see to the task that had brought me here in the first place. I needed to find the invitation list. A wisp of moonlight zigzagged in a sliver of illumination, making a jagged line over the rug, a chair . . . and a large writing desk.

Listening for the sound of anyone approaching, I set to searching the drawers of the desk. These weren't simple sliding drawers. It took me a few seconds to figure out I had to flip a switch that unlatched the drawer. Then it eased open with a soft purr. Blasted cognoggin thing.

It was too dark to see clearly, but I didn't dare chance lighting the wall sconces. Hopefully the invitation list would be clearly marked and in large enough writing for me to read. She must keep one, for how would—

A beam of light shot into the drawer I was rummaging.

"Needin' a bit o' glim there, luv? 'Ard t'see what yer buzzin' wivout a light."

I looked to my left. He stood there, cloaked in shadow. How had I not heard him? The man moved like a ghost! Only the hint of chin and cheek were visible from the shadows. He held some slender device that aimed light in a narrow beam. Right over my nosy fingers.

"Is that how you found what *you* were looking for?" I sneaked a sideways glance back down into the illuminated drawer. No invitation list yet.

"I warn't lookin' fer swag, luv," he said, shifting the light as if to give me a better view of his face. "But if ye don' believe me," he said, his voice dropping, "then yer welcome t'turn me over and look fer yerself." His eyes gleamed with humor and challenge. "Surely a bold one like ye'd 'ardly flicker a lash at the doin'."

"I suspect you'd enjoy it entirely too much if I searched you." Blast if my palms didn't go damp at the thought. "But I've no doubt you've found something of value to make off with from Lady Isabella's cache, and I suggest you return it immediately."

"Nay, luv, I ain't got nuffin' on me o' any value nor b'longin' t'anyone but meself," Pix replied, his Cockney so thick I could hardly understand him. "But ne'er say I ain't a gennulman at 'eart. Ye got a rum thin' goin' 'ere, Miss Stoker, but it ain't me place to be makin' like a beak an' judgin' ye on what yer after. I'm cer'n ye 'ave a good reason t'be weedin' through this 'ere desk. 'Low me t'elp ye."

His movements were quick and smooth, and he placed himself on the other side of the enormous desk. Out of my reach, for the moment.

"This drawer here," I said, turning the brass knob that set the mechanism into motion. As Pix beamed the light down, the drawer slid open. I allowed him to think

I trusted him enough to accept his assistance. Once I finished searching and his guard had dropped, I could . . . apprehend him?

That train of thought stopped as if it slammed into a brick wall. My throat went dry at the very idea of engaging in any sort of physical contact with him.

"Wot'sa matter, luv?" Pix asked. "Did ye find what yer lookin' fer?"

I returned my attention to the drawer. And there it was. My aimless rummaging had uncovered what looked like a guest list. I snatched it out of the drawer, giving thanks for small favors, and Pix obligingly moved the light closer.

I heard the sound of voices approaching. Someone bumped against the door, and then the knob began to turn. Pix extinguished his light. The door opened, and I ducked behind a long, heavy curtain. So did he.

What were the chances of us both ending up in the same small place? Unbelievable. But there we were, muffled together in close quarters. His strong fingers closed around my arm, and his solid, warm presence rose behind me. I focused on the fact that Lady Cosgrove-Pitt needed a new downstairs maid because the dratted curtain was really dusty. But overriding that musty scent was a pleasant smoky and minty aroma coming from the man behind me.

"Iffen I din't know any better," he murmured in my ear, "I'd be thinkin' you like slippin' into th' dark wiv me. Two nights in a row, is it?"

Right. He'd be so lucky. Still cloaked by the curtain, I moved as far away from him and his arrogance as possible. But I couldn't go far, because two people had entered the chamber. From behind the curtain, I couldn't see anything but a glow of light, which implied the new arrivals had no reason to hide their presence. They were also speaking with no attempt to keep their voices down. Servants. I could tell by their speech and accents.

Pix's soft, warm breath buffeted against my ear and temple, and I had to close my eyes against the distraction. It was almost impossible to keep my breathing steady and my heart from pounding. Drat him anyway.

Was that his mouth against my hair? Just above my ear? I bit my lip as warm sizzles rushed from my sensitive ear down through my body. When I got out of this situation, I was going to drag this rogue of a pickpocket down to Newgate and toss him into a cage myself.

"Ye smell nice," he had the effrontery to say. In my ear. *While there were people in the room.* "Ver' nice, luv. Like . . . mmm . . . lemonade."

Lemonade? I heard the laughter in his voice and wished I dared to expose him right then and there to whoever was in the room. Blasted man.

Desperate to put some space between us without shifting the curtain, I turned my attention to what was happening beyond the dusty velvet swags. By the conversation, it was obvious two maids had been sent by their mistress to retrieve something from the study. They found whatever they were looking for and left the chamber before Pix created any more mischief behind our curtain.

As soon as the door closed behind them, I flung the velvet panel aside and erupted into the cool, clean air. Thanks to Pix, my cheeks were burning hot. I turned back to confront him, and I heard a soft creak. The curtains moved, and then all at once, I smelled the fresh night air.

No! I got to the open window just in time to see a figure land on the ground one story below. He did a neat somersault and then disappeared into the shadows.

Incensed, I considered going after him. My ear still felt warm, and my palms were damp. I didn't care if I ever saw him again, except to point him out to Scotland Yard. But I still held the invitation list, and that was all that mattered. I had what I came for.

Two minutes later, I finished reading it, and I had at least one answer.

Mayellen Hodgeworth was on the list.

MISS HOLMES

An Unwanted Encounter

The day after the ball at Cosgrove Terrace, I was in my laboratory working on a new project. Like Uncle Sherlock, I spent a great amount of time conducting studies and experiments, and writing treatises. On this particular day, I was making notations for an instructional paper I intended to write regarding the residues of various powders and creams, in particular those found in a woman's boudoir.

Unfortunately, I found myself distracted by the events of the prior evening; in particular, the brazen actions of my partner. Miss Stoker's impulsiveness had endangered not only our persons, but our mission. I had no inclination to continue to partner with such a capricious person. And much as I wanted to speak with Miss Adler about the situation, the lady wouldn't arrive at her offices at the museum until two o'clock. Thus I had to wait until then to travel across town and apprise her of the events of last night.

I was about to set flame to a dish of geranium-scented Danish facial powder when I was interrupted by a knock on the door. I extinguished the flame and set the finger-size steam-thrower aside. "Come in," I called, raising my protective goggles.

Mrs. Raskill had learned early on not to heedlessly follow these instructions, but to enter the laboratory with care. Her hesitation stemmed from an incident several years ago when she'd walked in during an experiment with bees. I was properly protected, but she, alas, was not. The multitude of stings she acquired was one of the reasons she wasn't a particularly attentive chaperone. I could be in the laboratory for days, and she wouldn't notice, for she only bothered me if necessary.

"A parcel has arrived for you," she said, poking her head around the door as her eyes scanned the chamber for reasons to retreat.

A package? I was immediately suspicious and on guard. I had been expecting some sort of reaction or response from the Ankh—an abduction attempt or even a threatening letter. Possibly a *package*. After all, both my father and uncle regularly received such articles, and my uncle had been in perilous situations more than once.

"How did it come to be delivered?" I asked, eyeing it in speculation.

"It's from the Met," Mrs. Raskill told me.

My concerns dissipated in a rush of disappointment. It would have been interesting to determine how to open a package without setting off the bomb that might be inside. However, as the Met was a reference to the Metropolitan Police, my concerns were alleviated. There was no reason the police would send me a bomb. But nor could I fathom a reason they would send me a package of any type.

Apparently deciding it was safe to breach my inner sanctum, Mrs. Raskill entered. As always, her gray-streaked black hair was pulled into a no-nonsense bun at the back of her head. Not one tendril dared escape, even during her most active days. I often wondered whether she used some sort of shellac to keep it in place.

Although our housekeeper barely reached my chin, she managed to convey a sense of disapproval as she handed me a package about the size of a small book. I wasn't certain if today's disapproval was due to the disarray of my lab or the implication that I was involved with the police.

I took the parcel, examining it closely.

Atop: my name written neatly, but with many splotches and streaks of ink—*a bad pen, or someone in great haste. Left-handed.*

No other markings, and the wrappings were yesterday's newspaper; little clue as to the sender. I began to pull the paper off and the object slipped out and clattered to the table.

"What in land's end is that?" Mrs. Raskill exclaimed, moving closer to gawk at the sleek metal object.

"It's nothing of import," I said. But my fingers tingled as I picked up the device that had lately been in the possession of Mr. Dylan Eckhert. Why would he send this back to me after stealing it from my bedchamber?

Or had someone else sent it?

"I ain't seen nothing like that before," Mrs. Raskill said. Her tiny, rabbit-like nose was fairly wriggling with curiosity. "Is it a fancy mirror? What does it do?"

"It could be an explosive," I suggested, hefting it in my palm and attempting to appear concerned.

She edged away. "I'd best get back to the kitchen. The bloomin' Gussy-Maker's not workin' right again. I'll be havin' Ben comin' by to take a look at it later. Maybe you'll invite him to dinner."

Ben was Mrs. Raskill's cloud-headed nephew, and although he was quite competent when it came to fixing mechanical devices, he was not at all the sort of company I preferred for dinner. I didn't actually prefer any company for dinner—or any other meal, for that required me to relinquish whatever book I was reading or experiment I was conducting in favor of inane conversation on topics such as whether it had been foggy, drizzling, or foggy *and* drizzling today.

"Thank you, Mrs. Raskill," I said, still staring down at the device. Mr. Eckhert had said it was a type of telephone, but once again, I couldn't see how.

As the housekeeper took herself off, I picked up the newspaper wrapping to see if anything else was enclosed. Inside, I found a further message. It was short and simple: *Please come. I'm in jail.*

I considered whether I wanted to have further involvement with the young man who sneaked out of my house without so much as leaving a note in gratitude for my hospitality, *and* who sneaked into my bedchamber and stole this device from me.

Curiosity got the best of me, and I also appreciated the distraction from my aggravation toward Miss Stoker.

I made certain I wasn't followed during my journey across town, and no more than thirty minutes later, I was alighting from a street-lift at the lowest level of Northumberlandavenue. The police commissioner and his men entered the offices at Lower Whitehall No. 4, but the public came in through the rear entrance off Great Scotland Yard, which was how the police headquarters got its familiar name.

For all my uncle's complaints about the Met and the incompetency of its Criminal Investigation Division, the individuals I met inside were quite efficient in assisting me to find Mr. Eckhert. I'm certain my surname was an incentive.

Moments after my initial inquiry, I was escorted down a curving, dark staircase to a subterranean cell-lined hall. We passed several chambers, dark and dingy, scented with sweat, blood, and other unpleasant aromas, until at last we reached Mr. Eckhert's cell.

"Mina!" he said when he saw me. He clambered to his feet from where he'd been slumped on the floor in a shadowy, dismal space. Rushing over, he grabbed the bars with both hands. "Thank God you came!"

I concealed my surprise at his informal use of my given name as well as his language. Instead, I turned to the constable. "Thank you," I said, dismissing him. "I shall see myself out."

"What are you doing in here?" I said, turning back to Mr. Eckhert. "Did you come upon another murder scene?" I noted he'd stolen clothes from my father's closet.

The trousers were the correct length, and the shoes seemed to fit. But the coat and shirtwaist were too rumpled and loose, for, despite being slender elsewhere, my father has a healthy paunch. The prisoner had either lost his gloves and neckcloth or hadn't seen fit to obtain either from my father's wardrobe.

"Thank you for coming," Mr. Eckhert said, pressing his face into the metal posts as if he could somehow pass through. His nose and a small wing of blond hair protruded from between the bars. "I didn't know who else to call or what to do. Thank you."

"What happened?" I asked again, feeling a twinge of sympathy for the foreigner, despite my misgivings. Even dirty and a bit pungent, he was still very handsome. His blue eyes were soft and filled with admiration and gratitude.

I couldn't remember the last time someone had been so glad to see me.

"Can you get me out of here?" he asked. "I think . . . I think I understand that they'll let me out on bail. I don't understand your money system, but I sent you my cell—my phone. My telephone. As payment."

Something inside me shifted in the face of his obvious desperation and fear, and whatever hesitation I had about him evaporated. "Why have they arrested you?"

His forehead bumped against the bars, making a dull clunk and rattle. "They caught me trying to break into the museum last night. I was trying to get inside so I could look for the Sekhmet statue. I didn't know what else to do."

I lifted an eyebrow. "If you hadn't sneaked away yesterday morning without talking to me, I could have assisted you." I declined to mention I'd seen his Sekhmet statue only last night, and not at the museum.

"I know, I *know*," he said, bumping his forehead against the bars again. "It was stupid. But I didn't want you to ask me a bunch of questions, and I just wanted to . . ." He sighed. "Whatever. Mina, will you help me? I don't have anyone else, and . . . I want to go home. I don't belong here."

His blue eyes fastened on me. There was something in his gaze that tugged at me. At that moment, I realized I'd walk across a bed of nails for this young man.

I don't belong here.

How many times had *I* felt that way?

I tamped down the soft feelings welling inside and replied tartly, "Yes, I'll help you. I can arrange bail and release you, and even assist if charges are pressed. But I require two assurances in return."

"What? Anything, Mina. Anything."

"You'll tell me everything, and you won't abscond again."

"Abscond? Oh, yeah." He nodded against the bars. "I was stupid to run away. I've come to realize that if anyone can help me, it's Sherlock Holmes's niece. As weird as that might be," he muttered. "If you get me out of here, Mina, I promise you won't be able to get rid of me."

"Very well, then," I said, trying to subdue the burst of fluttering in my insides at his words. "I'll return as soon as I've made the arrangements."

I was just signing the last of the papers to release Mr. Eckhert into my custody when a familiar voice interrupted.

"What brings you to Scotland Yard, Miss Holmes?"

I managed to keep my handwriting from jolting. Nevertheless, I chose to finish authenticating the documents instead of turning to confront Inspector Grayling.

But the clerk behind the desk wasn't as circumspect.

"Why, Miss Holmes here, she's postin' bail for a real shady character what we got us in custody down below."

Grinding my teeth, I shoved the papers at the clerk, then turned to Grayling. "I'm quite certain, Inspector, that my presence here could be of no interest to someone as busy as yourself. Surely you're needed at some crime scene. Far from here."

Grayling ignored my comment. "Posting bail for a criminal? What's he in for, Fergus?"

My mouth opened and then closed, and I could feel my cheeks heat. He must have learned from the Hodgeworths how I'd obtained the invitation. Not that I'd done anything illegal; Mrs. Hodgeworth had given Miss Adler and myself permission to take the card.

"I believe I've misjudged you, Miss Holmes." Grayling's Scottish burr had become more evident, and his eyes were as cold as the sea in December. "I supposed you were merely playing at detective, trying to be like your uncle. But when you returned from the Star Terrace last night after an extended period of time in the dark gardens—and not alone, I wager—I can only assume you have placed yourself in untenable situations. What is your intention?"

By now I had drawn myself up straight [and bris]tling. "My intentions are none of your

His cheeks had gone ruddier, an[d his lips pressed in a] flat line. "Miss Holmes, when you ret[urned] your lengthy disappearance, it was quite of activities you'd been engaged. Your ha skirts were rumpled, and one of your g And now I find you here, at the Met, posti prisoner. You are obviously fraternizing wit of young men."

Incensed by his accusations and assump hardly keep from gasping in outrage. How dar have berated him in return, except that he was s

The clerk shuffled through the sheaf of documents and said, "Attempted robbery. Breaking, entering. Was appr'-hended trying to get into the museum last night."

Grayling's hazel eyes speared me. "So criminals are the sort you prefer to consort with, Miss Holmes?"

"Thank you, Mr. MacGregor," I said to the clerk, and snatched up the document granting Mr. Eckhert release. "I can find my own way to the constable." I lifted my chin and spun on my heels.

Despite my speed, I'd progressed only a short way down the passage when Grayling's long legs caught him up to me.

"Miss Holmes, I don't know what you've become involved with, but—"

"Inspector Grayling," I said, pausing at the intersection of two corridors as I tried to determine which way to go. "I cannot imagine why you should concern yourself with my activities. Should you not be investigating the murder of Miss Hodgeworth? Instead of attending Society balls?"

"Miss Holmes," he said, stepping closer. I backed up into the wall behind me. He was as close as he'd been last night when we were waltzing, and the very realization set me off balance.

"Miss Holmes," he repeated, "I am investigating the murders of two young women, along with the disapp—of a third—likely also murdered. Everythin—is my concern. Particularly since—ning in the place of on—

close to me. So close I might brush against him if I should express my deep anger as passionately as I felt it.

"Does your father know of your nocturnal activities, Miss Holmes? And what of your uncle? If he were aware, I wager he'd put an immediate end to them."

His statements were absurd. My father cared little for how I spent my time. And Uncle Sherlock was only slightly more interested in me, simply because he knew I was a loyal audience for his lectures and that, unlike Dr. Watson, I actu-ally learned from him.

"If you please, Inspector Grayling." My voice was clipped with fury. "I have more important things to attend to than continuing this offensive exchange. And I'm certain you do as well. Good day."

His eyes bored into me as I edged away. I could feel his angry stare between my shoulder blades as if he held the bar-rel of a Steam-Stream gun there. And of course, the moment I was out of his presence, I thought of all sorts of cool, smart things I could have said to put him in his place.

I was so discombobulated I went in the wrong direction, and it took me some time to relocate the constable who could release Mr. Eckhert. However, a short time later, the newly released prisoner and I retraced those steps on our way to the outside. We obtained his meager belongings—a small sack which I deduced contained his foreign clothing.

I decided to take Mr. Eckhert with me to the British Museum when I went to speak with Miss Adler, and as it was approaching two o'clock, I felt the necessity to make haste. But that was not to be, for as we rounded the corner, passing several policemen dressed in their blue uniforms and sturdy hats, we came upon a small cluster of people blocking the corridor.

In the center of the group rose two heads that made my stomach plummet. One of them was that of a tall Scot with a high forehead and curling, rust-colored hair.

The other . . . oh, *blast*.

"Alvermina! What the devil are you doing here?"

"Hello, Uncle Sherlock."

Miss Holmes
In Which Miss Holmes Gives a History Lesson

I looked up at the tall, spare man around whom the others had crowded. As always, he was clean-shaven and his dark hair neatly combed. He held a hat in long, slender fingers. His coat was brushed, and his trousers were without a speck of mud.

I tried not to think about the fact that he'd just announced my abomination of a name to the entire Metropolitan Police force.

"Greetings, Dr. Watson," I added. My uncle's cohort was shorter than he and of a stocky frame, but by no means chubby. He wore a close-trimmed mustache of chestnut brown and professional, yet out-of-fashion, clothing. Small round spectacles perched on his nose.

I avoided looking at Grayling, for I could only imagine the expression on his face.

My uncle had turned his regard upon Mr. Eckhert, who was staring unabashedly at him. My newly liberated friend exclaimed, "Sherlock Holmes! I can't believe it's really you!"

"You're living at my brother's house, I perceive," said my uncle. "Since arriving in London, you've been a vagrant and homeless. But my niece has taken you in and now has had to bail you out on a charge of breaking and entering. The British Museum, if I'm not mistaken."

Mr. Eckhert's expression turned to one of shock and bald admiration—both of which were common to people upon experiencing Sherlock Holmes for the first time. I wondered if I would ever have that sort of effect on people.

"How did you know that?" my friend asked.

"It's information there for anyone to see," began my relative in his aggrieved way. "One must observe—"

"Never mind," I interrupted. I was one of the only people in London besides my father who would dare do so. Even the shorter, less elegant but more approachable Watson was intimidated by his friend at times. "Uncle Sherlock, I'll be by Baker-street soon to return the item you—erm—loaned me. You must be on an important case, or you wouldn't be here at Scotland Yard. I shan't keep you any longer."

And then, as if it had been I who'd accosted him instead of the reverse, I excused myself to the rest of the group. In doing so, I caught Grayling's gaze before turning away. His eyes were narrow with wariness and aggravation, flickering from me to Mr. Eckhert and back again.

"I can't believe that was Sherlock Holmes. *The* Sherlock Holmes," Mr. Eckhert said in an undertone as he walked in step with me. "He really *is* as brilliant as in the stories."

I rolled my eyes. "I don't suppose it was that difficult for him to make those deductions. You're wearing my father's clothing—that, along with the ill fit, would indicate your vagrant state and the fact that I took you in. And as for the details about your bail, well"—I gestured with the paper I held—"I suspect my uncle read the details on your release document. He's notorious for reading upside down and backward, and he would recognize the type of document used for bail."

"Wow," Mr. Eckhert said, pausing to glance over his shoulder as if to catch one more glimpse of my famed relative. "And Dr. Watson too. They both look just as I imagined them."

"Mr. Eckhert, do you think you could cease fawning over them and hurry along? There's someone back there I would prefer to avoid. And we're going to the museum now."

I picked up my pace, and my companion fell into step with me. Although he was in need of freshening up, I decided it would be best to get to Miss Adler as soon as possible. There would be a place for him to wash up at the museum.

"London," said Mr. Eckhert as we walked outside of the building, "is so different than I remem—imagined. It's so . . . close. And tight, and dark. There's no grass or trees, and it smells. The buildings are on top of each other and so tall. Walking down the street isn't like being outside, it's like being *inside* a really massive building—like a huge shopping ma—uh. I mean, all of the bridges and walkways and everything. And those open elevators—what do you call them? Lifts? It's always so dark and foggy and gray. And what are those things up there? They look like huge balloons at the tops of the buildings." He pointed to the sky-anchors. A half dozen of them swayed high above our heads.

Before I could respond, I heard a familiar purring rumble. We both turned to see a steamcycle roar around the building and down the street. Gliding at knee height above the ground, smooth and sleek and fast, it blasted past us in a blur of copper and a tail of white steam. The long, flapping black coat of its driver fluttered in its wake, and he was bent over the handlebars, eyes protected by large goggles, hands by brown gloves. On his head was an aviator hat that I suspected covered ginger-colored hair.

"Sweet!" Mr. Eckhert exclaimed, stopping to gawk after the cycle. "What was that? A motorcycle?"

"It's called a steamcycle. Usually, they aren't quite so fast. Or loud. Or . . ." Sleek. Cognogged. "It's probably an illegal vehicle, at any rate." I made no effort to hide my exasperation. "I wouldn't be surprised if there was some electrical mechanism beneath that steam engine."

Mr. Eckhert had a strange expression on his face as I started in the direction of the museum, but then he paused and sniffed. Something delicious was in the air, and I couldn't remember the last time I'd eaten.

"Something smells good," he said. "The food they gave me in jail was disgusting."

"The best street vendors are on the middle and upper levels," I said. Since one had to pay to ascend in the lift, the better vendors knew where the most profitable customers were.

The enticing scents wafting down from the carts selling items like roasted apple puffs, vanilla-stick coffees, and flaming carrots were all the urging I needed to dig out five pence for our entrance to the street-lift. I had a particular fondness for the soft, sweet carrots on a stick.

Moments later, we stepped off the street-lift and heard the ornate brass door clang shut behind us. Mr. Eckhert led the way to a small cart of the flaming carrots, and I selected the largest of the offerings. I purchased two, as well as an egg biscuit for my companion, who claimed he was starving.

He said something about egg mick-muffins and ate the biscuit in three large bites as I held the two carrots on their sticks, waiting for the flames to burn out. I showed him where to throw the wrapping from his food into the sewer-chute and handed him his carrot with a warning: inside, beneath a thin sugary crust, the carrot would be soft, sweet, and steaming hot.

"What did you mean earlier about electrical mechanisms being illegal?" Mr. Eckhert asked, then was distracted by the sight of a Refuse-Agitator. The self-propelled vehicle was doing its duty far below at ground level by rolling through one of the small sewer canals, likely pulverizing the trash he'd just discarded. Little clouds of black smoke puffed from a duo of pipes as it chugged along.

"'The generation, utilization, and storage of electrical or electro-magnetic power is prohibited,'" I said, quoting directly from the Moseley-Haft Act.

Mr. Eckhert stopped there on the sidewalk and nearly got himself run over by a knife-sharpener and his motorized cart. "Are you saying that *electricity* is *illegal*?"

"Yes, of course. It's a widespread safety threat."

"That's crazy! Haven't you people ever heard of Thomas Edison?"

"Yes, of course I've heard of Thomas Edison. Everyone's heard of him. It's because of him and his unsavory activities that the law was passed."

Mr. Eckhert gaped at me. "What year did you say this was?"

"It's 1889," I said, finishing the last bite of my sweet, warm carrot. "Victoria is Queen. Lord Salisbury is the prime minister. Lord Cosgrove-Pitt is the leader of Parliament. Now, shall we walk? I don't wish to dawdle any longer, and, Mr. Eckhert, the sooner you get to a washroom, the—er—less attention you'll be drawing to yourself. Which I deduce was the reason you borrowed my father's clothing—so that you could blend in with other Londoners. Incidentally, a gentleman never goes about without gloves."

"Okay, I'm walking," he said, looking at his hands as if to see whether gloves had magically appeared. "Tell me about this law. I don't remember learning anything in school about a law making electricity illegal."

At his cryptic words, a funny shiver went through my insides. Despite the fact that I'd been immersed in the problem of Miss Hodgeworth's death and the Sekhmet mystery, questions about Mr. Eckhert and his origins had never been far from my mind. I'd analyzed the facts over and over and had only come to one conclusion.

An unbelievable conclusion.

But my uncle's favorite maxim had been pounded into my head from a young age. *When you have excluded the impossible, whatever remains, however improbable, must be the truth.*

I turned to answering his question. "Seven years ago, there was a time when it seemed as if the civilized world would adopt the use of electricity to power everything mechanical. But it became clear how dangerous it is when fifteen people were electrocuted by a wire in New Jersey during a rainstorm. Mr. Edison tried to cover up the incident, but Mr. Emmet Oligary, one of the foremost businessmen in London, made certain it was written about in the papers. The scandal was exposed, and it became obvious that widespread use of electricity was a real danger to society. Mr. Oligary led the charge to make certain all of England was aware of the insidious dangers of electrical power. His brother-in-law,

Lord Moseley, consulted with Parliament to craft and pass the law in 1884."

"Let me guess," said Mr. Eckhert as we approached the wide flight of steps to the British Museum. "Mr. Oligary had a bunch of factories running on steam engines." His expression was grim. "Probably manufacturing the parts to them, even."

"Of course he did. The steam engine was just becoming popular at that time. And now we use that technology for everything. Good afternoon, sir," I said to the guard at the door of the museum.

He looked with suspicion at the disheveled Mr. Eckhert, but when I glared at him with a level gaze of my own, the guard gestured us through. The heavy glass doors, framed in brass, clicked and whirred as they folded open. I led the way through the Banksian Room to Miss Adler's office. It was nearly quarter past two.

"Good afternoon, Mina," said Miss Adler when we were given entrance to her office. She was sitting at her desk, with a small mechanical device poised over an open book. It appeared to be a magnifyer of some sort and was clicking in a pleasant rhythm. "And . . ." She looked at my companion, then back at me and rose to her feet.

"Miss Adler, I have an abundance of information to share with you in regard to the events of last night, but first I'd like you to meet Mr. Dylan Eckhert. You might recognize him from our previous encounter, over Miss Hodgeworth's body. I've learned he came to London in an unlikely fashion. I am going to help him find a way to return home."

"Mr. Eckhert, I'm pleased to officially meet you." It was to the gentlelady's credit that she showed no reaction to his disheveled and aromatic appearance—which was such a contrast to her own neat, fashionable self.

"Hello, Miss Adler. Irene Adler. Wow," he said, his voice hushed. "This is so weird."

My heart was pounding, for I was about to take a great chance. I would either be correct, or I'd humiliate myself. But of course that was impossible. My conclusions were never wrong. They simply couldn't be. "Mr. Eckhert, perhaps you would be so kind as to tell Miss Adler where you're from. Specifically, from what *year* you've traveled."

The others looked at me—Miss Adler with unrestrained shock and Mr. Eckhert with something like relief.

"So you've figured it out . . . and you believe me," he said, looking at me with those blue eyes again. This time, they were filled with gratitude and enough warmth to make my insides go awhirl. He straightened up, closed his eyes, and then opened them. Exhaling a deep breath, he said, "I'm from the future. The year 2016."

For a moment I was stunned. Not because my conclusion had been confirmed, but because he'd come from so far—more than a hundred years ahead. Countless questions popped into my head. Where did one begin?

"What's it like?" I asked. "There, in 2016?"

"It's very different . . . and not so different. For one thing, it's not so . . . dim and dark all the time. And electricity isn't illegal," he added. "It's *never* been illegal. It's not a threat to society any more than—than steam. Or horse-drawn carriages."

More and more questions poured into my mind like sand funneling down through an old-fashioned timekeeper, but I ruthlessly shoved them away. I could interrogate him later—and I fully intended to do so. But now was not the time.

Miss Adler had been staring at my companion. And now she said, "Truly—2016?"

"Yes, for real. And, like, could you just call me Dylan? Or Eckhert, as my friends do? I can't deal with this Mr. Eckhert stuff."

"Of course, Dylan," Miss Adler said, seeming to recover herself. "If it will make you feel more comfortable."

"Mr. Eckhert traveled here with the help of an illuminated scarab on a statue of Sekhmet. At just about the same time Miss Hodgeworth was being murdered. It cannot be coincidence that those two events happened concurrently."

"Of course not," she agreed.

"He was arrested trying to break into the museum last night, presumably to try and find the Sekhmet statue so he could determine how to return home. I was able to get him released on bail, and we've come directly from the jail."

"I did hear about the attempted break-in. And what a traumatic experience you've had." Miss Adler still wore an expression of shock, and I couldn't blame her. After all, I'd had more than a day to come to the conclusion . . . and yet, I still couldn't fathom the concept. *Time travel?* "Perhaps you'd like to—er—wash up a bit, Dylan?" she suggested. "I'm certain we could obtain some clean clothing for you as well."

When our guest accepted the offer with alacrity, Miss Adler added, "Mina, perhaps you'd take a moment to read this passage while I show Dylan to a washroom." She gestured to the open book on her desk. "I suspect you'll find it enlightening."

As they left, I settled myself in her position at the desk and took note of the large book. The pages were old and yellow, held together not by the stitched leather binding we find on current publications but by large, looping leather thongs. The text was cramped and faint, and simple sketches broke up the blocks of prose. The words were handwritten rather than typeset and in a variety of colors and styles. The mechanical device on which Miss Adler had mounted the tome not only provided light, it also magnified the text and held the book open to the proper page.

The line drawing of a lion-headed woman drew my attention. Beneath it, in flowing, fading text, was a poem or song. It took me a moment to decipher the cramped, ornate entry, and even then, I passed over some words and phrases when they were blotched or unreadable.

> *Sekhmet, the Goddess of Death, shall be called back to life.*
> *Shall endow Her strength and power upon those deserving.*
> *Gather Her Instruments, meld them whole ——*

With the purest of sacrifices shall find the — power.
For the Power of Sekhmet shall rise in vengeance
For the weak and restrained.

A little shiver went down my spine. Last night, the Ankh had referred to "the Power of Sekhmet."

The day is nigh, the Ankh had said.

What were the instruments?

Gather Her Instruments, meld them whole . . .

I examined the pages, trying to find further reference to the instruments or to the Power of Sekhmet. From what I was able to glean from the book, it seemed to be a collection of Egyptian and Sumerian legends and writings.

After carefully turning one more crisp, browned page, I found an entire leaf devoted to them: *The Instruments of Sekhmet: Her Scepter. Her Diadem. Her Cuff. Her Sistrum.*

There were drawings of them all. First, the tall scepter with a lion's head. A detail in the drawing indicated a green gem for the feral feline's eye, and its long, smooth, mane running the entire length of the staff.

Sekhmet's diadem appeared to be a delicate, filigreed object—not at all Egyptian in appearance. It looked as if it were made from slender golden curves and twists, but upon closer examination, I realized it too depicted a lion. A feminine snout at the front of the diadem was combined with the leonine mane that curled and curved in an ethereal shape that would hug the crown of the head.

The cuff was a smooth, flat, metal band that enclosed the wrist. The drawing was faded and mottled, making it difficult to see much detail. With the help of the magnifyer and a bit of patience, I was able to discern that the fastener which held the bracelet closed was made of two almond-shaped feline eyes.

The sistrum, a small musical instrument, resembled an ankh in the drawings: it was cross-shaped and had a loop in place of the top, upright bar.

The door to the office opened, and in walked Miss Adler, accompanied by Dylan. He was clean, shaved, and dressed in proper English clothing, with the exception of gloves. I didn't bother to ask how she had arranged it; there was no sense wasting time on such trivial details.

He looked very British, yet he still seemed . . . different. With his long hair flipping up gently in random places and the slender, blue rubber bracelet he wore, along with the manner in which he stood and moved, he exuded foreignness. He reminded me of a cat reluctantly dressed up in child's clothing—subdued for the moment, but not in his natural habitat. Not terribly different from how I'd felt at Lady Cosgrove-Pitt's ball, dolled up and thrust into an unfamiliar environment.

Shifting under my regard, Dylan gave me a sort of lopsided smile and tucked a finger inside the collar of his shirtwaist, tugging sheepishly at the neckcloth.

"I trust you found the reading relevant?" Miss Adler said, redirecting my attention.

"Indeed. I have much to tell you, for this makes what I learned last night clearer." I launched into an explanation of the events surrounding the Roses Ball and our unexpected adventure. It was with great effort that I managed to keep an accusatory tone from my voice as I described Miss Stoker's foolhardy actions—from leaving me behind at the top of that long, dark, subterranean flight of stairs, to her bold accusation of the Ankh.

"Fortunately we were able to escape, thanks in part to Miss Stoker's physical capabilities," I said, keeping the begrudging tone from my voice with effort.

"The leader's name was the Ankh?" Miss Adler said.

"Yes. Clearly nothing more than a symbolic name. *Ankh,* of course, means 'life' and is a common icon in Egyptian culture." I could have lectured further, but Miss Stoker wasn't present, and surely Miss Adler was already familiar with the symbol.

"And you weren't certain of the individual's gender?" she asked.

"Even employing my powers of observation, I could draw no clear conclusion. There were moments when *she* seemed feminine, and others when I was certain *he* had to be a male. But aside from that, the most important thing we've learned is that there is indeed a society related to Sekhmet. I neither saw nor felt anything that indicated danger to me or anyone else, with the exception of when Miss Stoker drew attention to herself and they attempted to detain us."

What had also occurred to me, but I chose not to mention, was that the Ankh had seemed to easily make the connection of me to Miss Stoker—simply because we were standing next to each other.

"Thus, if I'm to revisit the Society of Sekhmet, which I intend to do, I must do so clandestinely." I went on to repeat—verbatim—what the genderless speaker had said during the meeting. "The Ankh promoted female independence, but not once did she speak of the right to vote."

"So it isn't merely a suffragette group," said Miss Adler. "But something more . . . and something that is endangering young women. I will report to Her Royal Highness this evening."

"The Ankh spoke of Sekhmet helping the young women. She said 'I, along with the Power of Sekhmet, will help you gain control of your lives in a manner such that women have never done.' *The Power of Sekhmet.* That same phrase is notated here in the book. And the Ankh spoke of women being repressed and controlled . . . and in the book, there is reference to the goddess's power rising up in vengeance for the weak and restrained."

"I believe," Miss Adler said, picking up her spectacles, "we have quite a lot of research to do. We must find out more about the Instruments of Sekhmet as well as this implication that she can be called back to life."

A week ago, I might have found such a conversation ludicrous. Calling a goddess back to life? Absurd. But the young man standing across the chamber from me had opened my eyes to the impossible becoming probable.

I turned to Dylan. "It would be helpful if you showed us where you woke and where the statue of Sekhmet was when you originally discovered it. Your journey and its disappearance—and perhaps this entire case—must be connected."

My new friend agreed, and we left the chamber. Miss Adler elected to remain behind, explaining, "I have a variety of resources that could assist us—papers, books, scrolls, and other antiquities. I'll begin to gather them."

Despite the fact that he'd traveled more than a century back in time, Dylan seemed to know his way through the museum. It was just after closing, so the exhibit halls were empty and silent except for the low rumble of distant cogworks and a sibilant hiss of steam. The lamps had been turned off and a smattering of external light filtered in through high windows.

As we approached the trio of Graeco-Roman salons, I observed the way a sliver of sun made a triangular highlight over the breast of the Ostian Venus. We walked through the first salon, past elegant statues of the Muses, Mercury, and the goat-eared Satyr.

Our footsteps made soft padding sounds as we passed through a little transept approaching the long, narrow Egyptian Gallery. This was where the famous Rosetta Stone, among other antiquities, was displayed. The stone itself was on a circular dais, and a revolving glass enclosure had been erected around it for safekeeping.

"They've placed an entire glass case around it now—er, in my time," Dylan commented as we walked past.

He led me through a darker salon and then to a small stairwell. This area of the museum was cluttered and dusty, with crates and boxes stacked in haphazard fashion. Presumably, it was one of Miss Adler's duties to unpack, arrange, and catalog the contents.

I have an excellent sense of direction, and even after several turns and descents, I still knew our whereabouts in the museum. So when Dylan paused outside a small, dingy room, I recognized that we were on the west side, two levels below the Assyrian Basement.

"In here," he said.

I pulled the slender illuminator from my reticule and flipped its switch. The beam of light created a large yellow circle that danced on dark gray walls and a low ceiling. A collection of small objects—a knee-high statue of Bastet, a vase missing a large chunk, a piece of rock, and other pieces of rubble and dirt—littered the floor. Some long-tailed rodent moved in the shadows, darting into the corner.

I spun the dial to set the illuminator on its brightest level and walked into the chamber.

"The statue was there." Dylan pointed to the far corner.

Bringing the light down with me, I hunkered on my hands and knees as I'd seen my uncle do at various crime scenes. This is much more difficult when you are a female, dressed in layers of crinolines and skirts, along with a restrictive corset. Nevertheless, I managed to do so with a modicum of modesty and commenced to examining the floor.

Faint scrapes on the stones—*something heavy had been moved.* Clean, no dust or dirt—*it had been moved recently.*

Suddenly, a strange noise blared into the silence. It sounded like nothing I'd ever heard before. A sharp, high, screeching sound that might have been attempting to be music.

Dylan, who'd been standing off to the side watching in fascination, jolted to attention. His eyes wide, he began to fumble through his waistcoat and then his outer coat and in his agitation and excitement, the sleek "telephone" erupted from the depths of a pocket and tumbled onto the ground.

He ducked to the floor and snatched it up, but by then, the noise had stopped. "Oh my God," he said, staring at the object as if he'd never seen it before.

The device had come to life—it was illuminated and I was close enough to where he was kneeling that I could see tiny words on the front of it.

BenBo text (3)
Jillian text (5)
Flapper missed call

"I've got *two bars,*" he exclaimed, looking around the small, dark space, then down at the shiny telephone. "How can I have bars? One bar. Now I only have one. How the *hell* can I have b—they're *gone!*" He stared at the device, shaking it, jabbing at it with his finger, bolting to his feet to point it in different directions. "They were there a minute ago. Did you see that? There's no way. *No way.*"

"What is it? What happened?" Leaving the illuminator on the floor, I gathered up my skirts and pulled to my feet.

I understood little of what he was talking about, but his emotions—excitement, disbelief, and hopefulness—were obvious. And then they gave way to despair. I'd never seen anyone with such an expression of bewilderment, hope, and sorrow.

"For a minute," he said, "for just a minute I was . . . somehow . . . connected with the future. My future."

Silence reigned as we both stared at the device.

I heard him swallow hard, and he looked away. His knuckles were white and his jaw moved, shifting from side to side. "I have to figure out how to get home," he whispered. "My mom and dad must be going crazy."

"Dylan," I said, groping for words I didn't have. Trying to manage emotions I didn't know. I didn't know how to act, to even be a friend. But at that moment, I *wanted* that connection. It wasn't just curiosity about who he was and from where he'd come. It was empathy: a feeling that was just as foreign to me as he was.

I'd spent much of my life feeling lost and out of place. An overly educated, brilliant young woman in a world owned and managed by men. Dylan seemed nearly as misplaced, and I wanted to help him.

"I'll do anything I can, Dylan. Whatever I can."

He nodded, his handsome face grim and his eyes bleak.

Then I did something I'd never done before, never even imagined doing. I opened my arms and pulled him into an embrace.

There was no awkwardness, no fumbling of words, no mortifying flush burning my cheeks. He was warm and alive, and I could feel grief and despair emanating from his body.

"Thanks, Mina," he said, his chin moving against my shoulder.

And inside me, something shuddered and cracked, like a door opening.

Miss Stoker
Miss Stoker Goes Hunting

Miss Holmes didn't contact me the day after the Roses Ball. Nor the next day, nor even the next. Her silence didn't concern me . . . in fact, I almost welcomed the rest from her bossiness.

But when it got to the fifth day after our adventure with the Society of Sekhmet and I'd had no word from her or Irene Adler, I began to wonder. What a nuisance.

Miss Holmes must be sulking.

I took out my aggravation on Mr. Jackson's Mechanized-Mentor, beheading his metal self in an explosion of gears. As I was picking up a dented cog before Florence came to investigate the noise, I was struck by an unpleasant thought.

What if my outburst had put Miss Holmes in danger with the Ankh and the Society of Sekhmet? What if she hadn't been in communication because something happened to her?

I wouldn't be worried for myself. But for Miss Holmes? The awkward, brain-beaked young woman spent too much time thinking and not enough time in action. She'd probably deduced herself into a trap.

Or maybe she was still sulking.

I supposed I'd better look into the situation.

However, that afternoon, Florence reminded me it was her day to stay in and receive social callers. She insisted I stay in and help her serve tea and converse with whomever came to visit. I was only able to beg off by claiming I had plans to meet an acquaintance at the British Museum and by forcing Pepper to accompany me so I wasn't going unchaperoned. I wasn't lying about my destination, and Florence was thrilled that I actually *had* a social engagement.

"Who are you meeting, Evvie?" she asked, arranging a vase of flowers in the parlor.

"Miss Banes absolutely *loves* the Greek Wing," I said.

"Miss Venicia Banes?" Florence perked up, her bright blue eyes widening. "The very eligible Viscount Grimley's sister?"

"Yes, she is," I said, adjusting my bonnet. I avoided looking at Pepper, who stood by, attempting not to giggle. She was just pleased she'd be able to walk to the livery and visit her beau while I was at the museum.

"Perhaps the viscount will be chaperoning his sister today," Florence said.

"It's possible," I called, rushing out of the parlor. "So I don't dare be late! Good-bye, Florence."

By the time I got to the museum, it was near closing. The guard warned me I had less than half an hour with the artifacts and antiquities as I breezed past and into the echoing halls.

I made two wrong turns, but I finally found myself at the Special Office of the Keeper of the Antiquities. Below the sign was the Royal Seal of Her Majesty the Queen.

"Evaline," said Irene Adler when she opened the door. She removed her spectacles, blinking as if she'd been reading for a long time. "Come in."

I stepped into the office. The last time I'd been there was the night Miss Holmes and I met, a week ago. Then, the office had been neat and organized, but today was a different story. Books and papers littered the large round table, as well as the floor, desk, and every other available surface.

"Have you spoken to Miss Holmes?" I couldn't imagine anything more mind-raking than sitting in this chamber, reading books and organizing them for hours. The bottoms of my feet felt prickly and uncomfortable at the very thought. But Miss Holmes would probably be happy as a pig in slop.

Miss Adler looked at me in surprise. "Of course. She's been—"

A door on the opposite side of the chamber opened and Miss Mina Holmes strode in. She had her nose in an ancient-looking book. Behind her chugged a small self-propelled cart laden with more volumes. It came to a halt with a little burp of smoke.

"Right, then. Are you moving the entire library into your office?" I asked Miss Adler.

The older woman smiled, and Miss Holmes looked up from her book. "Miss Stoker," she said. Her voice was cool but not quite rude. "How kind of you to join us." Now it had gone a little more frosty.

"I would have been here sooner, had you requested my help," I replied. Glancing at the never-ending piles of books, I thanked Fortune she hadn't.

"I wasn't suggesting you offer your assistance," Miss Holmes replied, her nose back in the book. "I was under the impression this was precisely the sort of endeavor with which you preferred not to be involved." She glanced up at me with a flash of chilly green-brown eyes. "My experience is that you're more inclined toward drawing attention to yourself so you can demonstrate your superior fighting skills, regardless of the dangers involved or the prudence of such activity."

Right. Definitely sulking.

"And, clearly, without any semblance of plan or organization," she added, thumping the book closed in emphasis.

I bit my lip. So I'd made a mistake. I hadn't *meant* to draw attention to myself. I was just . . . doing what I was made to do.

I cast a covert glance at Miss Adler to see her reaction, but the lady seemed engrossed in the book she was reading.

"I would have been here to provide my help with whatever you're doing. But I received no communication from you."

Miss Holmes sniffed. "I didn't realize you required a summons to your duty."

My spine stiffened. "I—"

"Perhaps," Miss Adler said without looking up from her page, "you might bring Evaline up to date on our discoveries and theories, Mina."

Miss Holmes set her book aside and looked up at me. "You might as well take a seat."

Her cheeks had tinged pink at Miss Adler's gentle direction. I noticed for the first time that her rich golden-brown hair was in nothing more than a loose knot at the nape of her neck. Dark patches under her eyes made her appear tired, and her dress was rumpled. Had something bad happened? If so, I hadn't been here to help. I'd been doing my own sulking.

"We've been researching Sekhmet's instruments for the last five days," Miss Holmes told me as I moved a pile of books to sit on a nearby chair. "I've not even left the museum and hardly slept—there are so many references to review. We believe that someone, presumably the Ankh and her Society of Sekhmet, is attempting to follow a legendary formula involving four items that either belonged to the goddess—which is unlikely—or somehow have some supernatural tendencies attributed to her."

"What sort of instruments?" I asked, thinking of pianos and violins.

"A scepter, a diadem or crown, a cuff or bracelet, and a sistrum, which is a musical instrument."

Right. Well, I hadn't been that far off.

I listened with growing interest as she described each of the instruments. They'd found several passages about them in a collection of books and scrolls, and they were even mentioned on a stone with hieroglyphics on it. This sort of puzzle, tinged with supernatural and otherworldly elements, reminded me of the stories from my vampire- and demon-fighting family tree. One of my family members had battled an UnDead who attempted to infuse a large obelisk with evil traits.

"What did the hieroglyphics say?"

My companion gave me a pained look. "Hiero*glyphs*, not hiero*glyphics*. The former is the text or the characters, the latter is an adjective. To wit, a hiero*glyphic* text."

I glared, and she continued, "The hiero*glyphs* clearly represented Sekhmet and her instruments, which gives credence to the writings we found in scrolls and papers that simply couldn't have existed—or at least survived—for the thousands of years since Sekhmet was worshipped as the favored goddess. Thus, we believe the instruments do, or did, exist. But other than that, we haven't found any further information about where the instruments were, where they might be now, and what they could be used for if collected together—which is the crux of the text that originally sent us off in this direction." Exhaustion showed in her face. "We could be completely wrong about this, and meanwhile, more girls could die."

"Wait," I said, my eyes widening. "A scepter?"

"A scepter, a diadem, a—"

"Some men were taking a large, heavy crate from the museum on the night Miss Hodgeworth was killed, and one of them also had a long, slender object."

"A large crate? Large enough for the statue of Sekhmet to fit in? Who was it?"

"How the blooming fish should I know? Someone who didn't want to be seen. Or someone involved with the Society of Sekhmet."

Did that mean Pix was involved? If so, why would he tell me about it? Was it possible *he* was aware of the Society of Sekhmet too?

"I don't know anything more, but I can try to find out while you continue to research more information." I didn't try to hide my delight. At least I could be doing something instead of poring over page after page of cramped, faded, archaic writing.

"Did you see the thieves? Do you remember anything—"

"No, I didn't see them. He said they went off southwise, though," I added to myself.

"He? Whom do you mean?"

"Some con artist who goes by the name of Pix. I found him lurking around the outside of the museum after you left that night, and he told me." I stood with enthusiasm. "I'll track down Pix and get as much information as I can."

I was nearly to the door when Miss Holmes spoke again. "There is one other situation of which you might like to be apprised, Miss Stoker. If you can bear to be detained long enough for me to do so."

"Carry on." The sooner I was out of the room and on the streets, the better.

"Mr. Dylan Eckhert is the young foreigner we found with Miss Hodgeworth's body," she said. "He's been staying here at the museum because he has an unusual problem."

"Why? Is he partial to hieroglyphs?" I couldn't help but ask. Miss Adler's lips twitched, but she remained silent.

"No," Miss Holmes said in a cool, affronted voice. "He's traveled more than a hundred years through time, back from the future."

Right. I blinked. And let the concept settle.

The rest of London would never believe it of their staid, gear-ridden, mechanized world. Vampires. Demons. Supernatural instruments supposedly belonging to an Egyptian goddess . . . and now time travel?

Fascinating and intriguing.

Because of this, Miss Holmes probably expected more from me than a nod of comprehension. But being a vampire hunter, I wasn't easily surprised by supernatural things. I simply asked, "Does he know how it happened?"

"He isn't precisely certain, but he believes it had something to do with a man-size statue of Sekhmet. He was near it, and there was an illuminated scarab in its base. When he touched it, something happened and he was transported back in time. When Mr. Eckhert became aware of his surroundings, he realized the statue was gone and he was in a different place and time. I have no theories as yet what caused such an event, but I continue to consider a variety of possibilities. In the meantime, Mr. Eckhert has been assisting us with our research. However, he prefers to spend an inordinate amount of time in the empty chamber belowstairs where he arrived so suddenly. I believe he's hoping something will happen to reconnect him with his world."

"Thank you for telling me." I was sincere. The poor sod. He'd been shuttled back in time to a strange place with no way of returning home? "I'll look forward to meeting Mr. Eckhert again at the first opportunity. But now I'm going to locate Pix and see if he can give me any more information."

"He's likely our only hope, for any footprints or clues outside of the museum would have been obliterated in the last week. If you had seen fit to tell me about this sooner, I would have been able to examine the scene."

I nodded, gritting my teeth. "You're staying here at the museum?"

"For now. It's more efficient than traveling back and forth, and I've had clothing sent over."

"Then I'll contact you here once I have news."

As I rode in a ground-level horse-drawn hackney back to Grantworth House, I mulled over the best way to locate a shadowy thief in the dangerous London stews. Pix told me if I needed to find him, to ask for . . . Old Cap Anglo? Mango? No, *Mago*. Old Cap Mago. Who or what was that?

I went home to dress and arm myself for a visit to Whitechapel. Once home, I learned that Florence didn't have any evening plans. Blast it! She'd be in all night, making it difficult for me to sneak out . . . and she would also want to ask about my visit to the museum with Miss Bane. She would also be filled with gossip about Miss Hodgeworth's death. Even though it had been a week since the girl was killed, the tragedy was still a topic of conversation and worry.

I resigned myself to eating dinner with my family.

Naturally, Bram was at the Lyceum Theatre. But Noel, who was ten, ate with Florence and me. In fact, he managed to steal the last piece of apple bread right out from under my hand. He gave me a big, satisfied grin as my fingers closed over an empty plate. I glowered at him, but at the same time, I wanted to tousle his thick, dark hair.

"How was your visit to the museum, Evvie?" Florence asked, adding sugar to her after-supper tea. The Sweet-Loader whirred softly as its wheel turned and three lumps plopped into the cup. "Mrs. Yarmouth made a point of saying how much she missed you today. And last week as well." She raised an elegant brow meaningfully. "And your appetite seems to have returned."

"The museum was crowded. And Miss Banes didn't make it after all." I realized I'd eaten two beef short ribs, a large pile of roasted parsnips and potatoes, a generous serving of greens . . . and a piece of apple bread. I was going to have to loosen my corset before going out tonight. I eyed a plate of slivered pears.

"Mrs. Dancy asked after you as well," Florence said, hand-stirring her tea with small, neat circles. "She mentioned her son Richard. Apparently, there was a mishap with lemonade? At the *Cosgrove-Pitts'*." Her spoon clinked sharply against the side of the cup.

Drat! I forgot about the pears. "Uhm . . ."

"That's not a particularly polite or ladylike sound," my surrogate mother said. She speared me with her gaze. "I was under the impression you hadn't received an invitation to the Roses Ball, Evaline. You knew how much I was hoping to attend with you." Along with the displeasure in her eyes was a note of regret.

I bit my lip. "I'm sorry, Florence," I said, trying to think of an excuse . . . and a way to remove that disappointment. She loved parties and gowns and frothy things. "I . . ." The problem was, I never spoke a direct falsehood to her. That was why I'd hidden the invitation in the first place so I could tell her I didn't see it—because I hadn't actually opened and read it.

Being a vampire hunter who didn't lie was impossible.

"I know you don't care for those formal occasions," she said in a milder voice. "But it's a necessity, dear Evvie. Bram and I promised your parents we'd make sure you were taken care of, that you'd be married off well to a nice young man from a good family. One that could take care of you."

I could take care of myself. But Florence—and the rest of the world—would never understand that. "I'm sorry," I said again.

"I'm utterly confused as to why you attended the ball anyway, but without a chaperone. What if you had met someone completely inappropriate? What if something had happened to put you in a compromising position with him? Then what would I tell your parents—and Bram?"

An image of Pix rose in my mind. Could there have been anyone *more* inappropriate at the ball? Or a more compromising position than hiding behind a heavy curtain with a thief?

Thank St. Pete that Florence hadn't chaperoned me.

"I'm very disappointed in you, Evvie. To that end, I've asked Mrs. Gernum to save *all* of the mail for me in the future. And you and I will review *all* of the invitations and determine which ones we will attend. Together. I take my commitment to your parents very seriously. And your well-being too."

Right, then. How many vampire hunters got reprimanded about attending balls and being chaperoned? Surely I was the only one.

"Yes, ma'am." By now, my head was pounding and my stomach roiling, so it wasn't a lie when I said, "I'm not feeling well. I'm going to go lie down."

Florence gave me a shrewd look, then nodded. Her lips were flattened, once again reminding me how much I'd hurt and offended her. "Very well, Evaline. But I expect you to be awake and breakfasting by nine tomorrow morning. You'll be going with me to the milliner's and Madame Varney's."

Drat. Madame Varney was a seamstress, but going there was more of a social excursion than a shopping trip.

"Of course," I said. And fled.

Once in my chamber, I rang for Pepper, hoping she'd returned from her afternoon walk with her beau, Chumly. I needed assistance to prepare for tonight's excursion. I'd be leaving as soon as I could climb out the window, even though the sun wouldn't be setting for another two hours. She was the only other household member who knew about my secret life. She was clever and enthusiastic when it came to arming and equipping me for my dangerous tasks.

Pepper placed a two-finger-wide stake in its mechanized sharpener and flipped the switch. It whirred as the small wooden stick spun in place, a long peel like that of an apple falling away from the new point.

"M'great-gramma Verbena allays said to hide an extra stake in yer coy-fure," she said, sliding a slender wooden pike down into the mass of braids she'd already done up in a tight knot. "An' keep an' extry one in yer sleeve." She handed me the newly sharpened stake.

"I'm going to need more than stakes tonight, Pepper. I'm hunting a mortal, not an UnDead. Where did you put my pistol?"

My maid's strawberry-blonde hair bounced as she selected other implements to slide into my tool belt. She kept her hair cut short, because its wild, frizzy curls were impossible to confine in any sort of hairstyle. I wanted to cut my hair short, for long tails were a liability when in a fight, but my maid always argued otherwise. "An' where would I put the stakes if ye did that?"

She produced the pistol, and I slipped it in a holster beneath my man's coat, followed by a supply of ammunition. A knife went down inside one tall boot, and other useful items dangled from the insides of my coat.

Instead of wearing a tight corset beneath a split-skirted ensemble, I'd chosen to dress as a lower-class man in trousers and boots. I donned a loose neckerchief around my neck, arranging it beneath the open collar of a dingy shirtwaist. Tonight I wore a special corset that flattened my curves instead of enhancing them. A piece of string tied the coat together where the buttons would have been, and one of the cuffs was missing. The stake and another knife had been slipped inside the lining of each sleeve. A soft, slouching hat hid my tightly braided hair, which Pepper had pinned painfully in place.

Then she used a piece of burned cork to give my face dirt smudges and a hint of stubble. Powder lightened the color of my lips and the cast of my skin as well. A pouch of money completed my ensemble. I was equipped for anything.

Even Pix.

Warning Pepper to dissuade Florence, who might come to check on me, I climbed out the window. Moments later, I was down the maple tree, reveling in the freedom of trousers and low-heeled boots.

It was a long ground-level walk to Whitechapel and Spitalfields. They were the most violent and dangerous neighborhoods of London and where I would begin my search. In the interest of time, I found a hackney. But I got out at St. Paul's and walked the rest of the way so as to keep my disguise as an impoverished young man.

Big Ben announced it was eight o'clock. The sun was low, its glow hardly able to slip between the crowded London rooftops and chimneys. The ever-present black smoke clouds billowed into the darkening sky, interrupting the pale pink sunset. A gaslighter sang some happy ditty as he extended a long, mechanized arm to illuminate a streetlamp. It came to life with a small, pleasant pop.

The farther east I went, the dingier, closer, and more putrid the streets became. Here in Whitechapel, the sewer-chutes were almost nonexistent, and those that were there were often clogged and left to unclog themselves or fill up and over-spill. And in this area, the upper-level walkways were the more dangerous and dirty ones. One well-placed push could send an unsuspecting person tumbling off the streetwalk and down to the cobblestones. Because the streetwalks were narrow, mecha-nized vehicles were uncommon even at ground level. Horse-drawn ones passed through without pausing unless required to. People loitered on street corners, in shadowy alleys, and in small clusters near the steps of dark-windowed buildings.

It took only a few well-placed questions for me to learn that Old Cap Mago could be found at a public house called Fenmen's End.

The pub was small and dark, like everything else in Whitechapel. Its entrance was three floors above the ground level. I rode up in an old, creaky lift that had been jammed open and didn't require any toll. As I walked across the nar-row fly-bridge spanning the air-canal, I looked down and saw one man throw another into the overflowing sewer canal.

Inside, the pub was loud and smoky. In the corner was a self-playing piano attached to a small steam engine. The off-key notes could hardly be heard over the grinding, squeaking mechanism. Three large fans whirred from the ceiling. They seemed to just press the smoke down instead of causing it to dissipate.

I'd never been in a place like this before: filled with men drinking, smoking, and swearing. In the corner, a group of spectators cheered on two men who were arm wrestling.

For the first time, I felt a shiver of uncertainty. I didn't have a plan. I was used to walking along dark streets and waiting to be accosted by thugs, or seeking out vampires by sensing their presence. That was much different than having to pretend to be a man in a man's world. I could take care of myself as long as I wasn't outnumbered. But in here, in this crowded, confined place . . .

I'd have to keep my voice low and masculine, my cap on, and act like everyone else. With all the cursing and whooping going on, it didn't seem as if it would be too difficult.

I made my way to the counter, where a slender, bewhiskered man darted about filling drink orders. "I'm looking for Old Cap Mago," I said in a gruff voice.

The man flipped a thumb toward the arm-wrestling corner. "Over there."

The men were shouting and crowing, jostling each other to get a better view. Money changed hands, and bets were called out. Being short and slender, I could squeeze through the crowd to see the contest.

The participant facing me was tall and dark-skinned. His bald head gleamed in the light, and he wore a gold hoop in one ear. He was the size of a house, but all muscle and height. Moisture glistened over his forehead and a bare, tattooed arm. There was an anchor inked on his skin. I'm certain if Miss Holmes had been there, she could have given me the man's entire history at one glance.

His fingers curled around a tanned, more elegant hand than his ham-like one, and the muscle in his upper arm bulged like a small, dark melon. The bigger man looked as if he'd easily win the contest, but as I knew, appearances could be deceiving.

The opponent, whose back was to me, also had sleek, well-defined arm muscles, exposed by the rolled-up sleeve of his shirt. I could see his shoulders move and shift beneath the white fabric. A short, dark club of hair showed from beneath his cap. Even though he was in the midst of a tense battle, he laughed and talked to the spectators. When he turned to jeer at the other man, I caught a glimpse of chin and mouth.

Pix.

Well, now. I started pushing closer to place my own bet, but then I had a brilliant idea. Turning to the man standing closest to me, I said, "I want to challenge the winner."

He looked me up and down. "Ye wouldn't last a minute wi' either one of 'em, lad. And ain't no one gonna bet on a snakesman like ye."

"I'll take on all the bets," I said, thinking of the pouch in my pocket. "If I lose, I'll pay them all."

Pix had taken me by surprise twice already, showing up in unexpected places and catching me off guard. Then he'd slunk back into the shadows, leaving me gawking after him. Now it was my turn to set *him* off balance.

A loud roar erupted. "Winnah!" The small crowd surged closer and then retreated.

"Now, damme, ye made me miss it!" grumbled the man next to me. "Who won?" he shouted over the uproar, then turned away in disgust. "Damn. Pix lost me two pound notes this time!"

"Pix lost?" I couldn't help but grin with satisfaction.

"No, dammit, ye fool. 'E won. 'E always wins. I thought f'sure that bloke would have pinned 'is 'and down."

My grin grew broader. Now I was even more determined to play. Making sure my cap was low over my forehead, I pushed my way to the table. Between my disguise and the guttering, uncertain lights, I was sure not to be recognized. I was careful not to look directly at Pix or to give him a clear view of my face.

"I challenge the winner." I wasn't surprised when the men exploded with guffaws and jeers. Fine with me. To convince them I was serious, I had to pull the pouch from my pocket. When I loosened its ties and tossed it on the table, the crowd quieted as a swath of coin spilled out in the dim light. "My bet."

"Well, there, boyo. If yer wantin' t'give up yer gilt so easy, who's t'argue?" said Pix. Settled back in his seat, in a satisfied pose, he looked around the crowd, laughing. When he glanced at me, his smile was expansive, as if he were a king granting an audience.

I took care not to meet his eyes, pretending to flex my fingers in preparation for the contest. I knew my hands were too small and slender to be a man's, but I hoped I'd be mistaken for a boy. A foolish boy.

"Why ye want t'give us yer brass, there, lad?" asked a stout man behind me. He was standing so close, he bumped up against my chair. The others had also crowded in so much I found it hard to breathe. "Ain't no one 'ere ever beat Pix. Wha' makes ye think *ye* can?"

Uhm . . . right. I hadn't really thought that part through, had I? And drat . . . the last thing I wanted was to be recognized by my opponent before I slammed his wrist onto the table. Blast. "I—er—"

"The lad's got t'be sodding drunk," someone shouted before I could answer. "But he's got flim, so I'm after havin' a piece of it! The pansy wants t'give up 'is money and ye're gettin' soft about it?" A coin clanged onto the table, and all at once, others began to rain onto the scarred, dark wood. Someone began to collect the bets and separate them into two piles: mine, with only two small coins—and everyone else's.

Pix lounged in his chair, jesting with the crowd. My opponent seemed to know everyone. He had a small glass of some amber-colored liquid, which he brought to his lips more than once.

"Well, then, shall we, boyo?" he said when the bets stopped coming. He placed his elbow on the table and opened his hand.

Looking at that long-fingered, masculine hand and sleek, muscular arm, I felt a flock of butterflies release in my belly. "Aye, let's get to it." I hoped it sounded like something a man would say.

I rested my elbow on the table and reached for Pix's hand, hoping he wouldn't notice that my palm was slightly damp. Strong, warm fingers closed over mine, grasping firmly as his thumb settled on the back of my hand. A shock of awareness flashed through me as our palms touched intimately.

Gentlemen wore gloves at all times, and I couldn't remember a time I'd touched a man's bare hand, except that of my brother. There was heat and texture. His skin was rough at the tips of his fingers, smooth on the inside of his palm. I felt the coarseness of a smattering of hair where my fingers curved near his wrist. And strength.

"Ready . . . set . . . go!" someone bellowed, and I immediately felt the pressure against me.

It was nothing. Pix was testing me. He expected to be able to slam my hand to the table whenever he was ready, and I decided to allow him to think so.

I kept my attention on the sight of our two hands entwined, one square and brown, and one slender and pale, and I made my expression appear tense. I allowed him to ease my hand backward a bit. He was hardly putting any effort into it.

Neither was I.

Pix turned away from the table, still pressuring my hand. "I'll 'ave another one, Bilbo," he called, lifting his glass. There was only a small portion left, and he slammed it back with an enthusiastic gulp.

"Come on there, Pix! We ain't got all night. Finish it up so's we get our glim!"

"Nay," called another. "Two pence on the lad iffen he 'olds off Pix another two minutes. Put sumpin' into it, laddie!"

I hid the excitement in my eyes, staring down at the table as a whole new round of bets rained onto the surface. How long could "the laddie" keep him off? they asked.

And that was when I started to put more pressure back.

Slowly, slowly . . . just a bit, until our hands were upright again.

And then I pushed a little more, waiting for Pix to pressure me back. I knew he was playing with me, but he had no idea how the tables were soon going to turn.

Easy, easy . . . I tried to appear as if I were struggling.

I pushed, easing him ever so slightly backward as he talked and joked with the others. Then all at once, while he was in the middle of a sentence, it was as if a mechanism switched on: his muscles tensed, his fingers flexed against mine. And he stopped me cold. Just stopped, didn't push me back.

I fought back a smile. And I put a little more pressure against him.

His muscles tensed more as our palms ground against each other. He continued shouting out jests and even took a drink from his replenished glass as he held steady against my pressure . . . and shifted me back just a little.

And then *I* stopped *him*.

Smooth and steady, I increased the pressure. My muscles tensed as I eased his hand back toward the table . . . down . . . down . . . down . . .

The spectators noticed, and they were shouting now. Encouragement to me and jests to Pix. Pennies and other offerings tumbled into my betting pile, charging me to hold him off a little longer. No one expected me to win. They believed Pix was playing with me.

As if to confirm this, he increased his pressure again. His fingers tightened, and I could feel the tendons in his wrist moving against mine. He inched my hand up a little until our clasped ones were vertical again. I even let him tip mine over, backward.

He pressured me all the way down, down . . . until my knuckles hovered above the table. The spectators were hardly paying attention, talking among themselves, slopping their ale and whiskey about. They knew the outcome, and some were already beginning to gather up their winnings.

Wrong.

Deliberately, I began to ease Pix's hand back up. He increased his pressure, but I kept mine steady, and I was stronger. I advanced: solid, smoothly, effortless.

I could feel shock running through him when he realized I was pushing him back up—and there wasn't anything he could do about it.

His conviviality faded, and he turned from his conversations with the spectators. For the first time, he placed his other arm as an anchor on the table in front of him, where mine had been all along. Despite the fact that he continued to throw out an occasional jest or insult, he was now concentrating on the match.

By now, the audience had noticed the change. Whether they thought it was another ploy by Pix to draw it out wasn't clear. But he'd almost won just a moment earlier, and now I had his hand back up and over . . . and easing downward.

I could tell he was now employing all his considerable strength; it wasn't effortless for me to keep his hand from rising. I was having to work at it. But, inch by inevitable inch, I forced him backward. Down . . . down . . .

He'd gone silent and dark with concentration. His muscles trembled with effort, but he couldn't fight it. The crowd was quiet now too, and then all at once, there was a flurry of new bets flung onto the table. I hoped someone was keeping track of them, especially since my pile was swelling.

It was time to end it, and I eased his hand down . . . down . . . and then stopped. Just a breath above the table. Just enough that he knew he'd lost, but before the match was over.

For the first time, I raised my face. When our eyes met beneath the brims of our caps, I saw the shocked recognition in his . . . and then chagrin, followed by a flash of reluctant humor.

Having made my point, I relaxed the pressure, and he whipped my hand backward, up and over and *down*. My knuckles slammed flat onto the table.

"Winnah!"

MISS STOKER

Miss Stoker Is Paid with a False Coin

Congratulations, both genuine and jeering, abounded. Many hands reached out to grab their winnings, and a small pile was thrust in my direction.

I looked up and saw Pix shoving another healthy gathering of the loot: coins, small metal pieces, a slender gold chain, and a watch toward me. His gaze glinted with self-deprecating humor—an acknowledgment that I was the true winner.

That was the most fun I'd had in a long time. I grinned back and picked up the pouch to scoop in my winnings. I wasn't paying attention until I felt one of the coins. It was an odd shape, with a raised texture, and I looked down.

It was an Egyptian scarab.

Blooming fish! I snatched it up before anyone else noticed and turned it over. On the bottom was an etching; it was too dim for me to see the details, but I was certain it was a drawing of Sekhmet. Shoving it in my pocket, I stood, and Pix rose as well.

"An' 'ow about a word, there, boyo," he said. He reached out and closed his fingers around my arm as if expecting me to bolt. "Two ales over 'ere, Bilbo!" He made a gesture to a table in the shadows. "The lad 'ere's payin'!"

"Let go," I said as we made our way between the last few people of the crowd.

To my surprise, he released me, and we settled at a table in the quietest corner of the place. My medievaler heart appreciated the simple bare-flamed candle sitting on a saucer, but the warrior in me recognized the danger of an open flame in a place such as this. Its flickering circle of light illuminated the very center of the table, and from below, up onto Pix's chin, jaw, and mouth. I still didn't know what color his eyes were. Although this was the third time I'd met him, I'd be hard-pressed to pick his face from a crowd. That was probably the way he wanted it.

We settled in our seats as the man behind the counter brought over two tankards and slapped them onto the table. I caught the strong, bitter scent of ale as its foam sloshed over the top of my mug and wondered if Pix expected me to drink it.

Bilbo glared down at me. "Thought you was lookin' fer Cap Mago."

"I was," I replied in my gruff male voice. "But not anymore."

"Awright, sonny, then pay up. Five shillings."

I fumbled through my pouch and produced the money. When Bilbo left us alone, I looked over to find my companion watching me from behind his mug of ale. The expression in his eyes sent a sharp bolt of heat through me. I tore my gaze away as warmth colored my cheeks.

"So ye couldna stay away from me, aye, luv? 'Ad to come searchin' me out down in th' stews." He'd settled his elbows on the table, which brought his face closer to mine. "Were ye lookin' t'do a bit o' dabbin' up wi' me, then, luv?"

Although I wasn't certain what the phrase meant, I had a sneaky suspicion it suggested something improper. I wanted to dump my ale on top of his head, but decided he'd probably enjoy that too much. And I did need information from him.

"That must be your fondest wish, considering how many excuses you've made to accost me in the last week." My fingers curled around the mug, and I toyed with the idea of taking a drink.

Pix laughed, low and rumbly, sending pleasant shivers over my skin. "Go a'ead, luv, taste it. Ye paid fer it, din't ye?"

"I'm not here to socialize." Blast. I sounded an awful lot like the prim Miss Holmes. "And I certainly don't intend to get drunk. I need some information."

"Well, then, luv, ye've come to the right place. But I'm feelin' mighty regretful ye' ain't 'ere jus' 'cuz ye wanted t'swap a bit o' spit. I promise ye, it'd be a right more excitin' than turnin' around a dance floor wi' a dandy like Richard Dancy."

So that bothered him did it? I placed my elbows on the sticky table, putting myself close enough to him that I could see the actual whiskers beginning to show along his jawline. In this proximity, even nearer than we'd been while arm wrestling, I became aware of that pleasant, minty scent I'd noticed before. "Right, then, Pix. I'm wondering something."

"Wot's that, luv?" A wicked smile twitched the corner of his mouth, making him appear dangerous and delicious at the same time.

"I'm wondering," I said, forcing my voice to stay light as his eyes focused on mine, "if you have any idea how jealous you sound." I settled back in my chair as his smile faltered.

Then he chuckled and eased back as well. "All right, then, luv. Ye've lammed me twice t'night. Per'aps I'd best take m'lumps and stop now. Wha' can I do fer ye?"

"You told me you saw some men removing things from the museum the night we met. And that one of them was carrying something long and slender. Can you give me any other information?"

He retrieved his tankard of ale and took a healthy swallow. It looked so good that I reconsidered tasting mine. One sip wouldn't hurt. I lifted the mug and drank.

Bitter.

Oh, ugh, sharp and *bitter*!

But then I tasted the nuttiness and the full, rich flavor, and warmth rushed to my belly along with the ale.

His gaze was dark and warm beneath his hat brim. "Right, then, luv. The drink—it takes some gettin' used to. And so . . . ye want t'know about the thieves. There's no' much more t'tell ye, but they were movin' a 'eavy box. Bigger'n a man. It was goin' into a large wagon, wi' no markin's on it. "

"That's it?"

He shrugged. "I 'ad other things to be attendin' to, an' it ain't my concern wot them flimps was doin'."

"What were *you* doing there?"

"Now that, m'luv, is no concern o' yours. But I will tell ye I was lookin' for m'bloke Jemmy. 'E's gone missin', and the trail led t'that particklar crib. 'Twas just yer good fortune I 'appened to be there that night." His teeth flashed again.

I placed the scarab on the table. "Have you seen this before? Or anything like it? Someone tossed it in on a bet tonight, and there have been others found like it, related to . . . to the death of the girl who was found in the museum."

"I did 'ear 'bout 'at. Sad business." He picked up the scarab, holding it near the candle, turning it over. He had the perfect hands for a pickpocket: long, dextrous fingers and solid, strong wrists. The thought soured any soft feelings I might have begun to have for Pix. I was here to get information from him, and nothing more. I should *not* be enjoying his company, his jests and, most definitely, I should not be noticing the shape of his mouth. And the way the corner of it ticked up gently when he was amused. I straightened up in my seat.

"Well?"

"No," he replied, and handed the scarab back. "But ye say it was in the pot t'night? I can find out."

He lifted his fingers and gave a sharp, piercing whistle. Immediately, two men detached themselves from a group and approached.

Interesting. Pix, for all his easygoing ways, had respect and stature in this place. It couldn't be simply that he was the champion of arm wrestling.

By now I'd seen enough of his face to confirm my earlier guess at his age. Twenty, twenty-two at the most. But here was a man who carried authority in a pub of thieves and pickpockets, who could whistle and summon them in an instant. And he could make his way into a Society ball, groomed and dressed like a neat servant who knew his way around the house and his tasks.

He was aptly named after an ever-changing, always on the move, sprite.

I took another sip of ale and didn't wince at the bitterness this time. I listened as Pix spoke to the newcomers. Their slang-filled cant was English and mostly incomprehensible to me, but I understood he was sending them off to find out who had put the scarab in the pot. After taking a close look at the object, the two men nodded and left the table. I saw them make their way around the pub and assumed they were asking about the talisman.

Pix watched them for a moment, then took a drink. As he lowered the mug, I asked, "Why were you at the Roses Ball, sneaking around in Lady Cosgrove-Pitt's—"

He covered my hand with his and squeezed, silencing me. "Not s' loud, luv."

My interest perked up, for my voice hadn't gone any louder than before. "What were you after?"

"Now, why would I tell ye that? Ye already *know* wot I was after. Gewgaws an' jewels an' the silver, o' course. Wha'ever I could stuff in me pockets."

He was confirming exactly what I suspected, but I didn't believe him. "You're lying."

He tilted his head and looked at me with an odd expression. "Right, there, luv. An' a bloke's gonna 'ave some secrets."

"I suspect you have a multitude of them," I said. "Like where you hide all the loot you've stolen. And who knows what else."

"On'y me an' the good Lord know, that's f'sure." One of the men approached, and Pix, reading something in his expression, rose to meet him. They spoke for a moment in undertones, then Pix turned back to me and bent over the table. "Yer in luck, darlin'. Ferddie o'er there was the one wot put the coin in the pot. 'E got it from Bad Louie, and—"

"Who's that?"

"A bloke ye *don'* wanna know. 'E's been stealin' girls offa the streets fer years. Even ye don' wan' 'im catchin' a glimpse o' the likes o' ye, luv. Ye kin trust me on 'at." His expression was fierce. "Ferddie says Louie's got 'imself a right purty speck o' a girl in fine, rich togs stayin' with 'im. *Stayin'* bein' a kind way o' puttin' it, iffen ye get m'meanin'." He looked at me closely, his voice still low. "Ye wouldna know anythin' about a missin' Society gel, would ye?"

"If he got the beetle coin from the girl, then I would definitely know all about her." I rose. Even if it wasn't Lilly

Corteville, a Society girl—or any girl—had no business being held prisoner by the likes of Bad Louie. "Take me to her, Pix."

He sobered, eyeing me. "What's the chances you'd stay 'ere instead?"

"None."

Whatever he muttered under his breath probably wasn't a compliment. Resignation in his face, he gestured for me to stand. "Come on, then."

Pix's two friends accompanied us as we left the pub and descended to ground level. We went only a couple of blocks before turning down a dark, close alley. A bridge that had once connected across the third street levels sagged, untraversable, above my head. Pix glanced at my ready pistol and curled his lip. I could almost read his sneer: he didn't need a blooming pistol. "Stay 'ere. Wait. Watch. I'll be jus' a minute."

I complied, but only because one of the other men stayed as well. The night was filled with distant shouts and clanging noises, the rare rattling of carriages, barking dogs and yowling cats, the hiss of steam. Neither my companion nor I spoke.

I watched the area where Pix and his companion had disappeared. There was a dark building in front of us, and they'd gone in there at ground level. Then I heard a shout in the distance. And gunshots.

I sprang to attention, my gun in hand, and started to move. I couldn't wait to get my hands on Bad Louie. More gunshots and shouts echoed through the night. Light flashed in a small explosion as I started down the dark alley, hurrying in the direction Pix had gone.

But before I got more than a dozen steps, two shadowy figures appeared. They were running, and one of them had something large and heavy over its shoulder. I didn't need to see to know the runners were Pix and his friend.

"Run!" More shouts and gunshots filled the air.

I stayed with my companions as we dashed through a dizzying maze of streets and alleys, up flights of rickety stairs and over narrow bridges, down and up again until I was completely lost. We turned down a narrow street with dark sky-touching buildings and then ducked into the entrance of a large, black structure. There was a loud clang behind me, and the sound of a metal bolt being thrown.

Someone shoved me along in the dark, and I was propelled down some stairs. A man cursed, another person pushed and guided me, and finally I saw the faint glow of light. At the bottom of the stairs, I stepped into a completely different world than the dark, dingy, dirty Whitechapel streets above.

This was someone's living quarters, and very well furnished. Settees and rugs had been arranged in a large open space that looked just as comfortable as a parlor in any Society home. Gas lamps . . . no, *electric* lights cast cool, white illumination. Much sharper than the mellow golden glow that lit the rest of London. Something mechanical whirred softly in the corner.

Well, here was the answer to one question: where Pix hid all his stolen loot.

I turned to him. He was sliding the large, heavy item from his shoulder onto the settee. I realized his burden was a person he'd retrieved and carried all this way.

The clear light played over her face, and beneath the dirt and bruises, I recognized Miss Lilly Corteville. She was conscious. Her eyes fluttered and focused, then fear and shock filled her expression.

"Lilly," I said, kneeling next to her, yanking off my cap so she could see my face. The pins ripped from my hair and scattered. "It's me, Evaline Stoker. You're safe now."

I could have sworn I heard someone whisper *Evaline* behind me, as if testing out the name, but the chamber was filled with so many other sounds that I couldn't be certain.

"Lilly," I said again, looking at her cut, bruised face. The poor thing. What had she lived through? "You're away from that horrible man. Whatever happened, you're safe." I found one of her hands and closed my fingers around it. Her digits were cold and stiff.

Her lips moved, and I couldn't tell what words they formed, but I understood. "Water, and something to eat," I ordered over my shoulder. "Hurry. And . . . something warm. She's like to freeze to death."

I'd hardly spoken the words when a soft blanket was thrust into my hands. I tucked it around the poor girl, but not before I noticed her torn, filthy clothing. It had once been fine and expensive, but now it told the tale of her experience: blood and dirt stained, lacking ruffles, lace, and other embellishments that could be stolen and sold.

She'd been missing for weeks. She'd obviously been wearing the same clothing all that time. Had she removed the lace and ruffles to raise money, or had they been stolen right off her by Bad Louie or someone else? I burned to ask questions, of her and of Pix, but I knew the time wasn't right. The girl was in shock, and she needed to rest.

And as for Pix . . . He'd saved her from a terrible situation. And in spite of everything I knew or suspected about his criminal habits, I had to thank him for that.

After dabbing her face clean with warm water and a bit of soft soap I hadn't thought to ask for, I helped Lilly Corteville drink some thin broth. Her gaze skittered about, and she didn't release my hand until her eyes closed. At last she slipped into a restless slumber.

Extricating myself, I stood and found Pix watching me. The other two of our companions were sitting across the room, playing dice at a table. My host sat in a chair, lounging in his deceptively relaxed manner. But I sensed tension and an air of something I couldn't define emanating from him.

"You'll take good care o' 'er, now, won't ye, luv?"

"Right after I find Bad Louie," I replied. Now that I had seen Lilly and her condition, I understood just how *bad* that man had been.

"No need f'that," he replied. "Bad Louie won' be stealin' no more pretty girls."

"You killed him?" I had a moment of shock competing with disappointment. I'd wanted to have a hand in the man's punishment.

"Oh, 'e ain't dead. 'E jus' wishes 'e were." There was no humor in his words.

"Thank you for helping her . . . and me. But now I must get her home."

"Aye, I've made the arrangements. Now, will ye sit and take a sip o' tea wi' me?"

I took the cup he offered and settled in a chair between Lilly and Pix. The tea was fragrant and sweetened, without milk. Just the way I liked it. How did he know?

And how, I wondered not for the first time, had he known my name? My vocation?

"Better'n th'ale?" he asked, watching as I sipped.

"I think I could get used to the ale."

His lips curved. "Aye, I'd expect nawt less from ye. An' now I've a question for ye, luv," he said as, all of a sudden, I realized how exhausted I was. My eyelids grew heavy, and weariness rushed through my limbs. It had been busy night.

"What's that?" I replied, taking another drink of the soothing brew.

"Why did ye let me win?"

I smiled at the hint of aggravation in his voice.

"Because I could."

I set the teacup down, and despite the fogginess that had begun to swim over me, I added, "And so now you owe me one."

He chuckled in that low, rumbly way of his. "And so it is. Now, close yer eyes. I'll see ye and yer friend 'ome safely."

Blast him! "You drugged my tea!" I struggled to sit upright. But my muscles were loose and my brain was foggy.

"Now, luv, a bit o' laudanum ne'er 'urt anyone—so long's it's jus' a bit. An' I can't 'ave ye leavin' 'ere, and rememberin' where my crib is, can I? I'm not one for unexpected guests."

His dark gaze, focused on me from beneath the ever-present cap, was the last thing I saw before darkness enveloped me.

Miss Holmes

An Unsettling Interrogation

*T*he next morning, I received a cryptic message from Miss Stoker. Written on paper from Fergus & Fenrick's, it said

Lilly Corteville home and in ill health. Discovered in Whitechapel. Come as soon as able.

Aside from the fact that she didn't seem capable of using proper subject/predicate grammar, Miss Stoker's girlish penmanship was bothersome with its distracting flourishes. As it was hardly dawn when I received the note, I felt a detour home to freshen up was a good use of time and would keep me from arriving on the Cortevilles' doorstep at an unreasonable hour.

I had attempted to convince Dylan to accompany me, but he elected to remain in the small dark chamber with his so-called telephone.

"I'm going to have to figure out a way to recharge it soon," he said, looking at me with haunted blue eyes in the glow of the device. "I only turn it on when I'm in this room. But it's still getting low."

"Very well," I said, unsure of his precise meaning, but unable to take the time to further investigate.

I was worried about the young man. On the one hand, I understood his need to return home, to remain in the spot where he'd been shunted through time, in hopes that a miracle would happen and he'd get shunted back. But on the other hand, I suspected that keeping himself cloistered was only causing him more anguish. Before I left him in his dank dungeon-like chamber, I shared this opinion in rather passionate tones. He didn't seem to care; instead, he continued to stare down at his illuminated device.

I had no choice but to leave him there. Having been locked away in the British Museum on a self-imposed exile for five days, I found the change of scenery refreshing. The sun had chosen to show herself today, and I felt the welcome warmth of her rays seeping through my clothing. For a wild moment, I thought of removing my gloves or tipping back the brim of my hat, just to feel the sun on my skin. I'd already allowed my parasol to rest on a shoulder instead of fulfilling its purpose of providing shade.

Now, as I waited on the porch of the Corteville residence—an imposing, grand mansion in the elite area of St. James, not more than two blocks from Cosgrove Terrace and Miss Stoker's own Grantworth House—I became even more determined to help Dylan. Not just to return to his time, but to help him accept his current situation until we could get him home.

The door lurched open and instead of the butler I was expecting, I found myself face-to-face with Inspector Luckworth.

Drat.

"Miss Holmes," he said in an unwelcoming voice. "Why should I not be surprised to see you here." It was clearly not a question.

Patting my bonnet to ensure it was still in place, I stepped over the threshold and offered my parasol to the mechanized umbrella stand by resting it on a set of open mechanical claws. A soft groan emitted from the device, as if it were waking. The brass fingers closed over my accessory, then the Brolly-Keeper turned and slipped my parasol into a neat cubbyhole in the wall. Several other small cubicles contained parasols, umbrellas, and walking sticks.

"Good morning, Inspector Luckworth. Kippers and sausage for breakfast I see," I said, noticing the remnants on his collar. "Perhaps you should look into an adjustment on your mech-leg; it'll keep your hip from being so sore. And you should see to replacing the lamp to the left of your mirror as soon as possible."

He gawked at me as I sailed past him down the hallway, following the sound of low voices. They were coming from the parlor, outside which stood the butler I'd expected earlier.

"Miss Holmes," I told him, offering my calling card. "I'm expected."

He nodded and opened the door.

I paused before entering, adjusting my gloves and hat and patting at my hair again. Why was I suddenly nervous? I was dressed and groomed appropriately.

My skirt was a sunny yellow flowered *polonaise*, pulled back up into a bustle that exposed a cheerful gold, blue, and green ruffled underskirt. The tight-fitting basque bodice I wore over it was pale blue, trimmed with yellow, green, and white ribbons, making the ensemble bright and summer-like and complementing my golden-brown hair and hazel eyes. I would never look as elegant or stylish as Miss Adler or Evaline Stoker (neither of them had to contend with a nose like mine), but at least I was attired in clothing that befitted a visit to a home such as the Cortevilles'. Viscount and Lady Fauntley were of the upper crust of Society, and the latter, as Miss Adler had told us, was an intimate friend of Princess Alexandra.

When I stepped into the chamber, I took in the room and its occupants at a glance.

Miss Stoker sat on a chair nearby. She was dressed in ratty men's clothing, and her black hair hung improperly loose in long curling waves over her shoulders. I noticed the bulge of a pistol as well as a variety of other implements on her person, along with dried mud and offal on the edges of her boots. She appeared annoyed and restless, and when she saw me, she sprang to her feet.

"Ah, you've arrived," she said, hurrying to my side. "Took you long enough. I'll be off now." Before I could respond, she made her excuses and slipped out of the chamber, clearly glad to be leaving.

I turned back to the room.

Lady Fauntley was seated on a settee, speaking with two women. One of them was Lady Cosgrove-Pitt, and the other Lady Veness, the wife of another leading member of Parliament who'd more than once called on my father for assistance. They appeared to be soothing the distraught mother—although why they should be soothing her when her daughter was alive and safely home, I wasn't entirely certain.

Lilly Corteville was indeed home and safe—and by the look of it, she was also being soothed herself by none other than Inspector Ambrose Grayling.

It was a touching tableau: Lilly half-reclined on a small chaise, looking pale and weak, and Grayling had drawn up a chair so close it touched the upholstery of the chaise. He leaned toward her, holding one of her hands in his, speaking earnestly.

Tsk, I thought to myself in disdain. Neither of them wore gloves, and if he were any closer to her, I do believe he would be sitting on her lap.

I sniffed. If the lowly, working-class Inspector Grayling imagined he had a chance with the likes of Miss Lilly Corteville, daughter of a viscount, he would have a rude awakening.

Although . . . My attention slid to Lady Cosgrove-Pitt. He was related by marriage to one of the most powerful men in England. Perhaps his chances weren't utterly hopeless. Lady Cosgrove-Pitt looked up at that moment and gave me a nod of recognition.

"Lady Fauntley," I said to Lilly's mother, with a curtsey. "I'm Miss Mina Holmes. . . ." Just how was I to explain my presence here? After all, my involvement and that of Miss Stoker was meant to be clandestine and covert; I couldn't announce to the room the purpose of my visit.

"Miss Holmes, I'm pleased to meet you," Lady Fauntley said, taking my hand in both of hers. "Thank you for coming. Your presence means a great deal to me and my family at this time. Please, make yourself comfortable."

I blinked at this easy acceptance of my intrusion, but I realized Miss Stoker must have already made some sort of explanation for it. Perhaps even Miss Adler or Princess Alexandra herself had apprised Lord and Lady Fauntley of our involvement, though we'd been warned to keep it a secret.

"Thank you, my lady," I said. "I'm relieved your daughter has arrived home at last." I turned to Lady Veness and was introduced, and finally I faced Lady Cosgrove-Pitt. "I must apologize for retiring from the Roses Ball without taking your leave last week. I intended to say good-bye, but you were engaged at the time, and I didn't wish to interrupt."

The truth was, after returning from the harrowing experience with the Society of Sekhmet, I'd wanted to make a quick exit before anyone noticed my hair was in disarray and my skirt hems were a mess. I had seen Lady Isabella, but she'd been in an intense conversation with another woman on a balcony overlooking the ballroom.

"But of course, Miss Holmes," she said, her grayish eyes sparkling with warmth. "I should be the apologetic one for not being available to bid you farewell. I do hope you enjoyed the ball and that Lord Cosgrove-Pitt and I will see you at more functions."

"I did enjoy myself. Thank you. Now, if you'll excuse me, I'll say hello to Lilly."

As I approached the reclining girl and her companion, Grayling looked up. "Miss Holmes."

"Inspector Grayling," I said, resisting the urge to comment on the fact that he didn't stand to greet me. "I do hope you aren't getting a cramp in your side, bending over as you are. Hello, Miss Corteville. I'm Miss Mina Holmes. I'm very relieved you're home and safe."

As I looked at the supine girl, I could hardly keep from cringing. Her face—a very pretty one; breathtaking, in fact—was mottled with bruises and embellished with cuts. Her green eyes were veiled with pain and shock. Someone had obviously helped her wash up and brushed and braided her hair, but aside from that superficial attention, it was obvious she was still distraught over her experience.

"Thank you," she said in a low voice, and gestured to an empty chair that wasn't as close to the chaise as the other occupied one.

As I took a seat, I noticed Grayling had released her hand from his and eased back. I hesitated. I needed to speak with Miss Corteville about the Society of Sekhmet, but I didn't want to do so in his presence, and I didn't want the other ladies in the room to hear me.

But to my surprise, Lilly Corteville spoke unprompted. "I was telling Inspector Grayling what happened."

"Pray continue," I said. "I'd like to listen."

"Miss Corteville was explaining that she was in a hired hack on the way to . . . where was it, Miss Corteville?" Grayling asked. He reached into the pocket of his wool coat, which had been brushed and the buttons all tightened. He withdrew a small journal and self-inking pen.

I made quick observations:

Very close shave, no nicks, no leftover shaving soap—*a newly sharpened razor blade.*

The ticket stub from the Underground and a blotch of dark grease on his boot and staining his small fingernail—*reduced to using public transportation, likely because his steamcycle wasn't working properly.*

"I was going to attend a lecture. A salon," she said. My interest perked up, and I felt a sizzle of expectation, for the Ankh had referred to the Society of Sekhmet and the meeting of its salon.

"What was the topic of the salon?" I asked. "And, pray remind me, what day are we speaking of?"

"It was the twenty-fifth of April, and the salon was an evening gathering of friends. We enjoy discussing aspects of Egyptian culture. I hired a cab because I didn't want my mother to know I was going out. To be honest, I sneaked out of the house while she was at the theater." Lilly shifted on the chaise, her hands fluttering over the blanket as she glanced toward Lady Fauntley. "But I never arrived at the salon. The wheel on my cab broke—it must have hit some large stone or fell in a pothole and split. Either way, the wheel needed to be repaired, and I was required to alight from the cab."

Grayling's fancy writing implement, which had a large bubble-like reservoir of ink at the top, scratched busily in his journal.

"I decided to walk for a short distance and take some air. I was on the third level—I felt safe enough. I left the cab on Fleet-street, and there was a quaint little lace shop just closing up for the night. I wanted to stop in before I found another cab. But that's where it all went wrong."

Looking down at her fingers, which twisted in the crocheted blanket, Lilly continued, "Someone was following me. There weren't any cabs in sight, and I kept walking, trying to find one. I kept hearing the footsteps behind me, and it was starting to get dark. I was almost running, and I lost track of where I was. The next thing I knew, I went past St. Paul's and I was walking down Trinity, when I waved at several cabs, but they didn't stop. The moon was right there in front of me, just above the rooftops, but it barely gave any light. Then all at once, they were there. Three of them."

Her voice caught in a sob, and her fingers no longer played with the blanket, but instead trembled. "They . . . grabbed me and took me off and gave me to that man. B-Bad Louie. I don't know where he took me, but it was awful. Dark and dirty and frightening. I . . . I don't want to talk about what happened . . . there." Her words trailed off, and I could tell she was reliving the horror of her captivity. I could only deduce what sorts of pain and activities had been visited upon her, and my practical insides softened with sympathy as she continued. "He kept me there. For weeks and weeks."

I sat back in my seat, considering. Her story generated a variety of questions and emotions, many of which I wasn't prepared to share at the moment. The least of which regarded why she was lying.

Grayling's pen was poised above a page of his journal, and when she finished speaking, he paused, then rested it on his knee. "You've had a harrowing experience, Miss Corteville," he said in the kindest voice I'd heard from him. "Perhaps you might like to rest for a while. We can speak with you again when you're feeling better." The "we" in this last sentence clearly included me, and I stiffened at his presumption.

I was about to correct him about my intentions (if I wanted to continue questioning the young woman, I would certainly do so), when the door to the parlor opened.

Inspector Luckworth appeared and gestured to his partner. Grayling nodded, then looked at me. "Inspector Luckworth has retrieved the clothing Miss Corteville was wearing when she was abducted. Perhaps you wish to examine it, Miss Holmes?"

"Yes, I do." An examination could confirm my suspicions that she was lying about much of her experience. I was also aware of the real benefit to Grayling: I would not be left alone with Miss Corteville to continue the questioning without him. I was under no illusion that he was including me in the investigation for any other reason.

"If you would excuse us, Miss Corteville," he said, standing. He tucked away his journal and closed the cap on his pen before sliding it into his pocket.

Once out in the corridor, the door closed behind us, and Grayling, Luckworth, and I were alone.

"The housemaid is pulling the gel's dress and underthings from the garbage—they didn't realize we'd want to see them. Gonna be a ruddy—'scuse me—mess when they fin' it. Did you learn anything from the gel?" the elder inspector said to his partner.

"Miss Corteville gave me her story," Grayling replied as they walked down to the end of the hall and found a private alcove in which to speak. I followed, uninvited.

Grayling glanced up as I joined them, then pulled out his journal to review his notes. "She stopped to do some shopping after the wheel of her cab broke and needed repair, and then she got lost. Miss Corteville thought someone was following her, tried to elude them, and in the process became further lost in an unpleasant area of London, near St. Paul's. Then three men abducted her, keeping her captive in the slums of Whitechapel for nearly four weeks. It's quite a sad story," he said, flipping the book closed.

"She was lying," I could hardly wait to inform them. "There were several—"

"Of course she was lying." Grayling gave me a disgruntled look. "It's obvious to anyone that Miss Corteville has had a horrific experience, and one wonders if she will ever fully recover. But her story is riddled with untruths. She claims she saw several cabs on Vergrand-street that she tried to hail, but as it happened, on that day, that particular street was closed due to a flooded sewer canal. There was no traffic on that street at any level."

I sniffed. "I knew she was lying the moment she mentioned a lace shop on Mayfair. There's no such shop on Mayfair, or even in the blocks surrounding it. Aside from that, she claimed the moon was over the rooftops and gave off hardly any light, but on April 25, it was—"

"A full moon in an unusually clear sky," Grayling said.

"Not only that, but the moon rose high in the west that night, so it would have been behind her and very far above the rooftops, if she were walking away from St. Paul's on Vergrand—as she claimed."

We stared at each other, I with my lips flat and determined and Grayling looking down at me with that supercilious air. I found it aggravating that he was so much taller than me and *could* look down like that.

Luckworth, who'd been watching us volley back and forth, spoke at last. "Why is the gel lying?"

"I have my theories," I said before Grayling could speak.

"Please feel free to keep them to yourself," the Scot suggested.

"And I'll be investigating this case with them in mind. Good day, inspectors."

"Miss Holmes," Grayling said before I could slip back into the parlor, "I'd like to remind you that this is a very dangerous situation. Two girls have been found dead, and a third one . . . she's had a very harrowing experience. You're a civilian and not at all equipped to handle—"

"Thank you for your concern, Inspector Grayling. I'll take it under advisement. I'd like to examine her clothing when you've finished with it." Luckworth opened his mouth, and I added, "Please recall that I am here and investigating this case at the request of Her—er, in conjunction with Miss Adler. As she works under the auspices of the Crown, you have no authority to impede my work. Good day, inspectors."

I imagined I could hear the sound of Grayling's teeth grinding as I stalked back down the corridor, and it made me want to smile. Now I had to create an opportunity to speak with Lilly Corteville alone. If only I could find a way to get her out of the parlor, or to get her mother and her mother's friends out of the room. I suspected Lilly didn't want to talk about the Society of Sekhmet, which was why she'd made up the fanciful story about how she came to be in Whitechapel.

But why would she be so determined to keep it a secret? Did she fear retaliation from the Society members themselves—including the Ankh—if she divulged their existence? Or did she want to keep the group a secret for another reason? That made sense in the event my suspicions were correct that the Ankh was trying to harness the Power of Sekhmet.

As luck would have it, when I came back into the parlor, I found Lady Cosgrove-Pitt and Lady Veness preparing to leave. Lady Fauntley was seeing them out (presumably to have her own moment of privacy with them), which left me the chance to speak with Lilly alone. I wasted no time reclaiming my seat next to her chaise, and she opened her eyes when I sat down.

"Lilly," I said, "I'm here to help you, but I need the truth. You can trust me. I know about the Society of Sekhmet, and I need to know what really happened to you. We can speak before anyone else returns."

Her eyelids fluttered, and for a moment, I thought she was going to ignore my plea. But then she focused a clear gaze on me. "It tried to kill me."

"What tried to kill you? When?"

"The Ankh. It tried to kill me. It's trying to resurrect Sekhmet. It's going to come after me, I know it. It's going to try and kill me again."

"Lilly, I'm here because the princess has asked me to help you. You can trust me, so please tell me everything about the Society of Sekhmet and the Ankh. Quickly, before the others return."

"The Society of Sekhmet started out being just what I said—a salon where we discussed Egyptology. We used cog-nogged beetle medallions to identify those of us who belonged to the group because the membership is secret. It was an excuse to get out of the house, to go somewhere without our mothers, without having to be perfect and on show for a pos-sible husband. Then it became more. Exciting adventures and nighttime excursions . . . things we could never do if our par-ents knew about them."

I found myself nodding. It was just as the Ankh had said in the speech last week, and I understood how attractive it would be for young women who had no freedom.

"As time went on, the Ankh began drawing attention to how restricted we were, and talking about how if women ran Parliament, things would be different."

"Like a suffragette movement?"

"No. The Ankh didn't talk about women voting or women's rights. It spoke about taking control of Parliament and returning to the days of Cleopatra or Queen Elizabeth, when the governing forces were controlled by a strong female monarch. It spoke of how there were ways to get the husbands we wanted, not the ones our parents wanted us to have. How to attract the man we wanted, how to make him notice us. That was . . . that was what I wanted. I didn't care about the power. I . . . just want . . . *him*." Her voice ended on a little choked sob.

She closed her eyes and for a moment I could empathize with her, even though I could never imagine myself in her position. A beautiful young woman like Lilly Corteville, the wealthy daughter of a viscount, could have her pick of young men. And she was engaged to Sir Rodney Greebles. Why would she need the help of the Ankh? Did she want to marry someone other than Sir Rodney?

"And now he's not going to want me anymore," Lilly whispered, a pale hand curving around her white throat.

"Who?" What young man had she wanted so badly that she'd get herself involved in such a cult? Whoever it was, she fancied herself in love with him. What fools women can be over love! That was precisely the reason a Holmes would never descend to such base and irrational emotions.

The girl shook her head at my question, and I could see a tear glistening at the corner of her eye. "Jemmy. My darling Jemmy. He works for the Society, but he loves me. He wants to be with me, but the Ankh won't let him leave. We were planning an escape, to elope."

The women were still talking in the front hall; I could hear their voices. But it would only be another moment. "Lilly, can you tell me more about the Ankh?"

She swallowed, and I could hear the sounds of her dry throat working. I helped her sit up and sip from a cup of tea, all the while chafing at the delay.

She collected herself. "As the society expanded to more members, some of us were invited to prove our loyalty to the Ankh."

"And the Ankh is trying to resurrect Sekhmet," I said to direct her speech to the information I wanted. "How? Does it have something to do with the Instruments of Sekhmet?"

"How do you know about them?"

"I was an uninvited guest at a Society of Sekhmet meeting last week, so I've learned a little about them. I must urge you to continue, Lilly. I can hear the front door opening. Your mother will return momentarily."

"Those of us who proved our loyalty were brought into the Inner Circle. There were four of us." At last her voice was urgent. "Each of us was assigned to one of the instruments. Mine was the cuff."

"Mayellen Hodgeworth and Allison Martindale were two of the Inner Circle members," I deduced. "Plus you. Who was the fourth?"

Lilly nodded and thus confirmed my conclusions. "Yes. The fourth one of us, she died in a carriage accident with her parents before she was sent to retrieve her instrument. Her name was Gertrude Beyinger. As far as I know, she hasn't been replaced."

"How were you meant to acquire the instrument to which you were assigned? From what I have been able to discern, those items were the product of legend, and if they did exist, they would likely be buried or otherwise hidden in the sands of Egypt."

"The Ankh has been studying the legend in ancient scripts and scrolls for years, and located each of the instruments but for one. Two were in private collections, and one was in the museum. We were to prove our loyalty by retrieving the item, and in turn, we would be granted great privileges and power when Sekhmet was resurrected."

How could anyone be so gullible? Resurrecting an Egyptian goddess by locating her supposed personal effects here in *London*? I heard the front door closing. "Did you retrieve the cuff?"

"I stole it while the owners were on the Continent."

"From whom?"

Lilly shook her head. "I won't tell you that. I don't wish to be charged with any crime, and that's the only thing I've done wrong. Would that I'd never been so foolish as to become involved with all of this! Oh, Jemmy!" She was near tears by now, and I tried to head them off by offering her another drink of tea.

She sipped, seeming to take forever, and when she lowered the cup from her mouth, she continued. "I found the cuff and brought it to the Ankh the next day. It had to prepare the cuff before I could be inducted into the inner sanctum, and the Society was to meet again, on April twenty-fifth, for the ceremony. We were to meet where we always did, every week, and—"

"Did you go?" I realized my fingers were digging into the arms of my chair. "What happened?"

"I got to the place, and Jemmy met me at the door. He told me to run, to escape—that the Ankh was going to k-kill me. We tried to run away, but th-they were there . . ." She was sobbing by this time, clearly reliving the horror. "I d-don't know wh-what happened to Jemmy, but I ran and ran . . . and the n-next thing I knew, I was lost . . . and then the m-men found me. And t-took me to B-Bad L-Louie—"

"Where does the society meet?" Footsteps were just outside the door. "And when? Tell me, quickly!"

"At Witcherell's, at nine—"

She stopped as the parlor door opened.

Lady Fauntley came in and walked over to the two of us. "Miss Holmes, I'd like to thank you for coming. But my daughter needs to rest now. I'm sure you understand."

I knew I had no choice but to leave. "Yes, right, of course," I said. I'd learned much, but I suspected there was much more she hadn't yet told me.

Try as I might to catch her eyes, I was unable to do so. Lilly Corteville had turned away and clearly was unwilling or unable to speak to me any further.

The poor girl. I would have to come back at another time, but first I was going to be visiting Witcherell's to find out what I could of the Ankh's plans. For it was clear the society met every week on the same day. April twenty-fifth was a Tuesday.

And so was today.

MISS HOLMES

A Most Curious Device

O nce more at the British Museum, where I'd spent more waking time than at home since the first night I met Miss Adler, I hastened to her office.

Uncle Sherlock had impressed upon me from a young age that learning every streetwalk, road, alley, railway route, and business in London was imperative for him in his crime-solving capacity, and so I had taken it upon myself to study maps and become familiar with business districts and neighborhoods. I knew the schedule for every train, underground or otherwise, as well as the buses. One never knew when one might need to utilize public transportation.

Since it was still several hours before noon, she wasn't in residence. Fortunately, I'd acquired a key and was able to gain access on my own. I had preparations to make before I attempted to attend the Society of Sekhmet meeting tonight at Witcherell's Pawnshop.

Living in an age of great technology and scientific prog-
ress, I was skeptical of the legend of Sekhmet that the Ankh
promoted, but I also knew I couldn't fully discount it as being
an excuse for some other scheme—such as to terrorize members of the peerage through their daughters or overthrow the
government. After all, Miss Stoker was evidence that vampires
did exist. And, as had become apparent, so did time travel—
although one could argue the latter was a scientific endeavor
and not that of some supernatural force.

And, much as I tended to discount the idea, it seemed
that whatever the Ankh was doing with Sekhmet and its statue
had caused Dylan's leap through time.

I'd come to the museum to review the array of notes
and writings I'd collected during my week of research into
Sekhmet's instruments. If three of the instruments had been
located, I wanted to know as much about them as I could, as
well as about the fourth.

Lilly had retrieved the cuff herself. And based on Miss
Stoker's information that a figure had been running from the
museum the night of Miss Hodgeworth's death with a long,
slender item in hand, one would conclude that the second one
was the scepter. That left the sistrum and the diadem.

I sat at Miss Adler's desk and closed my eyes to review
what I remembered from the Society of Sekhmet meeting,
redrawing in my mind like a moving picture the Ankh's ges-
tures, the speech, and even the actions when she commanded
that we be apprehended.

Something about the Ankh niggled in my fertile mind, something I felt I should know or recognize. Something I was missing.

A thought lodged in my brain and my eyes popped open. I stared unseeingly into the room.

"Impossible," I said aloud.

Lady Cosgrove-Pitt had been at the ball when I returned from the excursion to the Society of Sekhmet's lair. I'd seen her myself, speaking with another person.

Still. There was something about the Ankh that reminded me of her. Or perhaps it was the other way around. Seeing Lady Cosgrove-Pitt today at the Fauntley mansion only served to remind me of it. It was the way she tilted her head, the way she moved her gloved hand.

And then there was the fact that, apparently, Miss Hodgeworth had received an invitation to the Roses Ball. And someone—Lady Cosgrove-Pitt?—had marked a secret message on that very same invitation.

The door to Miss Adler's office cracked open, shattering my concentration. A blond head poked around the opening.

"Mina," said Dylan, "I'm so glad you're here."

"And I'm relieved to see that you've emerged from your exile below," I said tartly, as a rush of warmth billowed through my middle. What was wrong with me that the sight of this young man would set me to fluttering?

"I realized you were right about what you said this morning—I can't just stay down there forever," he said as he came into the office and shut the door behind him.

I was acutely aware that the two of us were alone in a private room. "I'm glad to hear it. I intend to do anything I can to help send you back to your time, but until we can determine how to do that, I believe it's in your best interest to interact with the people and life here. After all, we don't know how long it could take." Gad, I was babbling, and I didn't seem able to stop myself.

He smiled, and my cheeks went warm. "I realize I've been a jerk, and I'm sorry. I was a little short with you this morning, and that wasn't right."

"Never mind that," I said, feeling both discomfort and pleasure from the way his gaze settled on me. It was warm and genuine—not at all like the cold gray-green stare of a certain detective.

"I'm glad you're here, because I just realized I might be able to help you. I feel like an idiot for not remembering before now. Do you know where my clothes are? My original clothes?"

"Of course." I'd brought them with me when I bailed him out of the jail, and they were in a cupboard in this very chamber. I produced the satchel and watched as he dug through it. I couldn't resist picking up one of the very odd rubber and leather shoes. It laced up like a corset, and the sole curved up and around the sides and front of the shoe. On the back in small letters, it said NIKE.

Of course, I knew who Nike was—the Greek goddess of victory. But I couldn't understand why Dylan would have her name on his shoe. I hoped he wasn't part of some sort of Society of Nike that came from the future. . . .

"Yesss!" he said, drawing out the sibilance of the last consonant in a sort of victorious sound. "I thought so."

"What is it?"

He was looking at a pamphlet of some shiny type of paper he'd just extricated from the pocket of his trousers. Although it was crinkled and worn, it was also very colorful, with the words *The British Museum* printed on the front, and a picture—

I reached out and touched the paper where the image was. I'd never seen anything like it. It must have been some sort of photograph, but it looked so real, so colorful, like a flat miniature of a building that I recognized as the very one in which we were standing—but different.

Dylan unfolded the pamphlet, and I could see that it was a description of the museum that came from his time. While I wanted to snatch it away from him and examine every last detail, I refrained and looked over his shoulder while he pored through it.

Then he stabbed a blunt finger at a page. "Look at this, Mina! Don't you think this could help?"

At last I was able to take the pamphlet from him, feeling the light, smooth, shiny texture of the paper myself. When I saw what he was pointing to, my heart gave a little flip.

The Cult of Sekhmet and the Twelfth Dynasty said the heading beneath an image of a delicate, filigreed coronet that looked very much like the drawing of Sekhmet's diadem. Excitement coursing through my veins, I read further, still fully aware of how close I was to Dylan.

The newest exhibit in the Egyptology salon (third floor, East Wing) is a collection said to belong to Amenemhat I, the Twelfth Dynasty pharaoh who created a cult around the goddess Sekhmet. He was so devoted to her that when he became ruler and moved the capital, the shrines and worship spaces of her cult were also moved. Found in the late 19th century in a forgotten room at the museum, this golden diadem represents the intelligence attributed to the goddess.

"I've never heard of Amenemhat," I said, my mind working through the implications. Time travel was a complicated concept. "His tomb must not have been discovered yet. There are many archaeologists excavating in Egypt right now, but it could be years. That means the Ankh couldn't have found the diadem either, which means whatever she's attempting to do with the legend of Sekhmet, she can't do it without the diadem."

"Wait, there's more. *I remember this!* We saw the exhibit and the diadem—you know, when I was in my time. And I looked it up, because the story was so interesting. Wait. I might still have it."

He fumbled in his pocket and pulled out the sleek telephone. "The battery's getting lower," he said, stabbing at the face of the device with his finger. "Damn. I'm going to have to turn it off for a while. But first . . ."

I watched in awe as he poked at it, slid his finger over the surface, and made the images change. Then all at once, there were pictures on there, *moving*.

Tiny people, *moving*. "What *is* that?"

"Oh, I hit the wrong app," Dylan said. To my relief, he didn't change it right away, and I looked down at the tiny moving pictures, with *sound* coming from them.

"What is that?" I asked again. They were dolls or people, maybe even mechanical devices, for they had oddly shaped heads—or else wore hats—and all wore the same clothing. They had long cane-like sticks and they were moving around very fast, hitting a small black object on a white floor.

"That's hockey, and that's me," he added, pointing to one of the characters moving around. "I play hockey. Back home. It's a sport, like . . . um . . . cricket?"

"Brilliant," I murmured, still watching the miniscule people. They crashed into each other, tumbling to the ground, and even began to hit each other. But the way they moved that tiny black disk around . . . it was almost magical.

"This is amazing," I said when he touched the surface again and the pictures went away, to be replaced by the rows of little square images.

"It can do a lot of other things, but it needs *electricity*. You know, that awful contraband. Electricity." He looked at me from the side, very close, his eyes twinkling as if it were some private joke between us.

My cheeks heated, and I found myself smiling back as my insides filled with butterflies. My organized thoughts scattered.

He returned his attention to the telephone. "I had looked up the information and I found a description . . . here it is." He slid his finger and stabbed at the glass. "It's still pulled up on my browser," he explained in what sounded like a foreign language.

"They found the diadem, packed away in the storage rooms of the British Museum. *It's already here.* The article says 'The diadem attributed to Sekhmet was found in a long-forgotten crate in the Archaic Room of the museum. Tarnished and bent, its delicate gold workmanship was nearly ignored because it had been thrown in a box with pieces of ruined statues and pottery. The diadem narrowly escaped being destroyed.'"

"It could still be here. The task for which Miss Adler was engaged by the museum is to go through and catalog all of the crates and shipments that flooded the country during the first part of the century. Sarcophagi and statues and countless artifacts were packaged up, shipped here, and then forgotten."

Dylan nodded. "I remember that. It was considered a terrible robbery of the Egyptian people, as well as becoming a lucrative trade for Egyptian grave robbers, who stole from their own country and sold antiquities to the Europeans. There was a show on the History Chann—uh, anyway. So that means it's still here."

"Or the Ankh could already have it."

We looked at each other, and for a moment, I couldn't breathe. He was so close to me, and our faces were almost at the same level, and he was so handsome, so fascinating . . .

Then I thought of my prominent nose and my too-wide mouth and how tall and clumsy I was, and the warmth that had begun to bubble hopefully inside me eased. I was an odd duckling, an awkward, plain-looking girl who didn't know when to stop lecturing.

A handsome, unique young man like Dylan would never—

"Mina," he said. His eyes hadn't left my gaze, and I realized his fingers were brushing against mine. "I think you're really cool."

I wasn't sure what he meant by "cool"—was that good, bad, or literal? My brain seemed to freeze, being this close to him.

Although my brain was frozen (and possibly whatever other "cool" parts of me he was referring to), my cheeks were not. They felt as if they were on fire.

Before I could say anything, there was a knock on the door, and then it flew open. I was startled and leapt guiltily away from Dylan, lest someone accuse us of anything improper.

"Did you speak to Lilly Corteville?" demanded Miss Stoker as she burst in with a swirl of pale blue skirts and a flower-laden bonnet. She brandished a white parasol.

"Yes, of course I did," I replied, refusing to look at Dylan. Now not only were my cheeks hot, but my forehead and neck as well. Had I been gawking at him like one of those silly girls I disliked? "I learned quite a bit."

As I willed my face to return to its normal shade, I divulged the results of my interview of Lilly, and then showed Miss Stoker the pamphlet Dylan had saved.

"Right, then. We must find the diadem before the Ankh does." Miss Stoker suggested the obvious.

"That's one course of action," I said crisply. "But for all we know, she—or he—could already have acquired it. Lilly Corteville didn't say which of the instruments is still missing." I decided to keep my suspicions of Lady Cosgrove-Pitt to myself for the time being. "I've already planned to pay a visit to Witcherell's this evening. At nine o'clock."

"I'll be going too," said Miss Stoker.

I gritted my teeth. I didn't want her to disrupt things again, and I saw no reason for two of us to attempt to gain entrance to the society's meeting place. One would be difficult enough.

"You need me to protect you," she added. My jaw was in pain as I fought to keep it closed. Instead, I settled for shooting her a dark glance.

"By the way, I'm Dylan," said our companion, breaking into the moment.

"It's a pleasure to meet you," she said, giving him a warm smile that set my teeth on edge. "Miss Holmes has told me all about your situation. I'm Evaline Stoker."

He looked at her, puzzlement and then comprehension crossing his face. "Stoker? As in . . . *Bram* Stoker? Didn't he write *Dracula*?"

Her brown eyes widened. "He *is* writing a book. About a vampire. Do you mean to say you know the book? From your time?"

"Oh, um . . . *crap*." Dylan stopped and looked at me. "I'm not sure if I should say anything about the future. It could really mess things up. Like in *Back to the Future*, this movie that—oh." He stopped again and huffed out a big puff of air that ruffled the long hair over his forehead. "Never mind. I shouldn't say anything."

"I agree, you probably shouldn't," I said, ridiculously pleased that he'd turned to *me*, that it was *I* he seemed to want an opinion from, instead of the pretty, vivacious Miss Stoker.

"Whatever the two of you are going to do," Dylan said, "I'm going to see if I can find the crate. At least then we'll know if the Ankh has already found the diadem."

"Excellent plan," I said. "If the Ankh hasn't found it, perhaps we can lure her into the museum and capture her that way. We can set a trap."

"Like Scooby-Doo," Dylan said with a grin that all of a sudden faded.

I turned to Miss Stoker. "In regards to our proposed visit to Witcherell's, you do realize that we cannot be *noticed*, and we cannot be *recognized*?" I said, in case she had any ideas about announcing her presence as she'd done the last time. "We're going to have to go in disguise."

"Right," she said. "And I know just the place to get whatever we need."

Miss Stoker

Of Crushed Cauldrons, Critics, and Characters

The public entrance to the Lyceum Theatre was at ground level on Wellington-street, but I brought Miss Holmes through the back entrance used by the actors and other personnel. I often visited Bram and knew how to navigate the backstage to his office.

It was just past noon, and the wings, prop closets, costume wardrobes, and dressing rooms were deserted. The actors and stagehands wouldn't arrive for several hours, having been up until well past two o'clock the night before. It was no wonder this was the quietest part of the day in the theater. Like vampire hunters and pickpockets, actors and actresses carried on their festivities until dawn.

My brother's voice boomed from his office as we approached. He was talking to someone, and he sounded bothered. I was used to Bram's moods, especially when he was working on his book. Miss Holmes looked at me in question, but I knocked on Bram's door.

The talking stopped, and the door swung open. "Evaline."

"I hope we aren't interrupting," I said, glancing around him into the office.

"No, no, come in," he said, gesturing us into the chamber. I could feel my companion's attention sweep over him. The only resemblance between my brother and me is our thick, curling dark hair. I'm petite and elegant, and he's rather stocky. He has a full beard and a mustache with an auburn tint in the growth nearest the lips.

I walked into the office and wasn't surprised to find it empty.

"I thought I heard you talking to someone." Props and papers were everywhere, along with costumes, a sword, and a crushed papier-mâché cauldron. The company was currently performing *Macbeth*.

"I was working on my book," he said, gesturing to a large typing machine. A paper protruded from its roll and was filled with words. Crumpled papers littered his desk and the floor. "You likely heard me cursing at the blasted thing. Writing a book is blooming difficult, even when ye know the topic of vampires and vampire hunters." His hair was a mess, as if he'd been pulling on it.

He noticed Miss Holmes for the first time, and I introduced her.

"Sherlock Holmes's niece, are you? You're being the intelligent one, then, aye? You don't go taking yourself off and doing dangerous things like my sister here, do you? Trying to find vampires, hunting them with supernatural strength," he muttered, glancing at the typing machine again. His brows drew together. "That's after being my biggest problem with this book. No one would believe it, Evvie. The critics would be laughing for weeks—a story in which a *woman* kills the evil, cunning vampire. It's not possible for a woman to outsmart and kill the powerful and intelligent Count Dracula." He looked at Miss Holmes and added, "It's the character of which I speak, of course."

"Of course."

"But you know it is possible," I reminded him. Why did he always have to bring this up?

"If you ever actually *kill* a vampire, I might be believing it. But it's no more than a legend anymore, Evvie. You've got the skills, but you've never actually staked an UnDead."

I stiffened and gave him a lethal glare. My face was hot. Bram was a blooming idiot. Drat him for blathering my secrets. Blast him for announcing my failure. "That may be the case, but I can, and I will. Someday."

At least he didn't know the details of that night. How I'd frozen up and nearly become a victim myself.

"Right. I do believe it, Evvie," he said, holding up his hand as if to ward off my supernatural strength. "But there aren't any vampires about to be killed anymore. And no one would believe a young woman could do it, even if there were. A *young woman*? Never. But what *would* they believe?"

"Perhaps the precise *opposite* of a young woman?" Miss Holmes said.

Bram must have missed the sarcasm dripping from her voice. His eyes suddenly popped wide open, and he stared at her. Then he pivoted toward the desk, then back to her again. Papers fluttered to the floor in the cyclone.

"But aye!" he said in a triumphant voice. "The opposite of a young woman is an *old man*. A brilliant old man who uses his brains to outsmart the count instead of a young woman who uses her strength and speed."

Miss Holmes and I exchanged exasperated glances. I saw vexation, obviously on my behalf, in her expression.

"I'm gratified to be of assistance," she said coolly.

"What did you say your name was?" he said, looking over his shoulder as he yanked the paper from its mooring in the typing machine.

"Miss Mina Holmes," she said.

"Mina," he repeated. He froze once more. His eyes glazed over as his mind slipped off somewhere again. "*Mina*." He stepped over to his chair and sat down this time, scrabbling through papers. "It's just the sort of name I need. She's a very proper, very intelligent young woman. Strong of character, not flamboyant. The epitome of the Victorian woman . . ." He was mumbling to himself as he flipped through sheaves of paper. "She even knows all the train schedules."

"*I* know all the train schedules," Miss Holmes informed him. "And the buses and underground as well."

Then he looked at us, obviously remembering we were there. "If you'll excuse me, I'll be returning to my work now." His eyes were alight with excitement and passion.

"Right, then," I said. "We'd like to borrow some of the costumes and makeup, Bram. May we?"

"Whatever you like," he said, flapping a hand in our general direction. "Wait," he commanded as we started toward the door. "Is that your given name, Mina? Or is it short for something?"

My companion paused, her expression turning to one of distaste. "Alvermina." She spoke as if it were a confession.

"Hell," Bram said. "You'll be pardoning me, but that's the most terrible name I've ever heard. I can't name a character *that*. But I do like Mina," he muttered, turning back to his typing machine. "Hmm. Mina. Philomena? Wilhelmina?"

His words followed us as we left him to his work.

ℳISS HOLMES

A Civil Conversation

After an hour digging through the makeup and costume closets at the Lyceum Theater with Miss Stoker, I had a generous cache of disguises. Apparently there was some benefit to having her as a partner. If I'd had to resort to raiding my uncle's stash, I don't believe I would have been as successful, because despite what some people might think, Uncle Sherlock doesn't have a large variety of female clothing or accessories.

Miss Stoker and I took a smooth, silent lift up to the highest streetwalk and made our way back to the Strand. I took my leave in front of Northumberland House after lecturing her about why we couldn't arrive at Witcherell's together without inviting comment. And I reminded her to keep her gloves on at all times tonight, for hands could be very telling about one's identity.

With traffic clogging the throughways at all levels, it took three quarters of an hour to travel home. But that was typically London, even during the later hours of the evening and night. It was impossible to move quickly from one area to another. By the time I walked into my house, it was after four o'clock, which gave me three hours to work in my laboratory before I had to eat dinner and assemble my disguise.

When I had been called to post bail for Dylan, I left my studies analyzing the different characteristics of ladies' powder and creams. Because I hoped that giving my mind a rest from the Society of Sekhmet case might produce some deductions when I returned to it, I was determined to finish the analysis of the imported Danish face powder before leaving my lab today. To that end, I donned a protective apron and strapped on my goggles, then closed the door to my work area.

However, the best-laid plans tend to be wantonly disrupted, and mine were no exception. I'd just set fire to the small dish of geranium-scented powder when there was a knock at the door.

"Yes?" I called, taking no pains to hide my displeasure. The powder was burning more quickly than I'd anticipated, and the floral scent was distinct.

The door opened enough to show Mrs. Raskill's sleek pepper-and-salt hair and small, inquisitive nose. "You've a visitor."

I gave an unladylike huff. Since I wasn't socially active, my visitor was likely her nephew Ben. "I'm quite busy," I said, poking at the now-smoldering ruins of powder.

The geranium scent was still strong in the air, and the powder had turned an interesting shade of honey. I lifted one side of my goggles onto an eyebrow so I could peer through a magnifying glass to determine whether there were any other physical changes to the residue. I had only a handheld glass, not one of the fancy Ocular-Magnifyers I'd seen Grayling use at the museum. This limitation necessitated awkward contortions on my part as I bent, peered, poked, and held the magnifying glass all at one time—while jotting notes.

"He insists on seeing you," Mrs. Raskill said. "I don't think he's going to leave until he does."

"She's quite right, Miss Holmes."

I nearly dropped the magnifying glass at the sound of a familiar voice. Had I somehow conjured him up? "Inspector Grayling, what the devil—I mean, what on earth are you doing here?"

Grayling was standing in the doorway, which was now fully open. At the sight of him, his dark cinnamon-colored hair almost brushing the top of the doorway, his broad shoulders filling the space in a dark blue wool coat with six brass buttons, my insides did a sharp little flip.

"I must speak with you, Miss Holmes," he said, walking uninvited into my laboratory. "What are you doing?"

He'd noticed my awkward position, not to mention the clutter all over my table. And . . . oh drat, the way I had lifted my goggles off kilter, covering only one eye and the other lens raised up to my forehead. I could only imagine how ridiculous I appeared.

"I'm studying the residue left by various articles of the feminine toilette," I told him primly, removing the goggles. I wasn't going to think about the dark red circles that would be around one eye and imprinted on my forehead. "One never knows when one might encounter such a clue at the site of a crime."

"Indeed."

"I'm very busy, Inspector Grayling," I said, raising my magnifying glass again and returning to the task at hand. That, I decided, was a better option than standing there like a silent fool, gawking at him. With random red circles on my face.

"Obviously."

He'd stepped into the laboratory, and Mrs. Raskill made her escape. The latter realization surprised me, for I would have expected curiosity to get the better of the housekeeper.

"I've an Ocular-Magnifyer that straps to the head," he informed me. "And it fits over the eye. I ken it would make your task much easier."

I gave up and set down the glass to give him my full attention. "What is so important that you found it necessary to travel to my home and interrupt your busy day?"

At that, his expression became serious. "I thought it best to bring you the news directly. Lilly Corteville is dead."

I gave a sharp jerk and knocked the magnifying glass to the floor. Even as it shattered at my feet, I was saying, "Dead? No! *No!* How? When?"

To Grayling's credit, he made no comment about my clumsiness. Instead, he suggested, "Perhaps you'd like to step out for a moment where we can talk."

I was aware of a terrible, heavy feeling in the pit of my stomach. "Lilly's dead?" It didn't seem real. I'd just been there, talking to her in her parlor, only hours ago.

Grayling nodded, his face still grave. "I thought it appropriate that you heard the information from an official representative of the Met instead of through other channels."

By now I'd made my way around the mess of glass, and I followed my visitor out of the laboratory. Conscious of Mrs. Raskill's sharp ears, I said, "There is a small park at the end of the block. Perhaps we could sit and talk there?"

As soon as I made the suggestion, I realized how forward it sounded. My dratted cheeks heated yet again, and I focused on the ground so that I didn't have to meet his eyes and see the surprise or distaste reflected therein. To my relief, he kept any arrogant comment he might have made to himself.

Instead he said, "A seat in the park would be most welcome. I've been inside all day with this business."

And that was how we came to be walking down the street together. He offered me his arm, which was proper and meant nothing but that he did have some habits of a gentleman. I took it, because there was always the chance that one might have to dodge a pile of something unpleasant while walking along the edge of the street, and being in heavy full skirts with hourglass-heeled shoes could make that difficult.

I didn't want a repeat of my tripping incident at the ball.

He seemed willing to be candid with me, and as we approached the park, he said, "Word came to Scotland Yard at one o'clock today. Miss Corteville was found in her bed-chamber at approximately noon, no longer breathing. She couldn't be roused, and there was a bluish cast around her mouth and nose."

"Poison or asphyxiation," I said immediately, then cast a covert glance at him.

"It appears to be poison," he said in a mild tone as we approached the park. "Evidence suggests that's the case, but we haven't finished the investigation."

The park was hardly more than a mechanized bench beneath a large tree with a neat garden of flowers planted around it. I'd occasionally seen a child or two playing ball on the small plot of grass, but they'd been toddlers, with a short range and didn't seem to need much space.

"What sort of evidence?" I asked, forcing myself to sound casual as I released his arm. I was still shocked at the unhappy news and cognizant that Grayling had decided I should be informed of it. Was he beginning to accept my involvement in the investigation?

Grayling gestured to the bench, which was currently motionless. But just as I moved to take a seat, he sprang into action, holding up a hand to stop me. He pulled a handkerchief out of his pocket and dusted off the surface, then stepped back as I settled myself and my bustle onto the bench. This was no easy feat on a seat with a back (there's nowhere for the bustle to go, so one is generally required to lean forward). However, I tend to wear smaller, more practical bustles, and as today was no exception, I was able to sit with relative comfort.

"Next to her bed was a small vial, uncapped, and empty. I smelled the essence of bitter almond," he continued as if there'd been no interruption in our conversation.

"Cyanide."

Grayling nodded, then after a brief hesitation, took a seat next to me. There was a good space between us, I at one end, he at the other. But, still, it seemed odd to be sitting on a park bench, speaking casually with Inspector Grayling instead of competing with him.

"Yes, I suspect it was arsenic. There was enough residue left in the vial to test it, so we shall know in short order. There was a note and another item that will likely interest you."

"An Egyptian scarab."

The expression that flashed on his face was gone as quickly as it came, but it was testament to the fact that I had surprised him once again. "Aye, you are correct. There was a scarab with a Sedmet, er, Sethmet—"

"Sekhmet."

"Right," he said. "An image of Sekhmet was visible inside, once the object opened. The scarab was on the bed next to the vial and the note."

"She wrote the note to make it appear as if she took her own life."

"All indications are that she did take her own life," Grayling said. But his voice wasn't argumentative. It was filled with the same suspicion that echoed my own thoughts.

And what about the scarab? Did Lilly have another besides the one that had been found in her room, or had someone—the poisoner?—left another as a warning or as some sort of message? There had been a scarab found with Mayellen Hodgeworth's body too.

All at once, one of those thoughts crystallized, and I actually started. *Lady Cosgrove-Pitt had been there, at Lilly Corteville's house, today.*

"What is it, Miss Holmes? You've thought of something, haven't you?"

"I . . ." I realized I couldn't voice my suspicions. Not to him, and certainly not without more proof. But the fact that Lady Cosgrove-Pitt had been there was somehow relevant. It had to be. There were no coincidences.

I was even more determined to go to Witcherell's tonight and see the Ankh. And, if possible, to unmask it.

Her.

"I . . . erm . . . suspect the note said something about not wanting to hurt her mother?"

Grayling fixed his eyes on me. At the moment, they appeared more green than gray, and their steady regard made me feel jittery. "Is that what you suspect?" he said in a mildly derisive voice.

"What did it say?"

"It did say something of that nature, in fact," he said, still watching me. From his inside pocket, he pulled out the journal and the self-inking pen with the bulbous reservoir on top. After flipping through the pages, he stopped at one, paused, and then read, "'I'm sorry, Mother and Father. I love you. But I can no longer live with this burden. Lilly.'"

I blinked rapidly, feeling the sting of unfamiliar wetness at the inside corner of my eyes. What burden had been so heavy that she couldn't bear it and had chosen death over life?

She made the choice to leave her parents. For whatever reason, she took the poison. *She left.*

My throat burned and my eyes stung, and I could feel the inside of my nose dampening. Why was I so upset? I hardly knew the girl. Yet, I must have felt something akin to rage—as well as grief—toward the poor wretch. For she'd *made the choice* to leave her parents. To leave them behind, to leave them wondering what they'd done to deserve being abandoned.

I knew what it felt like, being abandoned. Left behind with no warning, no chance to right whatever was wrong. It was *I* who'd been left by one of my parents.

In fact, for all intents and purposes, I'd been left by both of them.

Grayling thrust something into my hand, and I looked down to see his handkerchief wadded in my palm. I dabbed sharply at my eyes, mortified that I'd revealed this range of emotion.

"It's been confirmed," I asked, aware that my voice was rough and unsteady, "that the note is in her handwriting?"

"Aye," said Grayling. And even in that simple syllable, I could hear the thickness of his Scots burr. He wasn't as unmoved as he appeared.

I wiped my nose and then, instead of giving him back the soiled handkerchief, I stuffed it inside the hidden pocket of my skirt. *Never allow any form of emotion to color your investigation, observation, or deduction.* It was that excess of emotion, Uncle Sherlock claimed, that made the female gender unable to make rational decisions and deductions. Which I'd spent my entire seventeen years of life attempting to disprove. At least, in my case.

I forced myself to thrust away any influence of my emotions and review the facts. I knew there were others Grayling either hadn't noticed or hadn't provided, but I could draw three theories:

Lilly Corteville had written the note and taken the poison.

Or she'd been forced to write the note, and then the poison had been forced upon her.

Or she'd written the note under some other circumstances, and it had been used at the scene of her murder in order to imply suicide.

If it truly was a suicide, where had she obtained the poison?

After a long moment of silence, Grayling spoke. "I suspect Miss Corteville obtained the poison from whoever murdered Allison Martindale and Mayellen Hodgeworth."

"I would suspect the same," I agreed, wondering if I should mention the Society of Sekhmet. "In which case, this is likely murder. Or accessory to murder."

"I would concur."

I opened my mouth to tell him what Miss Stoker and I had learned about the Ankh . . . and then closed it. Through Miss Adler's direction, Princess Alexandra had insisted on utter secrecy about our work. She must have her reasons, and I dared not compromise them without permission.

We sat in silence for another stretch of time. It felt surprisingly comfortable, and I realized I was loath to disrupt it. But the clock at St. Bartholomew's struck five, and I knew it was time for me to return home to prepare for my evening excursion.

As if reading my mind, Grayling stood abruptly. He looked down at me and said, "Miss Holmes, I hope you aren't planning to visit Witcherell's tonight."

I was hardly able to control my surprise. Perhaps he knew more than he was telling me. Including about the Society of Sekhmet.

"It wasn't difficult to find out where Miss Corteville was going on the night of April twenty-fifth," he said in answer to my unspoken question. "She didn't lie about taking a cab; she lied about the wheel breaking. The cabdriver left her at Witcherell's and watched her walk inside. He remembered it because it was an unsavory establishment for a young woman of the gentry to be visiting. I suspect you gleaned at least that much from her during your interview, and I am just as certain that you're planning to investigate it yourself."

I felt a little like Uncle Sherlock must have when he realized Irene Adler had been one step ahead of him. "Inspector Grayling," I said, thinking of the variety of accoutrements I borrowed from the Lyceum Theatre, "you might feel it necessary to visit Witcherell's tonight, but I can assure you, Mina Holmes will not be sighted on the premises."

Grayling looked at me long and hard before giving a brief nod. Nevertheless, his expression was filled with suspicion as he offered me his arm for our return to my residence.

When I arrived, I bid him farewell and went inside to find that a message had been delivered in my absence.

Dylan had found what he believed was Sekhmet's diadem.

Now all we had to do was lure the Ankh to the museum so we could capture her.

Smiling to myself, I closed the door to my bedchamber and began the process of eliminating any resemblance to Miss Mina Holmes.

Miss Stoker

Miss Stoker Is Stymied

That evening, I approached Witcherell's Pawnshop on foot. Thanks to the resources Miss Holmes and I had plundered from the Lyceum's costume trunks, no one would recognize me.

Pepper had braided my hair tightly against my head and pinned a bonnet over it. I chose the hat because it was abominably ugly. With five long pheasant feathers sprouting from the back of the crown and miniature brown-speckled blue bird's eggs decorating it, I knew no one would believe it was fashionable Evaline Stoker under that brim. We pinned false red-gold curls underneath. Miss Holmes had suggested I wear clear-glass spectacles, which she claimed would help to disguise the shape of my eyes. I also wore flat shoes to make me appear shorter.

"Merely changing the color of your hair and style of dress isn't enough to hide your true identity," she lectured.

"And for heaven's sake, keep your gloves on at all times. One's hands are an excellent means of identification, and most people don't think to disguise them."

Thinking it might be fun to don our disguises together, I suggested we get dressed at Grantworth House. But Miss Holmes gave me a disapproving look. "We can't arrive together, even if we are in disguise. I will be at Witcherell's at nine o'clock."

I'd seen many disreputable storefronts and buildings, but Witcherell's was the dirtiest place I'd ever seen. Located at ground level several blocks from Haymarket, it was on the same street as a dingy pub, a sad-looking bakery, a second pawnshop, and an empty storefront. Just the sort of places a pickpocket or thief would frequent.

The street and walkway were busy. Yet when I glanced up and down the way, there was no sign of Mina Holmes— even in disguise. So I walked into the pawnshop.

The only person inside was the proprietor, a skinny man with protruding eyes and a bald head. His nose was a large triangular blade that made even Miss Holmes's look dainty. He looked at me as I came in. Was I to ask about the Sekhmet Society meeting? Unlike when we attended the Roses Ball, this time Miss Holmes hadn't given me any indication of how she expected to proceed.

And I hadn't thought to ask. Or to plan ahead.

Chafing with impatience, I looked around for inspiration. How on earth did this place stay in business? Every one of its offerings seemed to fall under one of three categories: filthy, broken, or filthy *and* broken.

A little tinkle of bells drew my attention from behind, and I turned to see a young woman walk through the door. Finally. A young woman would never be in a place like this unless she was planning to attend the Society of Sekhmet meeting.

She glanced around hesitantly, then edged her way toward the counter where the proprietor sat watching both of us like a large, silent toad.

I would have assumed the newcomer was my partner, but it wasn't. Miss Holmes's nose would have given her away immediately. This young woman's nose, although by no means delicate, was shaped differently. Her cheeks and jaw were round and pudgy, and her skin was an unbecoming ruddy color. Her dark hair looked as if it were about to tumble free of its haphazard pins. She obviously didn't have a lady's maid to help her dress, although her clothing seemed well made.

However shyly she moved, this young woman appeared to have a better notion of what to do than I. She walked with small steps up to the counter.

"Oh," she said, pausing to poke her fingers around inside a shallow bowl. There was a soft rattling sound, as if the small objects were being stirred up. Her voice was loud and a little squeaky. "These beetles are *just* utterly too, *too*!"

Beetles? I wasted no time edging my way toward the counter.

"If ye be likin' dem, missy, ye mun fin' more o' dem back 'roun' 'ere," said the proprietor. He flipped up a section of the counter and gestured the young woman through.

Despite my impatience, I waited until she disappeared into the back room. Then I approached and looked in the bowl. It was filled with Egyptian scarabs.

"I like these beetles," I said. "May I look at the others in the back?"

The proprietor looked at me balefully. "I ain't got no more dem *beet*-ulls," he said, and picked up a rag that might once have been white. "Dis 'ere's wot I got." He began to polish a metal cup, ignoring me.

What had I done wrong? Was I supposed to speak some sort of password?

Surely no one chose a password as ridiculous as "utterly too, *too*" . . . did they?

I stewed about the situation for a moment, wandering the shop. All the while, I watched the skinny toad out of the corner of my eye. Then I came back to the bowl and dragged my fingers through it again, disturbing the disk-like scarabs. "What cunning little things," I said, trying not to sound as ridiculous as I felt. "They're simply, utterly too, *too*!"

"If y'ain't gerrna buy nuthin' or sell nuthin', then ye can stop wastin' m'time," the shopkeeper snapped, setting the metal cup down with a loud clang.

"I'm looking for more scarabs like those," I said. "You sent that other girl to look at them. Why won't you let me through?"

He remained silent.

What in the blooming fish was wrong with me? I couldn't even get past the owner of a pawnshop. And though I waited, hoping Miss Holmes or some other Sekhmet Society member would arrive, the shop remained empty of anyone but me and the beady-eyed proprietor.

At last I had no choice but to leave. The door slammed behind me as if to punctuate my displeasure. It was nearly half past nine. If I didn't find a way into the back room, Mina Holmes was liable to get herself killed. Aside from that, she'd never let me forget it if she gained access and I didn't. She must have made her way past the obnoxious gatekeeper prior to my arrival. I could only imagine what she was doing in the midst of the Society of Sekhmet.

I should have insisted we meet up ahead of time. This was no place for someone like her to be on her own. For one thing, she'd probably trip and draw the Ankh's attention to her straightaway.

But there was more than one way to skin a cat. And a scrawny little toad wasn't going to keep me from my mission.

As I came out onto the narrow walkway in front of Witcherell's, I peered up at the tall stretch of building. It rose several stories, appearing to merge into the dark sky. High above was a fly-bridge connecting this building to the one across the air-canal. A tiny golden light winked on either end, and there appeared to be a small landing on either side of the fly-bridge.

There.

I hurried across the throughway opposite Witcherell's, and along the stationary walkway until I found a lift. For once, I had a small pouch of coins with me. I slid two farthings onto the money tray and shoved it in place. The brass gate clicked, then opened, and I slipped through onto the lift. The night air was cool and crisp at this height, and the heavy layer of polluted fog dissipated as I rose in the open-air conveyor.

I exited five levels above the pawnshop and at the same location as the fly-bridge. Up here, the buildings were so wide at the top that they were only a short distance across the air-canal. Looking overhead, I saw the air-anchors wafting gently in the breeze, outlined by a drassy moon and stars. Each anchor sported several tiny glowing lights on the balloon as well as on the line attaching it to the building as a warning for airships that might fly through.

I heard a distant clock strike half past nine. I had to move quickly or chance drawing attention to myself entering the meeting after it had already begun.

The fly-bridge shimmied as I hurried across. On the other side, I located the pawnshop down several levels and to my right. Just above, I could see a small ledge that angled around the front of the building to the side—and, hopefully, to the rear. The perfect entrance.

It was simple to descend to the ledge. I climbed down by using a shadowy flight of stairs and then lowering myself from one ledge to another. When I got to the ledge above the pawnshop door, I skirted along its narrow width until I found a dark window. Moments later, I'd pried the glass free and slipped inside. The unlit chamber was filled with trunks, crates, and covered furniture. It was so dusty my eyes watered, and I had to muffle a sneeze in my sleeve. I hoped the toad below didn't hear.

In the dark, I could make out the faint outline of a door. There were no sounds of voices or footsteps, so I pushed . . . but it wouldn't open. Blast. It was locked.

I hesitated. The lock wasn't an issue; I could use the weight of my pistol to smash it. But the noise would be a problem. Fishing out a small burn-stick, I snapped it in half, and a soft green glow from the algae inside gave me a moment of illumination and the opportunity to look at the barrier more closely.

But before I could attempt to pick the lock, someone screamed.

I dug the pistol from my pocket. The scream had been feminine, and it came from above and toward the back of the building. It wasn't repeated.

No longer caring about noise, I slammed the heavy weight of metal down onto the doorknob. It shifted as the wood enclosing it cracked, and I drove the pistol butt down once more with a powerful blow. The knob snapped off and tumbled to the floor with a thud, but I was already pulling at the door.

I found myself in a corridor just as dark and dusty as the chamber I'd left. Despite the urgency, I paused to listen and sense where to go. Chafing at the delay, I drew in a deep breath, feeling, straining my ears. Waiting. Finally, I heard another, softer but no less desperate shriek.

I ran.

The voices drew me—sharp ones, and a high-pitched desperate one, along with some other spine-chilling cry I couldn't identify. I followed the sounds: down the corridor, up dark flights of stairs, and through a hallway, and so on. I went as silently as possible while running pell-mell, my pistol in hand.

At last I came to a long, shadowy hallway that ended at a double set of doors. They were closed, but golden light spilled from beneath and around the edges. I stopped and, putting my ear to the door, I heard movement from the other side. The heavy, cloying smell of something sweet wafted from the cracks. Opium. Voices came from the other side, but they were soft and didn't sound desperate or troubled. Had the scream come from here or not?

I wanted to burst through the doors and take whoever was on the other side by surprise. A rush of excitement had my fingers closing over the knob. But a prim voice in my head suggested that I might not want to be so capricious. It was as if Mina Holmes had somehow invaded my conscience. *Capricious.* That was definitely a word she'd use.

I tried the doorknob, grasping it carefully to muffle any rattle, and turned it slowly. It wasn't locked, and the door loosened.

Now all I had to do was gently pull it open and peek inside. I had just begun to ease the door open when a hand landed on my shoulder.

Miss Stoker

By the Fog of an Opium Stew

"It would have behooved you to be more expedient and punctual in your arrival."

My fingers still on the knob, I spun around, taking care not to jolt the door open. It was the shy, ruddy-faced girl from the pawnshop who'd charmed the toadly proprietor into letting her into the back room.

"Who the blooming fish are *you*?" I demanded. Then I looked her in the eye. "*Miss Holmes?*"

"Who else would it be?" Satisfaction flickered in her expression, then she said, "You weren't going to simply walk in there, were you?"

"No," I lied. And eased my fingers away from the knob.

Her eyes narrowed as she followed the movement of my hand. "Right."

I sniffed. "You smell like opium."

"Brilliant observation, Miss Stoker. It resembles an opium den in there. I find it quite interesting, for, as you might recall, Miss Hodgeworth's hair smelled of opium the night we found her. I suspect we are going to learn the answers to many questions within." She gestured to the double doors, then made another sharp movement. Apparently *I* was to follow *her*. "This way. There's a side entrance that's not as visible."

Blast. I'd been in too much of a hurry to notice the heavy black curtains that hung along the corridor, shrouding a side door. "Have you been inside? What are they doing? I heard someone scream."

She led me through the door and into a small alcove. The opium smell was even stronger here. A gaslamp lit the area, and I realized it was a narrow passageway that ran parallel to the room behind the double doors. It was barely wide enough for us to pass through in our voluminous skirts.

"Yes, of course I've been in there." It was odd to hear Miss Holmes's precise tones coming from this young woman. I looked closely and saw the outline of a false nose and the layers of makeup. "I arrived punctually and gained entrance on time. I was only inside the meeting chamber for a short while, and then I came to search for you. I do hope you weren't wasting your time shopping in that filthy store."

"I was examining the exterior of the building," I told her through gritted teeth. "*One* of us should know whether there is another entrance if we need a quick escape."

She nodded in agreement. "A commendable plan."

"How did you know the password to get in? And why didn't you take me with you? The shopkeeper wouldn't let me pass."

"Password? I employed no password. I suspect," Miss Holmes said archly, "you were denied entrance because you clearly had no idea what you were doing there. I saw the scarabs and made an enthusiastic comment, which identified me as a member of the society. Had you done the same, I'm certain you would have experienced the same positive—"

"Someone screamed," I interrupted her lecture.

"Yes. A female individual had the misfortune of spying a mouse," she said. "It ran over her feet, and then someone else's. Hence the second scream. It was quite chaotic for a moment."

I rolled my eyes and then pointed to the wall which separated us and the double-doored room. "What's happening in there?" For someone so fond of lecturing, Miss Holmes had been surprisingly distracted about this topic. "Have you seen the Ankh?"

"No, I haven't seen it. *Her.* But the Society of Sekhmet is gathered, and they're . . . well, you must see it to believe it." She stopped and gestured to a small door that led into the chamber. "No one will notice us entering here."

She cracked it open, and light filtered into the passage, along with a gust of sweet opium smoke. I peered around the edge and confirmed that we were entering from the side of the chamber, well placed in the shadows. Lights glowed, but there were none near the door, and it was simple to slip in unnoticed.

My jaw dropped at the sight. This was nothing like the previous Society of Sekhmet meeting we'd encountered.

Lamps, one in each corner, gave off small circles of light. The thick cloud of smoke was heaviest near the ceiling but it made the entire chamber seem muted and foggy. Silky fabric in crimson, garnet, topaz, and rust rippled on the walls. Large cushions and other soft, round furnishings littered the floor. Shallow bowls sat on low tables in front of the seats. They each held glowing coals . . . no, burning opium crystals. The smoldering drug gave off a low light and the narcotic smoke. Mellow music from an unfamiliar string instrument resonated, making the room feel even more exotic.

The scene reminded me of a picture of the thieves' den I'd seen in *The Arabian Nights*. So where was the massive chest of jewels and gold spilling onto the floor?

A dozen young women were seated or half reclined on the cushions. They were arranged in lounging, unladylike poses. Florence would have fainted at such an improper display: loose hair falling over their shoulders, missing gloves, and stockinged feet. But it was the bare ankles exposed by their bunched up skirts that was the worst offense.

However, the most shocking sight of all was the young men in attendance. There were several who seemed to be serving the young ladies—offering them goblets, plates filled with food, and even long-stemmed pipes.

They were shirtless.

I gaped for a moment, counting a total of seven men wearing nothing but breeches and sleeveless, open vests. I'd never seen a male without a shirt, and I could not tear my eyes away from the sight. They looked so very different than we women do, with their broad, square shoulders and bulging arms. And the muscular *ripples* on *their torsos.*

Was the room tilting, or was it the effects of the opium? My brain went soft. I felt warm and tingly everywhere, and my knees weakened. If I sank onto the cushions, would one of those young gentlemen come over and serve me? The thought made my insides flutter.

Someone pinched me on the arm, then jammed something sharp and pungent beneath my nose. It smelled bitter and unpleasant, but it cleared the fogginess away immediately.

Miss Holmes pressed a vial into my hand, and I held it beneath my nose as I looked around again. The double doors through which I had originally meant to enter were at the far right. A guard stood there. He took turns watching the room and checking the door behind him. Another guard stood at a set of double doors across the room from his counterpart.

There was no sign of the Ankh.

"I managed to speak briefly with one of the women here," Miss Holmes said softly. We remained unnoticed in the shadows, pressing flat against the wall. "What she said made little sense, due to the influence of this," she said, waving at the opium fog. Then she took a sniff from her vial. "But it appears that the Inner Circle meets beyond those doors. Presumably with the Ankh." She pointed to the double doors at the opposite end of the chamber.

"Is this what their salons are normally like?" I found it difficult to pull my attention from the shirtless young men. No wonder the ladies wanted to be members. This was more exciting than going to the theater!

"Smoking opium is dangerous and illegal, not to mention addicting," she said in my ear, her breath hot against my false curls.

"Not the opium! The young men. They are very . . . handsome."

"Don't be a fool." Miss Holmes elbowed me, and I grinned in the darkness before my moment of levity faded.

I'd been joking, but it wasn't a laughing matter. Two girls had been killed, one nearly murdered, and those crimes were somehow related to what was happening here and with the Ankh's Inner Circle. I had a feeling smoking opium was the least of the dangers for these young women.

We had to get beyond those double doors without being noticed.

Just then, one of the serving men passed closer to us than any of them had yet. He was carrying a tray of goblets, but didn't pause to offer any to the waiting ladies. Instead, he moved quickly through the room as if heading for a particular destination.

His bare, sleek bicep caught my attention first. He wore a wide band, and I couldn't tell if it was a leather cuff or a tattoo. But as he drew nearer, I happened to drag my attention up from his arm, over his shoulder to his bare throat. When I caught sight of his face, I couldn't control a gasp.

"What is it?" Miss Holmes hissed as Pix met my gaze.

His eyes widened, and his stride faltered. How could he recognize me so easily? I was in disguise! But the hitch in his step indicated he hadn't expected me any more than I'd expected him. Yet he gave no other indication as he passed by.

"Ouch! Stop poking me," I snapped at Miss Holmes. "I'll tell you later." And I slipped away.

Taking another whiff from my vial, I followed Pix. He stopped to deliver a chalice to a young woman. She reached languidly to take the goblet, looking at him with a gaze that made me both ashamed for her wantonness and unaccountably hot at her expression. She beckoned to him to join her on the cushion as some of the other young men had done.

If he *dared* sit down next to her . . . I kicked him in the heel as I walked past. At least he had some sense, for he straightened up to accompany me.

At the first unoccupied cushion, I sank down in a pool of skirts and turned to glare up at him. Before I could ask what he was doing here, he crouched and grabbed my arm, demanding, "What in the devil are ye doing 'ere?" His expression was flat and angry, without the humor that usually lingered in his eyes.

"I might ask you the same question." My head was swimming, and I was getting warm. I needed another sniff from that vial. His uncovered torso was *right there*, exposed behind the open vest. He was sleek and taut and dark. . . . I fumbled for the smelling salts and brought the vial to my nose.

"What are ye doin' here, Evaline?" His fingers tightened, giving me a little shake. "I didn' spec ye as a damned opium-eater, ye fool."

I wasn't certain which startled me more: his use of my name or his accusation. "I'm not," I said, yanking my arm away. "Lilly was a member of this society. They're killing young women, and I'm trying to stop them. But *you're* here, Pix," I said. His eyes were sharp and clear, despite the heavy smoke. "And you—"

"I got *mates* in 'ere," he said. "M' mate Jemmy's been captured and forced to work for—"

Suddenly, a shadow loomed over us. I looked up to see one of the guards standing there.

"Problem here, miss?" he said, reaching for Pix as his eyes swept over me. "Who the devil are you?"

Was he talking to me or to my companion? Before I had the chance to respond, Pix stood. I wasn't surprised how easily he evaded the man's grasp. He was slick that way.

"No problem 'ere," he said with an ingratiating smile, his hands spread innocently. Then before I could blink, his arm shifted close to his body, then jacked up in a strong, abrupt motion. The other man stiffened, his eyes widening, then slumped.

Pix caught him and eased the guard to the floor next to me. "Good gad, is he dead?"

"Doubt it," Pix replied, slipping something long and slender into his pocket. "Ye need t'leave," he said, taking my arm again.

I bristled and pulled away. We were still crouched next to the hopefully-not-dead guard, and our faces were very close together. I could smell a hint of Pix's minty scent mixed with wood smoke under the thick layer of opium.

"What do you know about the Ankh?" I had to say something to keep from getting lost in his intense gaze.

"I know nuthin' but 'at there's blokes been disappearin'. She's been takin' 'em, an' I finally tracked 'em down—"

We looked up at the same moment to see my partner standing over us, glowering in the drassy light. "Miss Stoker, what the devil are you doing?"

I yanked her down next to us, then glanced at the other guard. He seemed oblivious to all our activity. Relieved, I turned to Miss Holmes. "I'm certain you have a plan." I saw no need to hide my displeasure. Why couldn't she just make things up as she went? It always worked for me.

"Of course I have a plan. We have to get through those doors there." She pointed to the double doors that led to the Inner Circle. "And we need a distraction. Who are you?" she added.

"Ne'er min' 'at," Pix said, but without his usual charm. "I—"

The double doors opened abruptly, and a bright light spilled into the dim, smoky chamber. A gentleman stood in the entrance, outlined by the light as if he were an image in some holy icon. He was dressed in a long, dark coat, white shirt and shirtwaist, and trousers. He was hatless, with short blond hair gleaming in the light. He had a full, neat beard and mustache of the same color.

He didn't look anything like the Ankh we'd seen only a week ago. But as soon as he spoke, he confirmed his identity.

"Welcome, my darlings," said the leader of the Society of Sekhmet. "I trust you all are enjoying your evening?"

A low murmur rumbled through the chamber. Many of the young women were fully reclined, sleeping or otherwise unconscious. An uncomfortable prickle slid over my skin. Something was very wrong. But what? I sniffed from my vial again.

The Ankh laughed in a genteel, husky manner. "Very well, then, please carry on with your pleasure. I shall have need of only two of you tonight to join the Inner Circle. Who shall be the fortunate ones?"

He stepped into the chamber, using a walking stick for emphasis, and was followed by the two identical women who'd been at his side during the last meeting. My partner's interest tensed through her body as we watched the trio walk through the lumps of cushions, stopping at one not far from ours.

"You," intoned the Ankh, gesturing with the walking stick. "You are worthy."

One of the servants bent and assisted a young woman to her feet. Rather than seeming apprehensive, the girl curtseyed unsteadily.

My companion hissed something under her breath, and the Ankh turned suddenly, looking in our direction. And then, as if pulled by an invisible string, he began to move toward us. One servant led the woman he'd already chosen toward the open doors while the second one accompanied her master.

I tensed as the Ankh came closer. I could leap up and attack. Easy to knock him to the ground and take on the servant at the same time. I glanced at Miss Holmes. She shook her head in a short, sharp movement. *No.*

What the blooming fish was wrong with her? This was our chance! I gave her a violent glare, tensing and ready to spring. My breathing steadied. I curled my fingers around the small pistol in my pocket as the Ankh came closer.

Then Pix's fingers closed around my arm. "Nay, luv," he breathed in my ear. "Look."

Him too? Bristling, I turned . . . then I saw what caught his attention. The two large men who'd tried to capture us at the last Society of Sekhmet meeting stood just beyond the doorway. One of them held a shiny, evil-looking firearm.

Drat and blast! Even I couldn't compete with a bullet. I settled back onto the cushion, trying to look unobtrusive. As he drew nearer, my pulse sped up again. Could there be a way? If he came close enough? Energy sang in my veins. I knew what to do. I could do this . . .

I cast a quick glance at Miss Holmes. She seemed hypnotized by the commanding person.

When the Ankh did the unthinkable, pausing next to us, I closed my fingers surreptitiously around the pocketed pistol again. Trying not to look directly at him, I readied myself. *One . . . two . . . thr—*

"You," said the Ankh. "Come with me."

ᴹⁱˢˢ Stoker

Miss Stoker Is Taken Off Guard

I wasn't about to let Miss Holmes be dragged off into whatever danger lurked behind those doors. I began to rise.

But she met my eyes, giving me a mute plea to *wait*. I stilled, even though every part of my vampire-hunting body wanted to do otherwise.

As she stood, Miss Holmes's expression changed into a slack, uninteresting, drugged one . . . like that of the other young women surrounding us.

It was difficult, but I forced myself to also appear drowsy and incoherent. The best course of action was to remain unnoticed and not to look at the Ankh directly. I didn't want to be recognized. But what had drawn him to Miss Holmes?

Then, as if he read my mind, the Ankh's stare settled heavily on me for a long moment. Every one of my muscles tensed and was ready. My fingers still gripped the pistol, and it was all I could do to keep from bolting up and brandishing it. It was Pix's presence and his unusual caution that kept me from doing so. From the corner of my downcast eyes, I saw Miss Holmes's skirts drag over the floor as she followed the Ankh's servant.

Would I ever see her again?

The Ankh turned and walked back toward the open double doors, nodding to the two large men standing there. I sneaked a whiff from my vial.

As soon as the doors closed behind the Ankh, I lunged to my feet. I reached the hidden side door before I realized Pix had followed me. "Wot do ye think you're doin'?"

"I'm going after her." I meant to go back into the hallway through which Miss Holmes had brought me, hoping there was another door into the room beyond. "I don't know what the Ankh is planning, but it can't be good. We've got to stop it."

"I can't let ye—"

I shook off his grip once again. "You can't stop me. I'm a vampire rozzer, remember?"

"Aye," he said, his eyes dark and serious. They looked like deep wells of ink. "That ye are. Every bit o' ye."

Pix moved toward me, his gaze holding mine. I felt the solid wall pressing against my spine and shoulders. My pulse leapt as he eased closer. I could hardly breathe as heat rushed over me and my knees threatened to buckle. Then his mouth covered mine, soft and firm and warm, sending a shock of pleasure jolting through my body.

His hands, those long-fingered thief's hands, slipped around my jaw, curving to cup the back of my neck as he kissed me. It was a sleek, gentle sweep of lips over lips . . . and it turned into a tender nibble at the corner of my mouth.

Then all at once, he released me and stepped back. My whole body was hot and trembly. My knees shook, and I could do nothing but stare at him for a moment, my lips moist and throbbing, my heart thundering like a runaway horse.

"Aye," he said, his voice deep. "Every bit o' ye, Evaline Stoker."

I swallowed and tried to find my voice. "How—how *dare* you." He was a thief and a criminal, and he was here in the middle of an opium den. Not at all the type of man who should be kissing a young woman like me.

Not at all the type of man a young woman like me should be *allowing* to kiss her.

Instead of being put off by my outrage, he grinned crookedly and stepped back. "I'll take care o' that one," he said, gesturing to the original guard, who still stood at the other end of the chamber. The one I'd forgotten about in the last few moments, when Pix had had the audacity to push me up against the wall and *kiss* me.

He'd *kissed* me.

I reached up to touch my lips, then froze. But he'd already started off and, thank the blooming fish, didn't see. I needed another sniff from the vial. Head clearer, I slipped the tiny tube into my pocket and let myself through the door back into the hidden side hallway.

In here, the air was cooler and clearer. The last bit of my mottleness faded. I had to find out what was happening with the Inner Circle, but more importantly, I had to drag Miss Holmes out of there before she got herself in trouble. There were times when one couldn't *plan* for things. I didn't know what Pix was doing here, but he seemed perfectly capable of taking care of himself.

First he kisses my hand, then he kisses *me*? Who did he think he was?

Right. Forget about him. I had a job to do. I focused on that.

I was correct: the side corridor ran parallel all along the chamber where the Ankh had taken Mina. But drat! The hallway was no longer unoccupied.

The woman and I stared at each other in the same frozen moment, but I recovered more quickly. By the time she opened her mouth to scream, I was flying through the air toward her.

We tumbled to the ground. The unexpected force knocked the breath out of her so that she didn't have the chance to cry out. I shoved her facedown on the ground, my knee pressing between her shoulder blades to hold her immobile. She was unable to draw a deep breath even to speak. I was just about to use the leather trim on my bonnet to tie her wrists together when I had an idea.

She was one of the twin females—either Bastet or Amunet—who'd led Mina and the other girl away. I decided I would take her place. Pleased with my plan, I tore a piece of my petticoat away and tied it over her mouth, then bound her ankles together.

Then I pulled her long, black, shapeless shift up and off and tied her wrists together behind her back. This left her clothed in a plain white chemise and her underthings. She might be a little chilled, but it wasn't completely improper.

It would normally be impossible to undress myself, with all the lacings and buttons that marched up the back of my clothing, as well as the ungainly petticoats. But since I was wearing a costume borrowed from the theater, it was made to be donned and removed more quickly and easily than a normal gown. Why didn't they make all gowns so simple to wear?

For the finishing touch, I placed my hat, with the red curls attached, on my captive's head. With my dark hair still pinned in place, anyone would mistake me for her from a distance for a few moments. I tucked my pistol, knife, stake, and other tools into the handy pockets of the tunic.

I was just about to enter the room where Miss Holmes was when I saw a shadow at the other end of the passage. Pix was back, and he looked satisfied. I took that as an indication that he'd "taken care of" the guard.

"No' bad," he said, gesturing to my prisoner and taking in the sight of me dressed as her.

I was still furious with him for taking liberties, so I glared. "What are you doing here?"

"Ye can't go in there alone," he said, pointing to the chamber.

"I certainly can. And you—if you want to do something useful, you can get all those young women out of here. I'm sure you'll find at least one of them grateful enough to allow you to kiss her."

He flashed a grin, then sobered. "Ye can't go in there alone."

"If you know who I am, then you know I'm *made* for this, Pix," I told him. "This is what I have to do. I'm not helpless. I'm stronger and more capable than any other man or woman—even you. But those young women back in there? They *are* helpless. *They* need help. I don't."

He looked at me for a long moment. Then he gave a short nod. His lips were a flat line. "A'right. I'll take 'em an' Jemmy an' the other boys out o' 'ere."

"What are all those young men doing here, anyway?"

Pix's eyes grew dark. "She—'e—whoever 'tis—lured 'em in t'work fer 'em. F'the Society. But 'twas a bait and switch, an' half o' 'em are opium-eaters now and canna leave. I come t'find Jemmy and bring 'im 'ome."

"That's what you were doing at the museum that night, weren't you? Trying to find him? They were there, weren't they? The Society and the Ankh."

"I 'ear things, luv. I 'ear lots o' things on th' streets and in th' stews. Not all of 'em are good. No' all of 'em 're true. But sometimes . . ." He shrugged.

"I must go. Thank you, Pix," I said, surprised how much I meant it. I couldn't help watching as he slipped off back down the passage. Then I opened the door to the Inner Circle.

No one in the room seemed to notice when I crept inside. I looked around, mentally marking exits, potential weapons, and traps. Unlike the other chamber, this one was well lit. The Arabian thieves' den decor was nonexistent. The walls were beige, and electric sconces lined the space. Part of the roof was open to the night sky, as if it had been folded back like the pleats in a fan. Above, floating like eerie dark clouds, was a trio of sky-anchors. And beyond them, high in the heavens, was a sprinkling of stars and moonlit gray clouds.

Beneath that opening in the roof was a small dais with four wide steps leading to it on each side. A white table stood at the front, and arranged on it was a long, golden scepter, whose knob was the head of a lion, and an object that looked like a long golden loop with three bars running through it. The sistrum of Sekhmet? Next to the altar was the large statue of Sekhmet we'd seen at the previous gathering. Had Mr. Eckhert really traveled back in time using that thing?

The Ankh stood on the stage. In front of him was a large, ancient book on a small podium, its pages held open by a set of metal fingers. To one side was another table containing several items: a gleaming golden bracelet and a crown; candles suspended in intricate brass and bronze holders contained flames that danced in the night breeze; and golden bowls, cups, flasks, and other utensils. Standing behind the table was a device that resembled a crude skeleton made from metal:

it had spindly legs and even spindlier arms. Wires protruded from its body.

Two male guards stood to one side. Although they weren't identical in appearance, as the female assistants were, the two men wore similar clothing and resembled each other in stance, height, and the darkness of their hair.

Miss Holmes stood nearby, her eyes darting about the room, obviously taking in every detail. She couldn't see me; I stood far back and to her right. The other young woman who'd been recruited from the opium chamber stood next to her . . . Della Exington, niece of Lord Ramsay. The remaining female attendant stood between the two young women holding a pistol.

The Ankh was reading an incantation, his voice ringing out in a foreign language I assumed was Egyptian. He had his arms spread and looked from the book up to the open night sky and back down again as he chanted.

I eased farther into the room as the Ankh took a pinch of something from one of the smaller bowls and crumbled it into the largest one. He poured a sparkling red liquid from one of the flasks and added another ingredient that looked like small seeds. By then I could smell the pungent scent of something exotic and indefinable. All the while, he chanted, imploring some entity in the sky above.

At last, he stopped singing and lit a tiny twig with one of the candles, then dropped it into the bowl in which he'd been mixing. A soft *pop!* and then thick, curling red smoke snaked up from the bowl, bringing with it a stronger rush of the exotic scent.

The Ankh took the bowl and walked around the statue of Sekhmet, pausing every two steps. There were small vessels on the ground circling the statue, and he poured some of the smoking contents into each of them. This created many spirals of smoke rising around the goddess like a fragrant red curtain.

Moving to the altar, the Ankh retrieved the scepter and the sistrum and brought them to the Sekhmet statue. He fitted the scepter into the hand of Sekhmet that was positioned to hold it, and then slipped the noose of the sistrum over the other hand, which was raised with its palm facing outward. The sistrum thus hung from the goddess's elbow.

"It is time," said the Ankh, looking at the two young women he had chosen. "The Inner Circle has been prepared, and you must be initiated in order to access the deeper power of Sekhmet."

Della Exington came alive and stepped eagerly onto the dais. "I am grateful and pleased to prove my loyalty to the goddess."

"Felicitations, brave one," the Ankh said, turning to Miss Exington. The beard and mustache obscured much of the Ankh's face, yet I could see the delight in his eyes. His expression was unsettling in its fervor as he told Miss Exington, "You shall bring to Sekhmet her divine cuff, and you will be forever bound with her and her power."

He gestured, and one of the guards stepped onto the stage. Under the Ankh's direction, he helped the young woman into the circle of red smoke and turned her to face Sekhmet. As she looked up at the figure's leonine face, the guard lifted her left hand, fitting her palm, wrist, and arm against Sekhmet's in a mirror-like position. With her other hand, Miss Exington grasped the scepter.

The Ankh brought the cuff and fitted it around Miss Exington's upraised wrist, using it to fasten her to Sekhmet's arm. Fascinated and yet disturbed, I watched as the Ankh used a slender golden thong to bind her other hand to the scepter. All the while, the pungent crimson smoke continued to filter through the open roof.

"You shall join with Sekhmet. You have brought her Sacred Instrument, the golden cuff, to her, and your life force will meld with the goddess."

Miss Exington looked up at the statue as if it were the goddess herself. "I'm ready."

Sharp discomfort prickled over my skin, lifting the hair from the back of my neck and along my arms. What should I do? I curled my fingers around the pistol I'd slipped in my tunic pocket and glanced at Miss Holmes.

She was staring at the scene with the same horror I felt. She also had a pistol barrel pressed into her side by my twin counterpart. The Ankh wasn't taking any chances that his other Inner Circle candidate would have second thoughts.

The guard brought the spindly mechanical figure over and positioned it behind Miss Exington. As I watched in morbid fascination, he lined up the device's "arms" and "legs" to mirror the position of Miss Exington's, and then fastened three wires to the cuff. Three more wires were attached to the scepter, and three to the sistrum. The eerie red smoke curled around them, cloaking girl, statue, and machine in its thick fog.

"What—what are you doing?" the captive asked, her voice quavering as she pulled at her bonds.

"Be still, my dear. Your life force is the greatest gift you can bestow upon Sekhmet."

For the first time since entering the chamber, I moved. I started toward the altar, and the Ankh noticed me immediately.

"Ah, Amunet, you've returned in time," he said, giving me a brief glance.

I had to *act* . . . but for once, I was hesitant to leap into action. The guards still loomed. And then there was the gun pressing into Miss Holmes's torso.

Miss Exington pulled more violently against the wires that bound her. "I—I don't think I—"

"Be still, my darling," said the Ankh from outside of the circle of red smoke. "You are receiving a great honor from Sekhmet. You will be well rewarded. Hathor," he said, gesturing to the man who'd been assisting him. The man stepped away from the stage.

Miss Exington seemed to acquiesce, and her captor turned to the device.

"So shall it be! Sekhmet, I call to you to return."

Before I could react, the Ankh pulled down on a lever. A brilliant yellow spark snapped audibly, and I could see a hot red sizzle zip along the wires, through the device, and then over to the cuff and scepter. It was almost like electricity . . .

"Stop!" I shouted as Miss Exington jolted and screamed, then went rigid.

The Ankh spun around. "*You!*" He released the lever and lunged toward the table, snatching up the curved knife. I saw the lever swing back into its starting position. The sizzling sparks ceased, and Miss Exington sagged, struggling weakly against her bonds. She was crying.

I launched myself toward the front of the room, vaulting over a table that stood in the way. The Ankh's arm moved, and something silvery spun through the air toward me.

Someone cried out, and I heard a low shout . . . and then something red-hot tore into my side. Despite the sudden agony, I landed on two feet on the other side of the table just as Hathor sprang to action. Energy flooded my body as I spun into motion. I yanked up the table over which I'd just leapt, holding it with the legs facing the man.

As he rushed toward me, I whipped the heavy piece of furniture through the air. It crashed into him, and he stumbled back and into his companion. They landed in a heap on the floor.

I whirled to see that the Ankh had returned to the lever. His hand closed around it, and his eyes danced. "You're too late."

I pulled out my pistol and looked down at it as I lifted it to aim. And saw blood.

My blood.

I felt as if I'd been plunged into an ice-cold pool of water. Everything stilled and slowed and became murky and mottled.

I couldn't make my lungs work. They were thick and heavy, my vision narrow and hypnotized by the slick red blood . . . everywhere. On my hands, my torso, the gun, the floor.

I tried to fight the images assaulting my mind . . . I was back there again, with Mr. O'Gallegh . . . his throat and chest torn open, the scent of blood everywhere, the burning red eyes of the vampire mocking me as I froze. . . .

I tried to breathe, I thought I heard Mina, but she sounded far away. Too far away.

I *had* to . . . move . . . I had to . . . stop . . .

I heard someone laugh. Triumphant.

I pulled my face upright, looking at the Ankh.

He was smiling as he pulled the lever.

Miss Holmes

Horror

M iss Exington screamed again, the horrible sound cutting through the chamber.

Frantic, I looked over at Miss Stoker. Her eyes were empty, her expression dull. The hilt of a dagger protruded from her side. A dark stain ate into the fabric of her tunic, spreading rapidly, and blood covered her hand. Her chest heaved, as if she'd been running. The blood-slicked pistol slipped from her grip and tumbled to the floor.

I returned my attention to the Ankh, and then to Miss Exington, who had gone silent in her agony, still straining at her bonds. Then I turned back to my partner, who still hadn't removed the knife. All the while, I was cognizant of the heavy, hard metal of a pistol barrel pressing into my side.

Unfortunately, that heavy, hard metal of a pistol barrel was just above the pocket which held my own heavy, hard metal pistol . . . currently unavailable to assist me.

I could do nothing but watch the grisly scene unfold.

And I realized with a sudden cold rush that this was what awaited me.

After what seemed like forever—and yet not long enough—Miss Exington's body went taut, vibrating rigidly. She convulsed against the statue as the vicious current continued to pulse through her.

The dull *thud-thud-thud-thud* was horrifying.

At last, the Ankh, her false facial hair gleaming golden, returned the lever to its original position, and the chamber fell silent. The only sound was my own heartbeat, filling my ears.

I focused and dared a glance at Miss Stoker. She seemed to become aware again and yanked the dagger out of her midsection. Holding it in her hand, she took one awkward step toward the Ankh, but stopped when her adversary swooped down, picked up the pistol, and pointed it at her.

Blood pooled on the floor at my companion's feet. *Splat. Splat. Splat.*

"I don't think you'll be needing this any longer, Miss Stoker," said the Ankh. She wiped off the pistol with gloved hands.

My attention riveted on those gloved hands. Something familiar . . . As the Ankh replaced her handkerchief in a breast pocket, giving it a particular tuck with an odd flutter of her fingertips, my breath caught. Lady Cosgrove-Pitt had done precisely the same movement this morning while speaking to Lady Corteville.

I'd observed our captor closely during the entire course of events, watching for familiar traits and movements. Instinct told me I was correct in my suspicions, even though the Ankh looked nothing like Lady Isabella—she was taller, for one thing. She also had a different shape to her nose and jaw—from what I could discern behind the false beard and mustache. Even her teeth were different, but I well knew the effects of theatrical costume. Her eyes were heavily made up and shadowed by the curling blonde hair falling over her eyebrows, making it impossible to observe their natural shape. Her voice wasn't right either; it was much too low and deep.

I was an excellent example of how makeup and theatrics can obliterate one's identity. But there were certain mannerisms one couldn't or didn't hide, even when deep in disguise.

"From a family of legend, but not quite legendary yourself, are you, Miss Stoker?" Our captor tipped her head just as she lifted her chin—in the very same way Lady Isabella had done this morning when she'd greeted me.

The Ankh was *Lady Cosgrove-Pitt.*

I was convinced, but now I needed to prove it.

My attention turned back to the room at large as our captor continued to taunt my companion. "I must admit, Miss Stoker, I was concerned when I recognized you during our last meeting. As you come from a family of vampire hunters, I expected you to be more of a challenge. I thought you might be a hunter as well . . . but I was clearly mistaken."

Miss Stoker's face twisted, her eyes burned, filled with loathing and guilt. "You killed her."

The Ankh's eyebrows lifted into a swath of thick blonde hair. I could almost see Lady Isabella's sneer behind the mustache. "I'm afraid you're mistaken, Miss Stoker. Miss Exington offered up her life force to the goddess Sekhmet. Did you not see how eager she was?"

"She begged you to release her."

"By then it was already too late. If she died as a result of her decision, it's no fault of mine. She wanted to raise the goddess as much as I do."

I could no longer remain silent, despite the gun pressing into my side. "What you did was murder. Just as it was with Mayellen Hodgeworth and Allison Martindale and Lilly Corteville."

The Ankh turned, her eyes scoring over me. She made a sharp gesture to my gun-toting guard.

Before she could grab me—and notice the firearm in my pocket—I snatched off my bonnet and its false hair. I no longer had reason to obscure my identity; I wanted her to know who I was. I peeled off the heavy dark brows, the rubber tip on my nose, and spit out the small clay pieces I'd held in my mouth to change the shape of my cheeks.

"Miss Holmes," said the Ankh, "are you attempting to live up to the reputation of your family as well? That plan doesn't seem to have worked in your favor."

Considering that I had a gun pressed into my side, my companion was wounded (possibly mortally), and no one knew where we were, even I couldn't make a convincing counterargument. Neither Miss Stoker nor I had done a particularly admirable job of carrying out our duties thus far.

Instead, I tried to think of a way out of our predicament, and for the first time, I felt a tremor of apprehension. The weight of the gun in my pocket mocked me with its uselessness. I eased away from my guard.

"It's fortuitous that you've both chosen to join me here tonight," said the Ankh, stroking her mustache with gloved fingers. "The two of you could be useful. Imagine what the life forces of a Stoker and a Holmes would bring to the resurrected Sekhmet. And what power I'll have when she's brought back to life."

"Don't be absurd," I said with great bravado. If the Ankh meant to give my life force to Sekhmet, I was no longer in danger from the gun poking my side. "You don't truly believe you can resurrect a goddess by . . . what? Collecting artifacts that might have belonged to her? I've never heard anything so ridiculous."

The Ankh didn't take my bait. "Believe what you will." She aimed the pistol at me and gestured to the woman at my side. "Bastet, attend to Miss Exington. She's in the way."

As Bastet moved away to do her mistress's bidding, I glanced at Hathor and his companion. They were watching, giving me no opportunity to pull out my firearm. I looked at

Miss Stoker. To my horror, she'd slumped to the floor and sat with her head sagging to the side. Blood soaked the wall and floor around her.

Was she dead? Hadn't she told me multiple times that vampire hunters had great strength, speed, and healing capabilities. How could she be *dead*?

I started toward my companion. "She's hurt," I said when the Ankh's cold eyes fastened on me.

"That was my intent," said our malevolent hostess. "But feel free to see to her if you like. The less blood she loses, the more useful she'll be."

"Miss Stoker," I said as I knelt next to her, "*Evaline.*" The pungent scent of blood filled my nose. "Let me help you." I began to feel around in an attempt to stanch her wound, but she closed her fingers around my wrist. Her grip was astonishingly strong.

I looked at her, able to see her face unobstructed for the first time. The fogginess had disappeared. Her eyes, downcast until now, when they fastened on mine, were as sharp as they'd ever been.

"Keep talking. I'm going to make a distraction," she murmured. "When I do, the door . . . it's in the back . . ."

"All right," I said, glancing over at the Ankh. She was rearranging the wires from the device as Bastet and Hathor moved Miss Exington's limp body away. The other guard watched me with a cold gaze. I manipulated myself so that the side with my firearm was out of his sight. "Miss Stoker, I—"

"I should have stopped it. I could have stopped it, and I didn't." Her voice broke. She looked down at the blood on her hand, dried and cracked. I wasn't certain if she was truly seeing it, or looking at something that wasn't actually there.

"Evaline," I began again. Trying to be inconspicuous, I pushed my gun out without putting my hand in the pocket. She turned away. Her beautiful face had become stone.

"Get away from her."

I jolted, looking up to see Hathor's companion standing over me, pointing a gun. It had enough gadgets and gears on it that I wasn't inclined to ignore his warning.

Reluctantly, I stood, using my foot and the cover of my skirts to slide the weapon firmly up against Miss Stoker. "She's badly hurt," I said as the guard gestured me to stand against the wall at what he must consider a safe distance from my companion.

"More's the pity," said the Ankh from her position behind the table. She looked purposefully at Hathor, who moved off the dais to stand over my companion. "I dislike being rushed. But we can't have her dying before I'm finished, so let us hurry with the preparations."

"Lilly Corteville escaped from you," I said. I could use my attempts to distract the Ankh by getting confirmation for my deductions. "She was meant to be attached to the cuff, wasn't she? But she got away before you could do it."

The Ankh looked at me, her shadowed, black-ringed eyes shining with dark pleasure. Even now that I knew she was Lady Cosgrove-Pitt, I still couldn't see it in her eyes.

"You *are* a clever one," she said. "Perhaps worthy of the Holmes name after all. Yes indeed, each of the instruments must be given the power of a life force in order to become reanimated. And it occurs to me that the stronger and more worthy the life force of the animator is, the more powerful Sekhmet will be. That is why I find it serendipitous to have two excellent candidates for the diadem. You and your companion."

"You took the life force from Mayellen and Allison the same way you did from Della Exington," I said as the Ankh made her preparations at the table. "Why did you leave their bodies where they could be found?"

"Surely you can deduce that, Miss Holmes."

"One can only assume it was to make it look as if they'd taken their own lives. If bodies were found murdered, then there would be a crime to investigate, and you could be discovered. If they were found to have taken their own lives, there would be no investigation. And even if the bodies were simply disposed of, there would still be an investigation into their disappearance. Mayellen Hodgeworth was the one who was attached to the scepter. You were witnessed leaving the museum with it—and the statue of Sekhmet—on the night she was killed. *After* she was killed. You did it there, didn't you?"

"Apparently my confidence in you wasn't misplaced after all," our hostess commented as she added some dried substance that smelled musty and old to the bowl. "There'd surely be a place for one like you in Sekhmet's court, once she's resurrected."

"I'm afraid I must decline."

"That wasn't an invitation, Miss Holmes. I was merely making idle conversation."

The Ankh picked up the crown, presumably the final of the four instruments. Except . . . according to the message I'd received from Dylan, he'd located the diadem. The *real* one, if his information from the future was correct. The one the Ankh held resembled the drawings I'd seen, but it wasn't identical. My mind began to click through the possible ways to utilize this information. I continued my interrogation. "And you left the scarabs near the bodies for what reason? Surely not to lead us here, to you?"

"No, not at all. The scarabs were meant to be a warning to the other members of my Society. Some of them were becoming unsettled and uncomfortable."

"Like Lilly Corteville."

"Lilly was a mistake. She was to be the first, and she escaped just as we were beginning the process. I couldn't find her after that."

"Until today." I looked toward her, trying to imagine what that face would look like without the heavy fringe of hair over the forehead, and the thick, obstructing facial hair. Her face was angled so that I still couldn't get a clear view of her eyes as I made this pronouncement. But I knew anyway. I was *certain*.

"I know who you are."

The Ankh stilled, then laughed low and deep. "Even if you did, which I'm more than assured is not the case, it won't matter now. You won't be able to tell anyone."

"Your plan isn't going to work. You must have all four of the instruments for Sekhmet to rise. All four of the *correct* instruments, or Sekhmet won't be resurrected after all, regardless of whose life force you use."

"What are you saying?"

"That isn't Sekhmet's diadem."

The Ankh had ceased her preparations and stood unmoving. I read the struggle in the stance of her body: she didn't want to believe, she didn't want to have erred . . . but nor did she want to take the chance of failing at such an important moment.

I decided to assist her along the path of uncertainty. "The real one is at the British Museum."

She gave me a chill smile. "You're mistaken, Miss Holmes. I've commissioned or searched every part of the building myself. This is the Holy Diadem of Sekhmet."

I forced myself to keep from looking at Evaline. What was taking her so long? If she didn't act, I'd run out of things to say—and I'd find myself attached to the statue.

Keeping my attention on my adversary, acutely aware of the proximity of my personal guard and his gun, I replied, "The fact that the crown you're holding looks nothing like any of the drawings doesn't lead you to question your certainty? A *woman* like you wouldn't want to take the chance of being wrong. After all your plans. If you were wrong . . . they'd all come to naught. And you would have lost your chance."

Silence reigned for a long moment. What was Evaline *waiting* for?

"And I happen to be the only one who knows where the real diadem is," I said.

ℳISS STOKER
Out of the Frying Pan

A t Miss Holmes's announcement, I did three things at once: surged to my feet, discharged the Steam-Stream gun, and yanked on a string I'd looped around the leg of the Ankh's table.

The guard who'd been halfheartedly watching me howled when I slammed into his chin with the top of my head. The table shifted and fell off the dais. Its contents tumbled everywhere. And the blast of steam from my gun seared into the guard next to Miss Holmes.

I met her eyes. "Go!"

She darted toward the double doors as I whirled to blast the gun at the Ankh. He ducked, reaching for a weapon in his pocket as I discharged the gun again. This time it caught Bastet, and the woman screamed as the steam burned through her tunic and into her arm.

Boom! Something had fallen off the preparation table and combined with an element it shouldn't have. Flames erupted, catching on the edge of a tablecloth, and jumped quickly to an upholstered chair. Soon the space would be engulfed.

I ran toward the door in Miss Holmes's wake, flinging a heavy table behind me. The guard whose jaw I broke wasn't fast enough, and the table caught him in the torso. He stumbled back and fell into the man I'd Steam-Streamed. In the midst of the chaos, someone's pistol discharged with a loud crack.

The flames spread near the front of the chamber, and as I turned back to blast one more wide stream of steam around the room, I heard a loud mechanical grinding. But I didn't wait to find out what it was; I shot steam at my pursuers and burst through the double doors into the opium room.

To my relief, the chamber was empty except for Miss Holmes, who'd paused at the opposite side. Why was she waiting for me?

"Go!" I couldn't stop, I couldn't allow myself to think. If I did, everything would catch up to me: the pain, the loss of blood, my cowardice.

I should have stopped them. I should have saved her.

My partner went through the double doors, and I was only seconds behind her. We bolted down the corridor, and just as we rounded the corner, a figure appeared.

Miss Holmes hesitated, but I recognized him. "Keep going!" I pushed her between the shoulder blades as I met Pix's eyes. "There's a fire!"

My partner was panting, not used to the sort of physical activity that came naturally to me. Pix seemed to understand, for he grabbed her arm and helped me tow her along. She didn't argue, but she was probably so out of breath she simply couldn't. When she stumbled again, he slung her over his shoulder just as he'd done with Lilly Corteville. And he continued to run, outpacing even me.

We were coming out onto the street when I remembered Amunet. Tied up and hidden in the side hall where I'd left her.

"Oh no," I said, taking one deep breath of cool night air. "She's trapped!"

It was one thing to leave the Ankh and his guards in the chamber to find their way out. But Amunet was helpless and no one knew she was there.

No one but me.

I dashed back into the building. I had time. The building was made from brick. It wasn't as if it was going to burn to the ground. But the smoke, and the flames . . . they would eat anything wooden or cloth.

Or human.

Using my small illuminator for light, I retraced our steps. Despite the growing pain from my wound and the renewed flow of blood, I managed to find my way back . . . back to the opium room, now filling with a different sort of smoke . . . back through the side door, where Pix had stolen that kiss from me right against that wall . . . into the side hallway, tinged with smoke. A dull, grating roar filled my ears.

Beaming my light, I ran up the narrow corridor to where I had left Amunet. The smoke had begun to filter through, but it wasn't as thick as I'd expected. Light flickered from . . . the open door.

Amunet was gone.

But I wasn't alone.

I looked up to find a gun pointed at me.

"Welcome back, Miss Stoker."

MISS HOLMES

An Unfortunate Miscalculation

I could hardly catch my breath, but the cool night air helped. Whoever the individual was who'd been carrying me dumped me unceremoniously onto my feet.

I looked around and didn't immediately see Evaline, although I'd watched her run out onto the street behind us. However, just a short distance away was a cluster of very confused, frightened young women. The Society of Sekhmet had been evacuated. She was probably in the midst of the girls. Just then, the sound of sirens screeching filled the air. The police or firemen.

The young man who'd carried me out, whose torso was bared by the vest that identified him as one of the opium servers, spun to look behind him. "Bloody 'ell! I'm gone." Before I could thank him for his assistance, he took himself off.

I stood there for a moment, still panting, and looked up. The fire in the upper floors would devastate, but the building wouldn't come down. It was brick. Surely someone as clever as the Ankh would find an escape.

Which meant that this wasn't over.

The sky-anchors swayed high above, large dark balloons bumping against each other in the breeze. As I watched, one of them detached itself from the others. It happened occasionally that one of the moorings loosened, and streetwatchers would announce it with cries of "Cut loose! It's cut loose!" and there would be wagers on how long it would be buffeted about in the sky and where it would land.

Then comprehension dawned. The stage, the entire stage in the opium den, had been a sort of airship. The steps, in all four directions, had actually been folded sides, collapsed onto the floor. Now they'd been raised and the entire stage lifted . . . and was being piloted up and out of the open roof. I watched with a combination of admiration and annoyance that I hadn't observed this earlier.

"Miss Holmes!"

A familiar peremptory voice had me spinning around.

"This is becoming quite a habit, is it not? Encountering you in the thick of criminal activity." Inspector Grayling stood there, radiating exasperation. "You promised not to come here tonight."

"I didn't promise any such thing," I told him. "I merely said—wait!" I cried, struck by a realization. "I must get to Cosgrove Terrace." This was my chance to catch Lady

Cosgrove-Pitt in the act—or, more accurately, *not* to. *She wouldn't be there.* She couldn't be. "Quickly!"

"What is it?" he asked, his pique easing in the face of my desperate entreaty.

"It's—it's a matter of life and death," I said. I couldn't explain it to him; he wouldn't believe me. He wouldn't *want* to believe the awful truth about his relative.

I'd have to *show* him.

It was to Grayling's credit—and I suppose mine—that he didn't hesitate. "This way," he said, taking my arm when I whirled to hail an air-bus. "It's faster."

With a little more force than necessary, he directed me to the large, gleaming steamcycle. It appeared even more dangerous at close proximity. I swallowed hard.

"Put these on," he said, shoving an aviator hat and a pair of goggles at me.

Then he climbed onto the machine, straddling it as one would a horse. His long coat split over the seat, falling in two black swatches. For the first time, I noticed how long and powerful Grayling's limbs were and I realized, with a sudden shock of heat and nerves, that I was going to have to sit behind him. And *hold on.*

I couldn't breathe.

"I . . ."

"Miss Holmes," he said with challenge in his eyes, "a matter of life and death cannot wait for you to build up your courage."

Drat. He was right. I had to get to Cosgrove Terrace to prove that Lady Cosgrove-Pitt was the Ankh. I pulled the aviator cap down over my head and arranged the goggles as he did something to the machine.

Its engine came to life with a spectacular roar, then settled into a rhythmic, metallic purr. Steeling myself, I climbed onto the seat behind him, thankful I had had the foresight to wear the new split skirts I'd had made, like Miss Stoker's. I couldn't imagine what a spectacle I would have made of myself otherwise.

"Hold on," he said, and the engine gave another loud roar. I could feel it charge and vibrate beneath me, and I realized he was waiting for me to hold on to *him*.

Thankful my face was hidden by the goggles and that I was behind him, I placed my hands gingerly at his waist, curling my fingers into his wool coat.

The cycle roared again, then surged forward. I jolted backward and, stifling a shriek, gripped his coat more tightly as I leaned toward him. The warmth of his body melded into me as a sharp wind blasted over my arms and skirted legs.

We rounded a corner at full speed. I slipped to one side on the seat and nearly tumbled off. Terrified, I gave up on propriety and gave in to practicality, changing my position to wrap my arms around his torso, grabbing my wrist with my other hand. This position required me to rest my cheek against Grayling's back, filling my nose with the pleasing aroma of wood-smoked wool.

I felt the muscles of his torso shift and slide as he manipulated the cycle, and only after what seemed like forever did I realize I had my eyes closed.

Cautiously, I opened them and peered down from behind the green-tinted goggles. The first thing I saw was my leg curved forward, directly behind his as my split skirt blustered wildly about. Thank Fortune I was wearing pantaloons beneath it. Beyond that, I saw part of the brass detail curving around the cycle. We were moving so fast that everything else, including the ground some distance below, was a blur.

I'd never traveled anywhere at this speed. Cool air roared over me as we slipped in and out of alleys and over canals, beneath air-lifts and among carriages with the dexterity of a cat. I even lifted my face away from Grayling's warm spine and eased my death grip around his waist. It was exhilarating.

And then, suddenly, there was a brick wall. Right *there*.

I closed my eyes and ducked instinctively as Grayling's arm jerked. The cycle turned, tipping to the side so acutely I had to cling even more tightly to him.

I kept my eyes closed, deciding it was better I didn't see where we were going as we zigzagged through the streets, the roar of the machine filling my ears, its rumble buzzing through my limbs.

At last, it slowed and the roar eased. I opened my eyes to see Cosgrove Terrace, and my heart began to race for different reasons. Grayling drove the cycle up to the front entrance and parked just below the rise of three main steps. This was a different entrance than the one we'd used during the Roses Ball, but just as grand.

I climbed off the vehicle. My knees shook, and my body vibrated as if I was still riding the machine. And yet . . . I glanced at the steamcycle. During the moments I'd had my eyes open, the speed and maneuverability had been exciting.

Avoiding Grayling's glance, I pulled off the aviator cap and goggles. I wasn't going to worry about the condition of my hair. After a long night of wearing a bonnet with a wig and then the ensuing altercation with the Ankh, I couldn't imagine that an aviator cap would have worsened the situation.

After all, Lady Cosgrove-Pitt had already seen me.

Grayling walked to the door with me and rang the bell. "Is Lord Cosgrove-Pitt in danger? Or Lady Isabella? Have you received some information from your father?"

Shaking my head, I waited with complacence. Thanks to Grayling's speedy vehicle, it would be impossible for Lady Isabella to have arrived at Cosgrove Terrace before we did, even if she had an inkling that I might come here. She wasn't going to be inside, and her absence was going to be the first piece of evidence against her.

The door swung open before I had the opportunity to respond to Grayling's question, which was a good thing, because what precisely was I going to tell him? That his distant relative had been murdering young women in order to resurrect an Egyptian goddess from the ether?

"Good evening, Dusenbery, I need to speak with Lord Belmont or Lady Isabella."

"It's urgent that we speak to Lady Cosgrove-Pitt immediately," I said.

"Of course, Inspector Grayling. And Miss . . . er . . . ?"
The butler stepped back, giving us entrance.

I didn't offer my name. I saw no reason to give Lady
Isabella or anyone else warning that I was there. When Dusenbery seemed to hesitate—perhaps waiting for me to do so—I
pressed, "It's quite urgent. Is Lady Isabella in?" Since it was
well into the early hours of the morning, it would be odd for
her not to be in, even if she'd attended a party or the theater.

"Lord Belmont is at his club," Dusenbery said, looking
at Grayling instead of me. I'm certain the only reason he was
so forthcoming with that information was because my companion was both a relative and from the authorities. "I shall
see if Lady Isabella will see you."

"We'll wait in the parlor," Grayling told Dusenbery.

"I'd prefer to wait here," I said. It would be easier to see
or hear anything else happening in the house if we remained
in the foyer.

"Very well," said Dusenbery as he turned, presumably
to hunt down Lady Isabella.

I chafed at the delay, yet at the same time, I felt a strange
calm settle over me. Lady Isabella wouldn't see us, of course,
because she wasn't here.

And even if she happened to arrive in the next few
moments—which in itself was unlikely; after all, she'd been
air-lifted from a roof on the other side of the city—she'd be

unable to change her clothing and otherwise hide the traces of her secret identity.

I was going to have to induce Grayling to search the house if Lady Isabella "refused" to see us—that is, when the butler found that she wasn't in residence after all.

"Miss Holmes," said my companion, looking down at me from his excessive height, "will you please provide me some explanation for this?" His hair was ruffled from the ride, and I couldn't help but remember how my legs had pressed into the underside of his. And how well he'd managed that monstrous machine.

I heard the sound of footsteps.

"Ambrose! Whatever is wrong? What are you doing here at this time of the night?"

My heart dropped to my feet at the sound of Lady Isabella's voice. I whirled, the inability to hide my shock surely evident in my expression. My whole body had gone cold and numb. "Lady Cosgrove-Pitt. You're here." My lips hardly moved.

Impossible.

"But of course I'm here." Her eyes went from me to Grayling and back again, a bemused, confused look in them. My face heated to a fiery temperature as the rest of my person remained icy. "It's nearly one o'clock in the morning."

I examined her desperately, searching for any sign she'd just been in the midst of a fire. She was wearing a long night rail and a loose housecoat, and her hair was braided in one single plait that hung over her shoulder. I saw no trace of makeup nor any debris on her slippered feet.

How could I be wrong?

"I'm sorry to bother you, Lady Isabella," Grayling said. I could hear the stiffness in his voice and feel his confusion as he looked at me. "Miss Holmes—er—we believed it was an urgent matter."

I found my voice at last. "I just learned about Lilly Corteville. I wanted to express my condolences. I understand you were close to the family." I could think of nothing else to say, and Grayling's heavy regard continued to weigh me down.

Lady Isabella looked at me. I looked back at her, searching in vain for something in her eyes, some sort of recognition that we'd been face-to-face less than an hour ago.

"Yes, indeed. What a tragedy that was," she said in a soothing voice that conveyed confusion. "That was your purpose for rousting me from my bed?"

"I—I apologize, my lady. I . . . er . . . didn't realize how late it was."

"My apologies as well, Lady Isabella," said Grayling. "We'll be off now. Please give Uncle Belmont my regards."

"Of course," said the gracious lady.

No sooner had the door closed behind us than Grayling gave me a long, inscrutable look. To my surprise, it was neither condemning nor angry. It was . . . exasperated and a little bemused. And concerned.

"If I didn't know any better, I'd think you simply wanted an excuse to ride on the steamcycle."

I couldn't look at him.

I'd been wrong.

Very wrong.

How could I have made such a mistake?

MISS HOLMES

The Game Is Afoot

Dazed by humiliation, I recalled little of my subsequent ride home. Grayling insisted he take me there and nowhere else. I was too stunned to argue otherwise.

I had no idea what time I let myself into a quiet house, but the night was still dark.

How could I have been wrong?

How could I have made such a mistake?

I found myself stumbling into my mother's empty room. A single beam of silvery moonlight traced the knotted coverlet on her bed, and I sank onto that cold but welcoming furnishing. A soft puff of air escaped from the coverings, and I caught the faintest whiff of my mother's scent.

My insides churned unpleasantly, and my throat hurt. I couldn't ever remember a time I felt so ill and lost and empty.

Except the day she left.

From my seat on the bed, I looked at her dressing table. The gray, drassy illumination highlighted the few articles that remained: a small silver jewelry box, a broken hairbrush, two mahogany combs, and a wrist-length piece of lace. I knew that her wardrobe was just as empty.

Why, Mother?

What is wrong with me?

I'd always thought she left me because I was too much a Holmes.

But after tonight, I realized I wasn't *enough* of a Holmes.

I woke, achy and parched, curled up on Mother's rumpled quilt. Mrs. Raskill said nothing as I stumbled into my own chamber to freshen up and dress, but I caught a flash of sympathy in her gaze. I ignored it.

A short time later, I found my way into the laboratory. The broken glass from my magnifyer still littered the floor. Had it been only yesterday that Grayling had startled me with the news of Lilly Corteville?

Yesterday, when I believed I could observe and deduce and that things would fit together.

Yesterday, when I'd been trusted by the princess to protect and serve my country.

Yesterday. When I'd watched helplessly as a young woman died.

I remembered again the horrific sound of her body *thud-thud-thud-thudding* against the statue.

I closed my eyes and willed myself not to give in to base emotions. I wouldn't cry. I wouldn't think of it. I must keep my mind clear.

I'd have to get a new magnifyer. But the thought didn't motivate me as it might normally have done. I looked around at my work: my notes, the charred Danish face powder, the other vials and dishes. Was it all for naught? Had all my studying been a waste?

Was Uncle Sherlock correct after all? That women couldn't remain separate from their emotions in order to make accurate and important observations and deductions?

I needed to report to Miss Adler. I'd have to confess my shameful miscalculation. I'd have to admit that the Ankh had escaped.

And she still had one more instrument to find. One more young woman to kill.

Someone knocked on the laboratory door.

"Come in," I replied dully.

"You've got a visitor." Mrs. Raskill poked her little nose around the corner as if sniffing for any sign of danger. "I don't know what's so importan' that you're gettin' packages from the Met, and letters from all over, and visitors. Every day, it's sumpin'. It's up to comin' like bein' on Bond Street, all these comin's and goin's."

I followed her out of the laboratory. The last person I wanted to see was Grayling, who I was certain had come to interview me about the events of last night. But to my surprise, it wasn't Inspector Grayling who stood just inside the front door of our house. I didn't recognize the male individual, who appeared to be no more than fourteen years of age.

Hat held carelessly in bare hands—*not intimidated by upper-class settings or people, but not of the upper class himself.*

Met my eyes with confidence but not improperly—*respectful of upper-class women.*

Underground ticket stub stuck in his cuff—*public transportation; limited funds.*

"May I help you?"

"Gots a message for ye." He proffered a folded packet. "Was tole t'wait fer your answer."

I took the offered packet and examined it briefly, my skin prickling.

Expensive, heavy paper—*from Inkwell's, where the blue ink had come from on the invitation to the Star Terrace.*

Faint, pungent scent—*the same smell from last night's events.*

My heart racing, I opened the missive.

The diadem in exchange
for your companion.

I read it a second time, noticing the penmanship (*a right-handed female*), aware of a sudden roaring in my ears and the prickling washing over my body.

The Ankh had Evaline.

How was it possible?

I shook my head. I as well as the young man who carried me to safety had seen her come out of the building last night. She was right there.

But I hadn't seen her afterward. I hadn't even spoken to her. I'd been too distracted by the need to prove the identity of the Ankh, and I'd left the scene.

What would have happened if I'd remained there, with the other young women, instead of rushing off with Grayling on a wild goose chase?

Was Miss Stoker's abduction yet another effect of my gross miscalculation?

I gripped the message, determination flooding through me. The game was afoot.

"Wot's yer answer, then, miss?"

"Who gave this to you? Where and when?"

He gave an awkward bow. "I canna tell you that, miss, as I don't rightly know. I was on th' underground, and someone come b'hind me and give it to me. 'E 'ad a gun at m'neck and tole me not to turn around. An' 'e give me the directions."

"But then how are you to bring my response?" I asked suspiciously. "You said you must wait for my answer."

He shrugged and said, "I'm to walk down Bond-street and to be wearin' my cap iffen ye said aye, and iffen ye said nay, I'm not to be wearin' it."

"Were you given any further instructions?"

"On'y that I'm t'walk down th' street as 'e said when Big Ben calls noon."

I glanced at the clock. It was almost ten. "Very well. My answer is yes, so you may wear your cap on your walk down Bond-street at noon today."

"An' I'm told t'tell you there's t'be further 'structions if yer answer's aye."

"I suspected that might be the case," I said dryly.

I released the messenger and contemplated following him. But that would likely have been an exercise in foolishness. How would I know who was watching Bond, the busiest shopping street in the city? There would be hundreds of people in the vicinity at noon.

I decided to make other plans. I'd wait here, of course, for the further instructions. In the meantime, I tried to quell my worries over Miss Stoker's condition. If she was being held for the ransom of the diadem, then she'd be safe . . . at least until I appeared with it.

Taking a deep breath, I contacted the museum and notified Dylan to come to my house and to bring "the item which he notified me about yesterday" posthaste.

Then I washed up and dressed, choosing my clothing carefully. Although I'd worn split skirts last evening, I'd found them heavy and ungainly during the activities of the night. Thus, today I disdained my normal corset and instead wore a much shorter and less rigid one, which would allow me to be more active without becoming short of breath in the event I had to run again. I dressed in slim-fitting trousers with a simple shirt and vest. I stuffed a variety of implements into a large satchel and twisted my long hair into a single braid that I wrapped into a knot at the back of my neck.

Despite my devastating setback last evening, I was still convinced the individual was a woman. And I still wasn't convinced that she *wasn't* Lady Cosgrove-Pitt.

I'd give her the diadem. And I'd rescue Evaline.

And I'd unmask the Ankh in the process.

Now all I had to do was to wait for the Ankh to make her next move.

MISS STOKER

In the Shadow of Sekhmet

I smelled fish and smoke and inhaled dust, and I couldn't move my arms. Slowly, I opened my eyes to find myself in an unfamiliar environment. For a moment I was confused . . . then the pounding in my temple, a dull ache in my side, and the sight of blood crusted on my tunic reminded me how I came to be here.

I had gone back in the building to help Amunet and came face-to-face with Hathor. He pointed a gun at me, and I launched myself at him. We collided and fell to the floor. His gun fired and missed, but by the time I scrambled to my feet, Bastet was there, helping me upright by yanking my loose braid. They dragged me out of the hallway and into the altar room. The chamber was engulfed in smoke and patches of flames.

The dais had walls, and a loud engine roared above. Heavy cables reached down through the open rooftop, pulling the steps up to become accordion-like walls. The gun pointing at my head forced me inside this alcove. I joined the statue of Sekhmet next to the altar. An unbound Amunet sat in a small motor-chamber above, piloting what had become an airship up and out of the roofless building.

The Ankh and the other male guard were nowhere to be seen.

There was a seam at the corner of two walls. I dove for it, but Hathor dragged me back onto the base of the "ship." He raised his hand, the metal of the firearm gleaming, and when it came back down, I didn't duck fast enough . . .

I had no idea how much time had passed since I'd been knocked out. I was no longer in the odd airship nor the building that had been on fire. No one would know where I was or how to find me.

To add to the situation, my wrists were bound in front of me and my ankles chained to . . .

The statue of Sekhmet.

The Ankh's intention was unpleasantly clear.

The statue loomed over me, gleaming faint gold in the dim light. As I looked up at the lion-headed goddess, I couldn't forget the image of a battered, devastated body, thudding and trembling helplessly against those golden arms.

Della Exington was dead.

And I'd been unable to save her. Not because I couldn't get there in time, but because I couldn't make myself do it. I'd been frozen and paralyzed. Weak.

I'd dragged myself out of it. But it had been too late by then. Remorse and guilt flooded me. Then deep, burning fury. Tears filled my eyes, bitter and stinging.

I had no right to call myself a Venator, a vampire hunter.

My great-great-aunt Victoria had sacrificed everything for her calling, even staking the husband she loved after he was turned UnDead.

I couldn't even ignore a bit of blood in order to save a young woman's life.

I shifted and felt the dull throb in my side. It had stopped bleeding even before Miss Holmes and I escaped from the opium chamber. But when I ran back through the building to help Amunet, it started oozing again. On a normal person, this wound would have been fatal. At the very least, debilitating. But for me, it wasn't the injury or even the pain that had caused my paralysis.

Footsteps approached and the sound brought me out of my stupor. A tall, slender figure cloaked in an enveloping black wrap appeared. This time, the Ankh was garbed in female clothing: skirts and a poke bonnet so deep it shielded his or her face.

"Miss Stoker. I'm delighted to see that you haven't bled to death."

I could reach him. Her. Grab her by the leg and yank. She had to be unsteady on those tiny hourglass heels. Though it was around my ankle, my chain was long enough to wrap around her throat, to subdue her . . .

She stepped back as if she'd read my mind. Blast it.

"Your knife-throwing skills are quite good," I said. "Traveling circus, perhaps? Was your mother the fat lady?"

The Ankh stilled, looking at me from behind the bonnet. "You'll be pleased to know your partner has agreed to bring me Sekhmet's diadem in exchange for your person."

"Mina Holmes is no fool. Once you have the diadem, then what? Who will be your next victim?"

I saw the flash of a smile and the impression of two gleaming eyes. "That is a concern, I must admit. Nonetheless, I'm certain some solution will occur to me." A low, grating laugh told me she already had one. And I wasn't going to like it.

Despite her clothing, I still couldn't settle on whether the person before me was a woman who dressed in male clothing, or a man currently garbed as a female. "And when do you plan to execute this wily plan?"

"Tonight. The timing is most auspicious, for today is the anniversary of when I first learned of the power of Sekhmet. Five years ago, I stumbled upon the artifact which sent me on this path."

If Miss Holmes were here, she'd probably try to lecture and deduce the Ankh into submission. My moment of wry humor vanished as quickly as it had come. How the blazes was I going to escape my chain before my partner arrived, and how was I going to bring the Ankh down with me?

"Very well, then," said my host. She carried something long and silver and slender and moved closer. "Now that I've ascertained your relative health, it's time to send for your friend. I intend to have a gracious welcome prepared for her."

Brilliant. Mina Holmes would walk right into that trap.

She gestured, and Hathor came toward me. I kicked and bucked. Sekhmet wavered after I yanked especially hard on the ankle chains looped around her, but the Ankh and Hathor steadied the statue before it tumbled over. Hathor swung out with a powerful hand. The blow caught me against the side of the face and, unable to brace myself, I slammed to the floor. My temple hit the ground hard, and before I could recover, Hathor grabbed me from behind. He forced me onto my knees so I couldn't kick, and held my arms immobile. One large hand covered my nose and mouth, smothering me into stillness. I gasped for breath against his sweaty, dirty hand but couldn't twist my face away.

Only then did the Ankh feel safe enough to get close to me. I let her see the triumph in my eyes.

When the Ankh bent close, something silver in her hand, my pulse jumped. Could she know my weakness? Was she going to cut me? Spill more blood?

She reached for me, my neck, and grabbed a handful of my hair. Twisting it viciously, she brought a silver object toward my face. I closed my eyes, steeling myself, waiting for the pain. My mind was clear.

You're a Venator. You're strong. Fight.

Then I heard the soft *snip* and a bit of my hair fell away.

ᴹISS HOLMES

An Impossible Choice

ᴰylan arrived at my house just before eleven o'clock, carrying a heavy satchel.

Ignoring Mrs. Raskill's muttering about more comings and goings, I brought him into the parlor so he could show me the diadem. He greeted me with a smile and seemed to be moving toward me as if to offer an embrace, but caught himself at the last minute. A light stain flushed his cheeks, and he stepped back.

"You're wearing pants." The way his eyes traveled over my trouser-covered limbs made me self-conscious about the way the fabric clung to my shape. I felt indecent and exposed, and the way his blue eyes filtered over me made my cheeks heat up.

"I . . . erm . . ."

He smiled and sat down without waiting for me to do so first. "I didn't mean to embarrass you, Mina. I was just surprised. You look really hot—uh, really good in pants. In my time, girls—women—wear them all the time. It's considered completely normal."

My discomfort eased in favor of curiosity. "Is that true? Women can wear trousers in the future without it being frowned upon?"

"And a lot of other things you'd find scandalous. Like short skirts," he added with a bashful grin.

I bit my lip, holding back more questions that bubbled to the surface. It never seemed the right time to ask him all the things I wanted to know. I'd have to save my interrogation for another time—when I didn't have a friend's life to save.

"Very well," I said. "Back to the matter at hand. I'm relieved you located the diadem. It's a most fortuitous discovery, considering the development of the last twenty-four hours." I explained the events of the night before, leaving out my disastrous detour to Lady Cosgrove-Pitt's house. "And so I'm going to deliver the diadem to the Ankh."

"And I'll be going with you," Dylan said. He raised a hand at my sound of negation, his blue eyes boring into me. "I've been stuck in the darned museum for almost two weeks, and it's time I did something besides sulk. You can't go alone, Mina. And it's not because you're a woman," he added when I began to fume. "Remind me to tell you about Amelia Earhart and Jane Goodall someday. Going alone would be crazy, especially after last night. You should have taken me with you, or at least told the police. And besides all that, if the statue of Sekhmet is there, I want to see it. Maybe I can find a way to use it to get home."

I had a variety of reactions to this pronouncement. First, I found I rather liked this Dylan who spoke with such strength and passion. Who didn't think that simply being a woman was a reason not to go alone. And who liked the way I looked in trousers.

And second, I had a sudden, brilliant idea with which only he could assist me.

And third . . . I felt an unexpected pang at the thought of Dylan finding his way back to the future. Just as I was getting to know him, to feel as if we had some sort of connection, he might be leaving. I hadn't felt such kinship with another person in a long time. Perhaps ever.

"Naturally I can't tell Scotland Yard about this," I said. "The Ankh is too smart; surely she'll be watching for us when we arrive to make the exchange. If there are any authorities in the vicinity, I'm certain the deal will be off. Will you show me the diadem?"

Dylan pulled the item out of his satchel, and I examined it eagerly. It looked exactly like the drawing in the text I'd been reading. There was no doubt that, regardless whether it had actually belonged to Sekhmet or not, it was the instrument of legend. Delicate gold filigree created a very un-Egyptian-like crown. Two topazes were set in such a way in the front of the crown that they appeared to be lion's eyes, and the slender gold was wrought in the shape of a lioness's snout and whiskers.

"It was where we thought it was, wasn't it?" I couldn't allow the Ankh to have it. There had to be another way.

I'd make a copy. I had the equipment in my lab, and we had at least another hour before my acceptance of the Ankh's arrangement was delivered.

"Do you have your special telephone with you?" I asked, my mind working again on the half-formed plan I'd already been considering.

"Yes, although it's low on battery, so I've had it turned off for most of the last week. I have to find a way to charge it. But I can still use it."

"Can you force it to emit sounds and noises at will?"

"I sure can."

"Come into the laboratory. I'll tell you my plan while I work." I needed something to occupy my hands as well as my mind while we waited to hear of Evaline.

Time crawled, and it was well after five o'clock when Mrs. Raskill interrupted us.

"It's your visitor again," she said, poking her head around the ajar door. "Lands!"

Finally. I'd been unable to contain my growing apprehension for Evaline and her safety.

"At last we'll find out how to make the exchange," I said to Dylan, gesturing at the false diadem. It required only a few more adjustments, and I was confident it would easily pass muster as the instrument in question.

I hurried out of the laboratory, wiping my hands on a rag, and then stopped short. "Inspector Grayling." Drat!

"Good afternoon, Miss Holmes," he said, his voice cool and unemotional as he held his hat in a large, freckled hand. His eyes widened fractionally, however, as they swept over me in my masculine garb, bringing a warm flush to my cheeks.

Dylan might be accustomed to seeing women in trousers, but Grayling was not.

"How may I help you?" I asked as Dylan appeared from behind me.

Grayling's attention went to him and his expression turned stony. "I've come to take your statement regarding the events of last evening." He spoke to me, but seemed unable to pull his attention from Dylan.

"I'm rather busy at the moment."

"Obviously," Grayling replied crisply. He returned his attention to Dylan. "Have you been notified when you'll stand trial for the attempted break-in?"

I gawked at him, shocked by his rudeness, but Dylan didn't seem to mind. "I've been lucky. The museum isn't going to press charges, thanks to Miss Adler. She took care of it all before she left town." He glanced at me. "I meant to tell you earlier—Miss Adler had to leave unexpectedly."

I nodded and quelled an unfamiliar moment of uncertainty. My mentor was gone, and I was on my own. I'd already made one grave error. . . .

I stopped those thoughts and turned to Grayling. "I have a rather delicate project I must finish today. Perhaps we could make an appointment to speak tomorrow?"

That was assuming I'd be alive and able to speak tomorrow.

I shoved that thought away.

He fixed me with a steady look, then gave a short, sharp nod. "Very well, Miss Holmes. Good day."

We'd hardly returned to the laboratory when Mrs. Raskill thudded on the door yet again. "It's. Another. Visitor. Ye. 'Ave," she said, clearly capitalizing and punctuating each word. And the fact that she'd dropped the *h* in *have* indicated her extreme exasperation.

The same messenger who'd come earlier stood at the front door. "I've got 'nother message fer ye."

My attention swept over him once again, noting several changes to his appearance.

Gray dusty grit on the outside of left shoe only—*he'd been on Pennington-street since he was here last.*

A shiny dark green stain low on his trousers, the faint scent of algae—*he'd been at the dockyards within the last hour.*

A red-and-green paper wrapper peeked from his trouser pocket—*he'd recently patronized Shertle's Meats for one of their meat pies.*

"May I see the message?"

The folded packet's exterior was identical to the first. However, inside was a lock of dark, curling hair. There was no doubt to whom it belonged—Evaline's curls coiled in a clockwise direction and were a deep, shiny walnut color of this precise hue.

I turned my attention to the message:

> *You have until nine o'clock this evening to bring*
> *the diadem to Fannery's Square.*
> *If you do not, Miss Stoker will*
> *embrace Sekhmet for all eternity.*
> *If you do not come alone,*
> *the deal is defunct, and she'll die.*

"Are you to wait for a response again?" I asked.

"Nay, miss. Except I'm told ye'd pay me fer my troubles."

My mind was so busy analyzing my observations that I didn't have the attention to spare for being vexed by this assumption. I paid the young man, sent him on his way, and then returned my attention to the message and Miss Stoker's hair. I sniffed both the letter and her curls, and examined the latter on a piece of white paper.

"Where's Fannery's Square?" asked Dylan, who'd been reading over my shoulder.

"She's very clever. Oh, the Ankh is *quite* clever," I said, mulling over all I'd absorbed since the young man returned. "Fannery's Square is outside London by one hour. But the only way to get there is to take the train. The next train leaves at seven, and there is one more today at half past eight. The latter would get us to our destination too late, so we must take the seven o'clock train."

"How long will it take us to get to the train station?"

I pinched my lower lip.

The strange churning I always felt when I was getting close to something fascinating had begun in my belly. "This means the Ankh wants to ensure we're on the seven o'clock train, for some particular reason. That's why she waited so late in the day to send the message. She wants us in a particular location or on a particular route at a certain time. And everyone knows the Fannery train is precisely on time, so one must be at the station *before* seven."

I paced the room. The churning had grown stronger, my belly tighter. I recalled my observations of the messenger, and the churning turned into more of a warning prickling.

I didn't like it.

"Our messenger—who had to have received this message from the Ankh or someone close to her—was nowhere in the proximity of the Fannery line train today," I said. "He was at the docks. He spent at least the latter part of the day there, because Shertle's Meats never serves their pies until after half past four. And his trousers—the gray debris on the left shoe indicates he was walking on Pennington-street. It's the only location that sort of concrete is being poured this week—I read about it in the *Times*. That's one block north of the Yeater

Wharf. He didn't have time to go from Bond to Pennington and Shertle's after walking along there at noon, for the algae on his trousers is fresh. It hasn't yet dried."

Dylan was staring at me as if I were speaking in some slang that was just as incomprehensible as some of the things he'd said to me. "So what does this all mean? In plain English?"

"It means that I have a decision to make." I realized the churning, which was normally a comforting feeling, had turned into something akin to nausea. "I either follow the instructions herein, or I go where our messenger was—and where he received this message. That's where the Ankh is."

Suddenly the image of last night, with Lady Cosgrove-Pitt in her housecoat and her bemused expression rose in my mind like a terrible specter. Along with Grayling's exasperated, rigid face. The nausea grew stronger.

"I think."

I don't believe I'd ever said or even thought those words before. *I think.*

Dylan watched me. "So you're thinking we ignore the message and track down the Ankh somewhere . . . where? By the wharf? How will we know what building?"

"I can narrow it down to a block," I said, thinking of the particular smell clinging to the lock of Evaline's hair. "The one with the fish-smokers on New Gravel Lane. And as for which building? We'll look for the one with the airship coming out of the roof. Surely the Ankh won't risk leaving her Sekhmet statue behind."

I glanced at him, my palms damp and my insides heavy and rock-like. That was what the facts told me.

But the message—directions from the desperate woman who held my partner and who wanted the diadem above all else—commanded me otherwise.

Yesterday, I wouldn't have hesitated. I'd have listened to my deductions and ignored the message.

But today . . . I had to decide whether to follow my instincts and my conclusions . . . or to follow directions and possibly put myself into a trap.

But if I didn't follow the directions, I risked Evaline's life.

Last night's mistake had been nothing more than mortifying and inconvenient.

Today's decision was a matter of life and death.

I looked at the clock, my insides roiling. After six. I had to make a decision.

"I can't risk it. We're going—" I drew in a deep breath, fighting my logical mind. I made the decision and immediately felt ill. But I soldiered on. I couldn't afford to be wrong this time. "We're following the directions. We're going to Fannery's Square."

ᴍᴍ Miss Stoker

Miss Stoker's Decision

With the Ankh gone, I investigated my prison, limited as I was by the length of my bonds. I was looking for weapons or at least something to unlock the chains.

One option was to pull the heavy statue over and unloop the chains from around her. While that would free me from that massive anchor, it wouldn't unlock my ankles or wrists. I'd still be trussed. And whoever was below would hear the sound of Sekhmet crashing to the floor. There had to be another option.

Two huge floor-to-ceiling windows offered dirty light, but I couldn't get close enough to draw attention to myself. The roof was closed to the sky, but I could tell it was near twilight. Chairs and tables lined the space, and an empty fireplace yawned in one wall. The faint glow of coals cast an eerie red light in the darkening chamber. A bookshelf and a desk were arranged at one end of the room. This had been an office at some point, but now there was a pile of clothing in a corner, as well as a trunk.

The smell of rotting fish and the distant sounds of water told me I was near the wharf, in a completely different area of town than Witcherell's Pawnshop. I wondered if Pix considered these streets and docks part of his domain.

Surely he was back in the stews, arm wrestling with his friends. From what I understood of his brief explanation in the opium den, he'd come to rescue his friend Jemmy from the Ankh. And in the meantime, he got caught up with Miss Holmes and me. He *had* helped the other girls to escape too. And he'd taken advantage of my confusion and stolen a kiss as well. Although Pix seemed to care about my well-being, he would have no way of knowing where and how I'd come to be here, in the captivity of the Ankh.

I looked around the room and at the altar. There was no doubt what the Ankh had planned for me. The mechanical device, with all of its wires, waited, eerie and foreboding, next to the sleek Sekhmet.

Miss Holmes was going to bring the diadem, the real diadem, to trade for me, and then the Ankh would have it. She'd have all the instruments.

She'd also have both of us.

I wasn't a fool. No matter how intelligent my partner was, the Ankh was the one giving the orders. Setting up a trap.

It didn't matter whether the goddess could be reanimated, or if her power could be harnessed. The Ankh didn't care. She'd keep trying. She'd already killed too many young women. She wasn't about to stop there. She'd keep killing and killing until she managed to raise Sekhmet. . . .

My path became clear. Crystal and absolute.

I had to stop the Ankh before Miss Holmes stepped into the trap.

I looked up at the statue of Sekhmet and then over at the mechanical device, its ugly wires a portent of what was to come.

Yes. That was it. A feeling of calm and rightness settled over me. I'd never been more certain of anything in my life.

I was bound and restricted by the length of my chain, but I still had some range of motion. I inched toward the mechanical device and used my body to shift its position. It had to be in the correct location, and I could only hope the Ankh didn't notice.

It was difficult work. I had to use my considerable strength to tug the massive statue a little closer to the device, taking care not to tip Sekhmet over. *Not yet.* By the time I got everything into position, I was out of breath but satisfied.

No sooner had I finished with my arrangements than I heard the sounds of voices and footsteps. Quickly, I scooted my bound body back over to the opposite side of the statue and tried to appear docile and hopeless.

"The girl didn't go to the station," someone said as the door opened. "We waited, and she didn't appear."

The Ankh swept in, and I could feel his rage. He had changed clothing again, and this time was attired in trousers and a shapeless dark tunic. A low hat was settled down to his eyebrows, and a mask covered him from eyes to nose. A short dark beard shadowed his jaw and mouth.

"What does she mean to do?" the Ankh said as he stalked into the chamber. He was followed by Hathor, Bastet, and Amunet.

They couldn't find Miss Holmes. She'd done something unexpected. Was she coming or not?

I wasn't certain whether to be relieved or offended.

"It's nine o'clock." The Ankh looked over at me, his eyes dark and furious from behind the mask. "Your friend has recanted on our agreement. She's leaving you to die."

"She lied, you know," I said. "She doesn't have the diadem. She intended to trick you all along."

The Ankh swept over to the table. "I'll find her and show her what happens to one who tries to trick me. She might have caused a delay, but in the end, I'll win. As for tonight—I shan't wait any longer. I have everything I need." He looked at me and then at the crown Amunet had placed on the table. "This one will work. I'm certain of it. And if it doesn't . . . I'll continue to search for the real one."

I kept my eyelids hooded. I didn't want him to see I was ready. And willing.

Because I was taking him with me.

The Ankh conducted the same preparations as last night, and soon red smoke curled throughout the chamber. Hathor dragged me to my feet and, as Amunet kept a gun pressed into my side, he unbound my hands and one ankle, leaving the other still chained to the statue. If I made any sort of move, they'd shoot me . . . but not to kill. I was meant to die another way, and the level of agony was up to me.

The Ankh continued with his work, reading another chant to Sekhmet. This time, he didn't direct his words to the sky, but toward the large window. I could see Sekhmet's reflection in the glass as the sky darkened outside and the fire-light inside our chamber glowed more brightly.

I was forced to stand facing Sekhmet just as Della Exington had done. With a sharp wrench, Bastet forced my arm to mirror the statue's. The gold was cool and smooth against my bare skin. I kept my breathing calm as a thin wire running from the mechanical device was wrapped around my arm. It cut into my skin.

I was going to die.

And I was at peace. This was what I was meant to do, what my family legacy required of me: bravery, strength, and sacrifice. For the good and safety of all.

I drew in a deep breath and looked at the gear-ridden, wired device. It was still where I'd placed it.

Hathor tightened another wire around my right arm, positioning it against Sekhmet's scepter, and then Bastet brought over the false diadem. I trembled a little as she posi-tioned the crown on my head. I mentally reviewed the steps of my plan. *Me.* The one who never made plans. If only Miss Holmes were here to witness my brilliance.

When the Ankh began to pull the lever, I would have a few brief seconds to lunge to the side. I'd pull the heavy statue over with me . . . down and onto the Ankh.

We'd fall into the mechanical device together, and thus entwined, the Ankh and I would together give our life forces to a Sekhmet who would never rise.

My pulse was faster now. The Ankh placed the dishes of smoking coals around the statue, and the fog rose around me like a red curtain. It was time.

Which was worse? Knowing what was to come—the searing, sharp agony? Death? Or to be ignorant of it, as Della Exington had been?

"I'm not certain whether to be offended or pleased that you began the festivities without me."

The familiar, pompous voice carried across the chamber. Mina!

A soft little pop of warmth spread through my chest . . . then *drat!* She was here. She was going to ruin everything!

"Well, well, my sweet. So you've graced us with your presence after all," said the Ankh.

I shifted in my restricted position to see Mina standing in the doorway. She was holding a cloth-wrapped parcel, and . . .

Bloody hell. She'd got herself captured. And the diadem too.

Hathor's counterpart prodded my partner into the chamber with a complicated looking weapon. Whatever it was—gun, Steam-Streamer—it looked lethal.

I met Miss Holmes's gaze. Either she was too stubborn or too distracted to see the message I sent: *Get out of here!*

"Please come in, Miss Holmes. I'm delighted that you've arrived in time to see your friend share her life force with my beloved Sekhmet. We were just about to begin. Osiris?"

The attendant followed the implicit command by taking the parcel from Miss Holmes and ushering her into the chamber.

"I'm sorry I didn't follow your directions," my partner said. "I wasn't fond of the idea of being taken by surprise or otherwise abducted while on my way to Fannery's Square, which was, I'm certain, your original intent."

"Pish," said the Ankh. He sounded delighted. "But you are here, and it truly doesn't matter how that happened. You won't be leaving anytime soon, and Osiris would have made certain you came alone."

At that moment, I heard a soft sound to the right behind me. As if something was sliding across the floor. Miss Holmes had a sudden coughing attack, meeting my eyes over her hand. I turned to look in that direction, on the other side of Sekhmet, but no one was there.

"Very well, then," said the Ankh. "Where were we? Ah, yes," he said, moving to the machine. His hand rested on the lever, which I had positioned so he stood in the perfect place for me to bring the statue down on top of him.

I craned my neck, trying to look at Mina, but she was too busy making some odd expression at me. Her eyes bugged out and her mouth was twitching.

The last thing I wanted to remember seeing before I died was Mina Holmes, silently lecturing me about the mess *she'd* gotten herself into.

I heard another soft, skimming sound of something going across the floor. I looked over as the Ankh began to lower the lever.

I focused, waiting for the right moment . . . waiting for the first sensation of shock. I must act before it paralyzed me.

The lever shot down and I propelled myself toward the Ankh.

ℳISS HOLMES

A Disembodied Voice

I watched in horror as Miss Stoker jolted in pain, then all at once, she was falling—toward the Ankh.

The massive Sekhmet statue teetered ominously. I saw what was going to happen, and I screamed a warning, but it was too late. All three of them tumbled to the floor with a metallic crash that echoed through the chamber. A sizzle of power zapped from the machine, then fizzled into orange sparks.

"No!" I shouted, heedless of the firearm pushing into my back. "Evaline!"

Suddenly a loud noise filled the space. A blaring, blasting, screeching noise the likes of which I'd never heard before, but the sound of which was a relief. My plan was working! If only it weren't too late.

Osiris whirled as the Ankh's other servants bolted into action, confused at the distractions from every direction. As they spun around in panic, the second element of my plan was executed: a low, rolling *boom!* erupted from the fireplace.

In seconds, the chamber filled with heavy black smoke. I heard the sounds of footsteps and shouts, followed by a disembodied voice—"You're surrounded! Stand where you are!"—and knew that Dylan had fulfilled the third and final element of the plan.

But, good gad, *Evaline!* Was I too late? What had she done? How could she think I'd appear without a plan?

I ducked away from Osiris and dashed through the thick fog toward Miss Stoker and the Sekhmet statue, terrified everything had happened too late and she was dead—crushed under the heavy weight or electrocuted.

I coughed and then remembered to pull up the mask I had around my neck, covering my nose and mouth as I crawled along the floor. How much easier it was to do so in trousers than a bundle of skirts! I touched the base of the Sekhmet statue first, then my frantic hands encountered something soft and warm.

It moved, and as I attempted to wave away the smoke, I felt the statue shuddering and shifting against my leg with someone's effort to move it. I heard the sound of metallic clinks and clanks nearby. More shouts filled my ears, smoke stung my eyes, and I heard the sound of glass shattering. A rush of fresh air burst into the chamber.

"Stop her!" cried a voice I recognized. *Evaline!* Evaline was alive! She was a heap on the floor, a mass of clinking chains and struggling limbs, but she was alive.

But the Ankh was getting away! I bolted to my feet in time to see the slim, dark-clad figure stumbling toward the broken window. I stumbled after her, but tripped over something and fell hard on the ground. My palms landed on something sharp and painful. "Stop her! Dylan! She's getting away!"

The sounds of pounding footsteps and shouts—real ones this time, not from Dylan's useful device—came from the floor and stairs below. "Stop! Scotland Yard commands you to halt!"

I lurched toward the Ankh again. I wasn't about to let her get away. "Oh, no, you don't—" Someone or something slammed into me from behind, and I thwumped to the floor once more. My cut palms screamed as I struggled to remove myself from beneath the hindrance of something heavy, I watched the shape at the window.

The Ankh's slender figure shone against the opening, now jagged with glass in the drassy moonbeams. She looked at me from across the dim, smoky chamber, and I fancied our eyes met in acknowledgment and understanding. Then, outlined by the silvery light, she gave a condescending lift of her chin in my direction. Infuriated, I started toward her again. I couldn't let her get away. *I had to find out who she was!*

The door burst open behind me with a flood of light. I recognized Luckworth's voice shouting orders. "Stop! Halt! Scotland Yard!"

At the window, the Ankh froze, an arrogant yet surprised silhouette. . . . I shouted, finally erupting unencumbered to my feet, but it was too late. My nemesis gave a flippant wave—a clear farewell—then tipped backward, tumbling out into the night.

"No!" I charged toward the jagged black window. My foot caught on something, and I hurtled through the air. Screaming, I clawed at where the window should have been. Just before I crashed through into midair, two hands grabbed me from behind.

I flew up and back, and landed on the floor in an ignominious heap of gangly trousered limbs and sagging hair. I saw Dylan's relieved expression, then looked up into the furious face of Inspector Grayling.

ℳiss Holmes

Wherein Our Heroines Learn the
Meaning of the Word "Debrief"

"If you'd just waited a moment longer, everything would have been fine," I said, eyeing Evaline with unconcealed resentment.

It was three days after the events above the fish-smokers' shop at the docks.

"If *you* hadn't shown up, *my* plan would have worked perfectly," she retorted, folding her arms over her middle.

"Yes, and *you* would have been *dead.*"

"That might be the case, but at least we'd be certain of the Ankh's identity. Thanks to your ridiculous, overly complicated plan, we still don't know who she was."

I opened my mouth to argue, then I saw the glint of humor in her eyes and relaxed. "Quite true," I conceded, and exchanged a glance with Dylan. Our plan had been perfectly wrought and flawlessly executed . . . but in the end, the Ankh had had her own victory.

That was the only thing that continued to niggle at me.

We still didn't know who the Ankh was, or precisely why she (at least I'd been correct about the gender) had collected young women. Had she been trying to stir up their independence while attempting to raise a goddess's powers, or had that merely been a byproduct of her mad plan? I still found the concept absurd, but then again . . . Dylan Ekhert's time traveling was a testament to events and concepts beyond my understanding.

We did have a body . . . but it was bloated and nibbled beyond recognition. Pulled just this morning from the canal where it met the Thames, the dead woman had been dressed in dark trousers and a loose black tunic—just as the Ankh had been. I hadn't been given ample opportunity to examine the deceased, thanks to Inspector Luckworth's insistence that girls had no reason to be so morbid, but one thing was certain: even from my brief look, it was clear that the body didn't resemble Lady Cosgrove-Pitt.

Aside from that, the lady in question had been seen leaving London yesterday with her husband, bound for their country estate. It was still inconceivable that I'd been wrong about the Ankh's identity, but unless the body wasn't actually the villainess in question, the unthinkable was true: my deductions were incorrect.

No one could have survived the fall from that window, three stories off the ground. As I would have been such a casualty myself if it weren't for Inspector Grayling and Dylan both grabbing me at the last minute (how humiliating), I'd examined the area below quite carefully. Someone tumbling from the window would either have crashed to the cobblestones or landed in the canal. No body was found or witnessed on the street, which left the canal. And although it took three days, a corpse matching the description of the Ankh as we'd last seen her had been dragged from the sewage.

Thus, as far as Scotland Yard was concerned, the case was closed. The only reason I wasn't completely convinced was because in accepting that, it would mean I had been irrefutably wrong. And that I probably owed Lady Cosgrove-Pitt, as well as Grayling, an explanation. And an apology.

I turned my mind away from that unpleasant thought and looked at Evaline. I might have made a deductive reasoning error, but I must admit: she had done something much more heroic. "You were ready to die," I said. "You *would* have died. Willingly."

Our eyes met, and I saw wariness there, and another emotion I couldn't identify. Surprise? Gratitude? Shyness?

Evaline shrugged, but I could see how much it cost her to appear casual. "And you ignored the directions on the message from the Ankh. You didn't go to Fannery's Square. Instead, you risked your life to find me. You saved my life."

I remembered again how utterly tied in knots my insides had been after I reversed my decision to go to Fannery's Square. They didn't relax until I saw Sekhmet through the high window above the fish-smokers' shop. Only then was I certain I'd done the right thing. And only then did I send for Grayling and Luckworth. "In the end, I had to listen to my instincts."

"I'm rather glad you did."

That was when I realized that, somewhere along the way, she'd ceased being Miss Stoker and had become Evaline.

Not quite a friend, but no longer a stranger.

The unfamiliar sensation of camaraderie made me smile. "And I'm quite certain the remaining Society of Sekhmet members would have been just as appreciative of *your* sacrifice if you'd actually been able to make it."

A loud throat-clearing drew my attention to Miss Adler. She, Evaline, Dylan, and myself were sitting in her office, engaging in what our friend from the future oddly called a "debrief."

Miss Adler looked around at us, her eyes tired but pleased. I wasn't certain when she'd returned from whatever had called her away so unexpectedly, but yesterday morning I received communication from her to meet at the museum today. "The important thing is, you're all safe. Perhaps in the future, you'll learn to work together more easily instead of relying only on yourselves." She looked at us meaningfully, and I felt my cheeks warm. "Nevertheless, you've completed your first task for Her Royal Highness. She is very pleased, as am I. You undertook a complicated, dangerous mission and came through mostly unscathed and . . . I am inclined to believe . . . a bit more willing to recognize your limitations as well as your strengths."

Evaline and I exchanged glances.

"But no one's found any of the Ankh's papers? Her hideout? Anything she left behind about her plans? Any evidence at all?"

I looked at Dylan. Defeat showed in his face, and I understood why. He'd hoped that once we stopped the Ankh, we'd be able to find *something* that would help him. Something about the statue's history, her research . . . anything. We'd found Sekhmet, of course, and Miss Adler had made arrangements to have the statue delivered here to the museum.

We all hoped that once Dylan was in the presence of the artifact again, he'd be able to use it to return to his time. But when we replaced it in the cellar chamber in which he'd first appeared, nothing happened.

"There was a scarab in the base," he said, pointing to a deep indentation where the beetle had once been. "It was glowing, and when I touched it, that's when and how it happened. But I'm not sure how."

"It must have had something to do with timing of the Ankh performing her ceremony. The one when Mayellen

Hodgeworth died. She was conducting her activity here at the same time you saw the glowing scarab . . . a hundred years from now. You touched it, and . . . it happened."

"There's no way to send me back, is there? Replacing the scarab won't work?"

"The ones we found from Lilly and the others don't fit in the spot," I said, placing my hand on his shoulder. His muscles trembled beneath my touch, and I felt his breath hitch. I waited for a long moment for him to regain control of his emotions. "But there must be one. Somewhere. Or we'll find another way."

"I guess I won't be going home anytime soon," he said. His voice was strangely muffled.

When he stood, I wrapped one arm around him in an awkward embrace and patted him on the shoulder. I knew a little how he felt, a stranger forced to be part of a world in which one didn't quite fit. He was warm and very tall against me, and I realized I couldn't remember the last time I'd touched another person with affection.

Or was touched.

I experienced a sudden momentary relief that he wouldn't be leaving after all. That he'd be here a little longer, someone who was even more of an outsider than I. Angry with myself for such selfish thoughts, I pushed them away.

"I'm sorry, Dylan. I promise, I'm going to find a way to help you. Perhaps one of the Ankh's assistants might know where the missing scarab is. Since the Ankh is dead, they may be willing to help us now. There's a way. There *must* be a way."

Osiris and Amunet were in police custody. The explosions, noises, and general altercation—even for a location as rough as the docks—had brought not only the authorities but also other witnesses. Even so, Hathor and Bastet had managed to escape, but enough witnesses had seen fugitives running from the rooms above the fish-smokers' shop that I was optimistic that they'd be apprehended. I'd been down at Scotland Yard several times to give them my story . . . but I hadn't seen Inspector Grayling.

I considered that very fortunate.

Thank goodness I hadn't told anyone—even Dylan and Miss Adler—my suspicions about Lady Cosgrove-Pitt.

Dylan was looking hard at Evaline. "By the way . . . I've been trying to figure out how that all worked. The Ankh actually did move the lever, right? So, like, why didn't you get zapped? Or did you? What happened?"

"I felt a low, buzzing sensation just before I knocked us over. But it evaporated as we fell, and I hardly felt any shock at all."

"I suspect it was because the Ankh wasn't using the true diadem," I interjected. "Only the true diadem would extract the life force from the individual. If one believed in that sort of thing."

"Or," Evaline said, "the lever could have bounced back when we fell to the ground. And then everything went into chaos."

"And it was Dylan who created this distraction?" asked Miss Adler.

"It was all my plan, but he was the one who made it possible. I knew his telephone could make loud odd noises, and he arranged it so that it would do so at a certain time."

"I set two alarms," he explained. "One to go off first and to make a siren sound, and then another one to sound off later, with police voices shouting that they were surrounding the building."

"But the sounds came from across the room. No one was there," Evaline said.

I couldn't control my complacent smile. "Yes. That was precisely the point. We were able to employ Dylan's particular skill called . . . hockey—is that correct?"

"The game is called hockey," he said. "It involves shooting a puck across the ice—well, anyway, I'm really good at it and I can shoot exactly where something needs to go. Fast, straight, and smooth. That came in handy when I had to slide the phone across the room without anyone seeing it. The phone's about the same size as a puck. I sneaked in after Mina, and no one noticed me standing in the dark corner. And then I shot a smoke bomb into the fireplace without anyone seeing me either. It was like scoring two perfect goals."

"I heard it," Evaline said, turning to look at him. Interest shone in her eyes. "Both times, I heard it going across the floor. And then Mina started coughing, I suppose to warn me . . . but I didn't see anything to explain what was happening."

"But now," Dylan said, pulling the device from his pocket, "it's completely out of battery. I'm going to need to find a way to charge it again if I ever want to use it. Isn't there any way to get some access to electricity?"

"I know someone who could probably help." Evaline's face turned an interesting shade of pink. "His name is Pix."

That afternoon, I returned to my empty house. I felt bereft now that the adventure was over. I could return to my work in the laboratory and finish my treatise, but that no longer seemed as interesting or compelling.

Perhaps Princess Alexandra would contact me—us— again for another task.

Or since the Ankh had never been unmasked, perhaps Her Royal Highness wouldn't consider the project fully complete, despite Miss Adler's praise.

An unsolved mystery, riddled with my deductive error and an embarrassing incident with the Parliamentary leader's wife. I shuddered.

I might be discharged from working for the Crown before I'd hardly begun.

Depressed and irritated, I almost didn't see the package sitting on the kitchen table.

My name, in a dark, scrawling penmanship—*written by a man, confident and perhaps even arrogant.*

Inexpensive brown wrapping—the sort that could be purchased at any stationer or apothecary—*the sender was practical and tight with funds.*

Twine from a butcher shop—

My pulse increased as I unwrapped the packet.

A small note was attached. It read:

To replace the one which was broken.

It was signed with a firm, solid *A. Grayling.*

Inside was a very cognogginish, head-mounting glass magnifyer.

ACKNOWLEDGMENTS

As a writer, sometimes I think I do the easy part when it comes to publishing a project. There are so many people who have been involved in *The Clockwork Scarab* from the basic concept through the volume you are now holding, and I want to thank them all.

First, Maura Kye-Casella, my hardworking and *patient* agent for seizing on this concept in its very early stages and helping me muscle it into something better than the original one.

I also thank Mara Jacobs, Holli Bertram, Jana DeLeon, and Norah Wilson—some of my best writer friends—for reading one or more versions of the book.

There were several experts in the field of young adult fiction who took the time to read and give feedback on the book. I'm indebted to Rachel Wagner, Christiana Eisenhut, Jessica Nietzche, Cameron Martin, Sarah Pierce, Amy Pelizzaro, and Rebecca Moxie. Your thoughts and feedback were appreciated and taken to heart.

An extra special thanks to Emma Schulte for coming up with "cognoggin." Absolutely brilliant!

My peers and friends Kady Cross, Rachel Hawkins, Sophie Jordan, Kristi Cook, Leanna Renee Hieber, and Leah Cypess took time out of their own creative processes to read *The Clockwork Scarab*. Receiving positive feedback from such talented ladies is something I treasure greatly.

I've published more than two dozen books, and I am blown away by the amazing and creative team at Chronicle Books. I value the dedication from everyone in the production process and for including me in all aspects of the design, packaging, editing, and marketing for *The Clockwork Scarab*. In particular, my hardworking editor, Kelli Chipponeri, has gone above and beyond the call of duty with her time and effort spent on this project. I do believe she could recite the book by heart if asked. Ariel Richardson has been up to her elbows in the project as well, and if Kelli missed a word reciting the book, I'm sure Ariel would be able to fill in. These two women have been instrumental in making this project the best it could be. Thank you.

And finally, as always, I thank my husband and children for putting up with having a creative person for a mom and a wife. There are days when it's fun having an author in the house, but there are other days when we order take-out or I can't do a family movie night or I'm only half listening because I'm trying to work out a plot point. I love you all so much for your patience and acceptance and support.

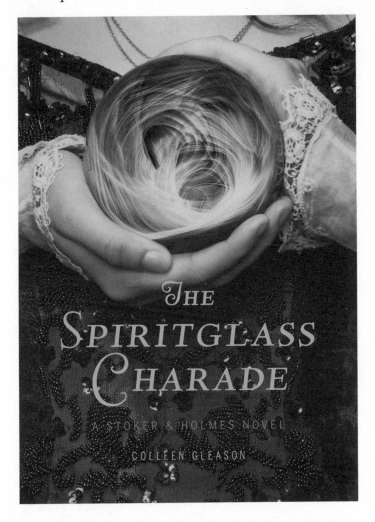

ℳiss ℋolmes

Miss Adler Is Tardy

I reside in the very modernized London of the fifty-second year of Her Majesty Queen Victoria's reign. Our Prime Minister is Lord Salisbury, and Parliament is led by the esteemed Lord Cosgrove-Pitt.

My nation is besotted with science, evolution, and invention. If a device can be conceived, someone somewhere is determined that it should be built (which is the only explanation I have for the unfortunate Hystand's Mechanized Eyelash-Combe).

This proliferation of invention and scientific practice is why I found it both amazing and disappointing that no one had yet invented a working time machine. And the reason I felt this disappointment looked up at me with deep blue eyes.

"Good morning, Dylan," I said as I closed Miss Irene Adler's office door behind me.

Though I'd expected to find the attractive dark-haired woman sitting at a large desk in her Darjeeling-scented chamber,

I confess I wasn't at all disappointed to find the young man instead. In fact, to my chagrin, my cheeks heated and my insides gave a little flutter the instant I saw him.

Such a base reaction can be excused by the fact that, aside from being charming and kind, Dylan Eckhert was one of the most handsome young men I'd ever seen. Not much older than I, Dylan had thick hair in every shade of blond. It was unstylishly long, falling into his eyes and covering his ears, and winging up a little at the tips. He had a strong square chin and jaw, perfectly straight, white teeth, and a clear blue gaze that turned pleasantly warm when he was happy or amused. Unfortunately, more often than not, that cerulean gaze was tinged with sadness or despair—a condition which I meant to help eradicate.

If I could help him find a way back home.

"Hi, Mina." He was holding a curious device. It was a slender, sleek object, slightly larger than my palm. Silvery and mirrorlike, the rectangular item was capable of making loud, erratic noises, lighting up at unexpected moments, and showing amazingly tiny moving pictures.

According to Dylan, it was a telephone. And apparently, this sort of mechanism was very common where he came from . . . more than one hundred and twenty years in the future.

Hence the requirement of a time-traveling machine.

"I expected Miss Adler to be here," I said, sitting in one of the chairs on the other side of the desk. "Her message said ten o'clock sharp." My impatience could be excused, for I had been waiting for nearly a month to be summoned to this chamber again.

My mentor's office was deep inside the British Museum, for Irene Adler was, among other things, the current Keeper of Antiquities at the institution. Or, at least, that was what she told curious-minded people. But there was more to her current occupation than simply unpacking and cataloguing long-forgotten treasures from Egypt and the Far East.

One couldn't tell it from her work area, however. The chamber wasn't particularly large, but it was well-organized and elegantly furnished, with a circular table in the center and the large desk at one end. Bookshelves lined the walls and a Tome-Selector had halted in the process of using its slender mechanical fingers to replace—or remove; one couldn't necessarily tell—a copy of *The Domesday Book*. A stack of newspapers sat at the corner of the desk, and one of them was mounted in a Proffitt's Dandy Paper-Peruser.

Behind Dylan was a credenza, on which I observed a new addition to the chamber: a charming copper teapot. It appeared to be a self-heating one, for it sat on a small cogwork dais from which I heard the emission of soft clicks and whirs.

Mingled with the scent of Miss Adler's favorite tea (the aforementioned Darjeeling), as well as a hint of her preferred perfume (gardenia), was also the faint odor of antiquity and even a little mustiness, though my mentor was meticulous about keeping her office dusted and swept. At the moment, the set of tall, narrow windows that looked out onto a small patch of grass on the north side of the Museum were unshuttered. The openings revealed the usual dull, grayish London weather at midmorning, and in the distance, I could see the shiny black spire of the Oligary Building.

Before Dylan could respond to my query, the door flew open. The pile of newspapers fluttered, the teapot's top rattled, and I actually felt a breeze announcing the late arrival.

"Good morning, Mina. Hello, Dylan," said Miss Evaline Stoker. The energetic young woman was my reluctant partner and occasional companion. Presumably, she'd been summoned as well. I wouldn't go so far as to call her an intimate friend, but I suppose since I'd saved her from being electrofied and she'd dragged me out of a fire, we'd progressed beyond mere acquaintances. "Miss Adler isn't here? Where is she?"

"Dylan was about to tell me before you—er—bounded into the chamber," I told her, watching as she settled gracefully, but no less quietly or slowly, into a chair across from me.

Miss Stoker was an attractive woman of seventeen with thick, curling black hair, lively hazel eyes, and perfect features. Unlike myself, she was petite and elegant—and also unlike myself, she was social, capricious, and a member of the peerage.

And while I, a member of the famous Holmes family (the niece of Sherlock and the daughter of Mycroft), was blessed with brilliant deductive and observational skills (not to mention the prominent Holmesian nose), Miss Stoker had been endowed by a very different family legacy. According to legend, she was supposedly a vampire hunter.

Or at least she would be if there were actually any vampires to hunt.

"I don't know where she is," Dylan replied, picking up his silvery telephone-device again. "Evaline, didn't you say you knew somewhere I could get electricity?"

"*Dylan.*" I glanced at the door, which was still tightly closed.

"Yeah, I know. Electricity is illegal here. But Evaline said she knew someone who might be able to help me charge my phone."

"Right. Yes. I . . . believe I do." Miss Stoker held out her gloved hand matter-of-factly, but of course I noticed the heightened color in her cheeks. "I'll take it to—uh—I'll get it charged for you."

He hesitated handing it over, and I was certain I knew why.

Even though Dylan had accidentally traveled here from London in 2016, somehow that singular device occasionally—*very* occasionally—was able to connect him back to that time if he stood in a particular area of the Museum. I suspected he was afraid of allowing out of his possession the one thing that might help him return—or at least communicate with—home.

Dylan had uncertainty written all over his face. "I don't know if I told you this, but there have been a few times when

I've been in the room where I first appeared that my cell phone seemed to connect to the Intern—I mean, to my time."

"I believe it happened once while I was present." I found the small mechanism fascinating and yet eerie.

"Last night, I was down there in that basement room and it connected for a *long time*. Almost three minutes. I texted—I mean, I sent a message to my parents to let them know I was okay. They're back home in Illinois, and as far as they know, I'm still at school here in London."

He drew in a deep breath, as if to collect his thoughts. "I also had the chance to do some quick research on time travel, to see if there was anything science had discovered from my time that might help. There's this thing called string theory, which says that space and place are always constant, always the same. But time is different—like strings hanging in one space. So we're each on a string that hangs or floats or whatever, in our time. It seems like I might have gotten bumped over to your string, which brought me from my time to this time, but kept me in the exact same place."

I nodded, understanding the elements of what he was saying (unlike Miss Stoker, whose blank expression indicated how little she comprehended). "And the question is . . . how did you move from your string to ours?"

"Exactly. If we figure that out, maybe that's a way to send me back. Scientists in my time say time travel is impossible. But . . . well, here I am. Proof that it isn't. Unless it's all just a bad dream." His expression sobered and the light faded from his eyes. "It has to be some sort of mathematical calculation, I think. That causes a vibration or something that makes the time-string move. . . . I don't know. I don't understand much of it. And I know you're working on it, Mina," he said earnestly. But that sadness lingered in his eyes.

I bit my lip. "But perhaps not as hard as I should be. Instead of studying face powders and—"

"Don't feel bad." He reached over to pat my arm. "If the greatest scientists of my time can't figure it out, I don't know how *you* could expect to in only a few weeks. But that's why this is really important to me, and why I need this thing charged." He turned to Miss Stoker.

"I'll take good care of it. But I can't let you come with me. It's too dangerous—not only because it's in Whitechapel, but also because I have to protect my . . . um. . . ." Her cheeks turned a shade pinker.

"Your source?" Dylan supplied.

"Right. My *source*. I like that word." Evaline smiled and held out her hand once more. "I'll protect it with my life. I promise."

I had misgivings about Miss Stoker's ability to keep the device safe, for she's an impetuous young woman who doesn't often think before she acts. Not only that, but she had more than once given me the impression she would rather seek out danger than find a more thoughtful, logical, *safer* way to solve a problem. But I didn't see how our friend had any choice other than to entrust her with it. After all, the device would no longer be useful to Dylan if he didn't get more electricity for it. And since the use or generation of that dangerous commodity had been criminalized by the Moseley-Haft Steam Promotion Act, such a source of energy was illicit and highly illegal.

Just as Dylan allowed the object to slide slowly into Miss Stoker's palm, the door opened once more. This time, it was the expected, elegantly garbed woman who entered.

Irene Adler is an attractive American woman of stage talent (mostly song). She is more famously known, at least to myself and my family, as the only woman to ever outsmart Uncle Sherlock. Thus, he calls her *the* woman.

To commemorate the occasion, he keeps a picture of her on his mantel—along with several other mementos of previous adventures. The photograph was the only compensation he accepted for the case, which had involved a scandal with the King of Bohemia.

Miss Adler subsequently married Godfrey Norton, at least according to what was published in the papers. However, during the time I knew her, she was always Miss Adler rather than Mrs. Norton, and she never referred to her husband. I suspected there might have been a divorce . . . or perhaps he never even existed. Regardless, for unknown reasons, the vivacious Miss Adler left the European stage (where she had quite a following) to take on the role of the Keeper of Antiquities for the Museum.

"My apologies for being late," Miss Adler said as she swept briskly around to the seat behind the desk. Dylan had vacated the chair as soon as she appeared, and now he stood, leaning against the wall. "One of the cog-carts blew a gasket and stopped traffic in the Strand. And now we are behind schedule."

"Do you have a new assignment for us?" Evaline asked before the poor woman had even settled into her seat. I glowered at my counterpart, but she didn't seem to notice.

"Perhaps," Miss Adler replied, seeming not at all non-plussed by my companion's impatience. She turned her arm to check the wide-banded wrist-clock she always wore. "But we must leave immediately. It's later than I thought." She hadn't taken a seat at the desk, but instead reached behind it to pull out a small reticule and an umbrella, then marched back around toward the door.

"Where are we going?"

"You might join us as well, Dylan." Miss Adler slung the umbrella's curled handle over her pristinely gloved wrist and eyed him critically. "You're dressed well enough to be presented to Her Royal Highness, now that you've put on the new clothing I bought you."

"Her Royal Highness?" A prickle of interest and excitement swept over me. "Are we going to Marlborough House?"

During our first meeting, Miss Adler confessed to Evaline and me that, although she was employed by the

Museum as prescribed, she was also using her contacts and expertise in Europe to work for Alexandra, the Princess of Wales and daughter-in-law of the Queen, on a variety of tasks related to royal and national security.

That was how Evaline and I came to be called into service for our country as well. Miss Stoker and I had been approached because of our family legacies, and because we were young women. In short, no one would ever suspect *us* of working as secret agents for the Crown. Young women, claimed Society's conventional wisdom, lacked the intelligence or the skills for anything other than marrying and raising children.

That school of thought was a delicious joke, in my opinion. After all, weren't England's two greatest monarchs— Queen Elizabeth and now Queen Victoria—women?

A faint smile curved Miss Adler's lips, but I observed weariness and shadow in her normally bright eyes. "Indeed. The Princess of Wales wishes to meet you and Miss Stoker, and I suspect she may have something else about which she wishes to speak to you. And as we have an eleven o'clock appointment, we are in danger of being late, so we must be off. One cannot keep a princess of the realm waiting."

"No, of course not." I rose, aware of a sense of relief and anticipation that Princess Alexandra wanted to see us.

My first (and only) assignment with Miss Stoker had been thrilling and dangerous—and it had been completed more than a month ago. When neither Evaline nor I were contacted by Miss Adler in the weeks that followed, I couldn't help but wonder whether the near-disaster that occurred during the

Affair of the Clockwork Scarab (as I'd begun to call it) had soured our royal sponsor on the concept of pressing extraordinary young women like us into service. I'd tried to ignore the crushing disappointment—the fear that I'd bungled my first assignment and would be relegated to working alone in my laboratory and poring over books day after day in my father's silent study.

Miss Stoker elbowed me as we followed Miss Adler out of the office. "All that worrying for nothing," she muttered. "We're going to meet the princess so she can thank us herself."

When we left the Museum, we were obliged to employ umbrellas—a not uncommon occurrence in our dreary London. However, today the dampness in the air was hardly more than a drizzle, and I could almost feel my thick chestnut-brown hair begin to tighten and kink beneath my hat like the bric-a-brac that trimmed my gloves. I patted the tight coil at the nape of my neck, hoping it wouldn't appear too disastrous by the time we arrived at Marlborough House.

I sat next to Dylan, in the carriage, and he seemed to take up quite a bit more room on the seat than I expected, for he was very close to me, and our arms brushed companionably. If it weren't for the layers of petticoat beneath my narrow skirt, surely I would have been able to feel heat from the side of his leg pressing against mine. I confess, I didn't mind his proximity in the least—although when I noticed Miss Stoker watching me with knowing eyes, that dratted flush warmed my cheeks again.

"London can be so dark and gloomy, even in the middle of the day," Dylan observed. Despite the drizzle, he'd unlatched the carriage window and nearly had his head poking out the opening as he watched the sights. "It's like dusk all the time, with the buildings so tall and close together and it being rainy and foggy almost every day. What's that tall black one over there, with the spikes on top?"

I knew which structure had prompted his comment. "The Oligary Building. Mr. Oligary's factories are the premier manufacturers of steam-cogs and gears. He manages his business from the offices in that building. Incidentally, Miss Adler—did you hear the news about Mr. Babbage's Analytic Engine? There's to be a small exhibition in the lobby of the Oligary, displaying all of Mr. Babbage's notes and prototypes."

"I would find that quite fascinating," replied my mentor. "When is it to open?"

"The article in the *Times* said it opened today. Perhaps we can make a detour and stop there on our return."

Miss Adler nodded, but once again I noted her tight, drawn expression. She appeared pale beneath her expertly applied rouge and was more subdued than usual. I wondered if she was ill or merely tired.

"That's a creepy-looking building, if you ask me," Dylan commented. "It looks like something out of Mordor. Tall, black, and shiny."

I was used to Dylan's references to unfamiliar places and people, as well as his odd vernacular. "I find the structure rather interesting in appearance. It's very different from the rest of London, with our flat-faced, rectangular brick buildings lined up in a row like uneven teeth, gears and chimneys protruding from their roofs."

Dylan turned from the window and grinned at me—an event that, I'm ashamed to admit, made my insides go soft. "And you didn't even ask me what Mordor was," he said in a low, teasing voice. "Surely you haven't lost your sense of curiosity, Miss Holmes?"

My insides squished more. I hastily turned my attention back to the cityscape, studiously avoiding Miss Stoker's gaze.

"Of course not," I managed to say calmly. "For if I asked what you meant every time you made a reference I didn't understand, we'd never finish a conversation. And look— there's one of the new vendor-balloons. They make it easier for the merchants to travel without clogging up the streetwalks."

Thus distracted, Dylan gazed out the window at the neat elliptical balloon with its small cart beneath. His thick blond hair ruffled in the breeze as drizzle splattered the windowsill, and I couldn't help but admire his handsome features.

Unlike with Evaline Stoker, young men never teased me. They rarely even spoke to me, and certainly not with such familiarity and ease. Nor did I feel comfortable enough around them to do more than converse in a stilted fashion— or, worse, launch into some babbling lecture.

Despite the fact I rather enjoyed feeling Dylan's solid arm jolting against me as we traveled through the clogged streets, I was impatient to arrive at Marlborough House and be apprised of the princess's intentions.

We finally alighted from the carriage. Once ushered into the palatial home, we were directed to the princess's private parlor. This entailed taking three steps from the threshold of the grand foyer, then stepping onto a slow-moving circular platform. When we came around to the proper direction, we stepped off the dais and onto one of three moving walkways that led to different wings of the palace. A page stood at the junction of each walkway and the circular platform, offering the assistance of a gloved hand to make the transition easier for each visitor.

The boy who handed our group off onto the walkway was wearing yellow livery, down to his gloves and shoes. Through simple observation, I noticed the young man had a fondness for caramels, had recently had his hair cut, and was left-handed.

"Notice," I murmured to Dylan as the walkway rumbled along beneath our feet, "the pages here are dressed in yellow because they attend Prince Bertie and Princess Alexandra. The personal servants of the Queen always wear red, white, and blue."

"Queen Victoria." Dylan's tones weren't quite as circumspect as mine had been, but such wonder blazed in his eyes I didn't have the heart to admonish him for it. "The *real* Queen Victoria. Do you think there's any chance we might actually see her?"

"Not here. She is currently in residence at Buckingham Palace, and I can think of few reasons for her to come here. She is a grand lady, and very imposing, as one would expect. But she hardly ever leaves the palace anymore."

"And . . . uh . . . who exactly is Princess Alexandra?" Dylan asked, this time in a more subdued voice.

"She is the Princess of Wales and her father is the King of Denmark. She's married to the Queen's son, Prince Albert Edward, informally known as Prince Bertie. Everyone loves Bertie and Alix, as she's often called. They're much more popular than the Queen—the princess especially."

The end of the moving walkway approached, and I took Dylan's arm (for he hardly ever remembered to offer it, claiming that simple courtesy was hardly ever done in 2016) as we stepped off. A yellow-gloved page was there to assist on this end of the journey as well.

A tall set of double doors confronted us. The page pulled an ornate copper lever and the entrance parted like a theater curtain, revealing a surprisingly small and cozy parlor. Because of the dampness and the princess's propensity for taking chill, a small fire burned at the hearth.

Surprisingly—or perhaps not, due to the nature of our visit—there was only one occupant in the chamber. Her Royal Highness was sitting on a dark red settee with thick velvet cushions. Its brass frame was fashioned like a tree trunk, with elegant branches arching into sidearms on either end. A mechanical bird perched on one gleaming branch, singing softly.

Princess Alexandra was forty-five years of age—making her at least a decade older than Miss Adler—and still a slender, extremely handsome woman. She had dark hair swept into a complicated mass of braids and coils, leaving a fringe of tight dark curls just above her brows. Her almond-shaped eyes were dark and lively, framed by thick lashes. She wore a bodice with a high, lacy neck meant, I knew, to hide a small scar from her childhood. Leaning against the settee within easy reach was a gold-knobbed walking stick encrusted with emeralds and topazes. I observed the princess had recently had her fingernails buffed and used a hair dye to keep her tresses ink-black.

"Irene." She gestured for us to approach. Her voice was warm and melodious, and she seemed much less stilted than her mother-in-law, to whom I'd been presented several times due to my father's work. "Come in and introduce me to these most amazing young ladies. And this handsome young man."

"I apologize for being tardy," said Miss Adler with a curtsy. She spoke a trifle louder and slower than usual due to the princess's partial deafness. "But you know how London traffic is."

"Not at all," our hostess replied with a tinkling laugh. "You know how terribly unpunctual I am! Now, please. I feel certain I've met this young lady when she was presented at Court. Evaline Stoker. You're a Grantworth as well, if I recall. And you must be the Holmes girl. Mina, is it? Your father has been instrumental in assisting the Home Office with a variety of situations. And your uncle! Miraculous in his solving of crimes, if I do say so. Make yourselves comfortable, ladies. This is an informal meeting. But who are you, young man?"

Evaline and I had taken our turns curtsying during Princess Alexandra's breathless speech, but now that the princess's attention had fallen on Dylan, Miss Adler gestured for us to sit as she introduced him. "He is helping me with a variety of tasks at the Museum, but Mr. Eckhert was also instrumental in assisting Miss Holmes and Miss Stoker in their last assignment."

"Well, then I must include Mr. Eckhert along with you two young ladies in my gratitude for investigating the business with the clockwork scarabs and discovering who was killing those poor girls. Thank you, most sincerely, from the bottom of my heart for stopping the Ankh before she hurt anyone else."

While I flushed with pleasure under her open regard and appreciation, it also made me slightly nauseated. For while Princess Alexandra was correct that Evaline and I had foiled the androgynous character known as the Ankh, I alone remained unconvinced that the female body that had been recovered and identified as the murderer's was in fact the villainous person we'd been chasing. Everyone else—including Scotland Yard—believed the case was closed.

I, on the other hand, had nearly accused Lady Isabella Cosgrove-Pitt, wife of the Parliamentary leader, of being the Ankh.

That had not been my finest hour. Particularly since it had been witnessed by one Inspector Ambrose Grayling of Scotland Yard.

"Thank you for giving us the opportunity to serve you and our country." Miss Stoker inclined her head in graceful acceptance of the princess's gratitude. "I speak for both Mina and myself when I say we are looking forward to our next assignment."

"Indeed." I was irritated for not having responded before Evaline did so.

"Excellent. Then I shall tell you why I have called you to attend me. But whilst I do so, if you don't mind, Irene, would you make certain your companions sample the truffles? As you know, they are not to be missed." The princess smiled, and a charming dimple appeared at the corner of her mouth.

"Most assuredly," Miss Adler replied, picking up the tray on the small table next to her. "Her Highness does not exaggerate. The chocolate truffles made by her Danish pastry chef are so delicious, even the Queen makes excuses to visit in order to have one."

Dylan and I exchanged covert glances and he waggled his eyebrows. I merely smiled and shook my head. It was simply inconceivable he'd meet the Queen any time soon.

Miss Stoker was already examining the tray of chocolates. They were each the size of a large cherry, and in a variety of unusual colors: pastel pink, robin's egg, daffodil, mint, and iced orange. Each was enclosed in a loose, springy swirl of spun sugar that glittered in the light, giving the truffle the appearance of being in motion. I could not conceive how the chef had placed the spheric chocolates inside each delicate coil without fracturing them.

"Now," said our royal hostess. "On to the matter I wish you to investigate. There is a young woman by the name of Willa Ashton. Her mother, Marta, and I were very close friends until Marta died, for she was one of the few ladies who came from Denmark with me. She married Ferdinand Ashton, the son of Baron Fruntmire. When I was ill with the rheumatic fever—goodness, twenty years ago that was—Marta sat with me nearly every day, and I came to love her dearly. Willa is just as charming and empathetic as her mother was, and I have summoned you today because I am greatly concerned for her mental and physical well-being."

When the princess paused to take a sip from the tea in her delicate china cup, I took the opportunity to slip one of the bite-sized truffles into my mouth. The sugary coil melted on my tongue, and the tinted exterior turned out to be a thin shell with an essence of citrus (I had selected one of the yellow ones). But inside. . . . It was nearly impossible for me to hold back a sigh of delight, for the interior of the sweet was like nothing I'd ever tasted. Light and fluffy, chocolaty without being too rich, buttery and decadent with a hint of crunch.

"Do you not agree they are the best chocolates you've ever tasted?" asked the princess, obviously noticing my reaction.

As my mouth was still filled with the ambrosia, I could only nod vehemently.

"Marta died five years ago," continued our hostess. "Before that, she and Willa often accompanied me on my visits to London Hospital. Willa has continued to do so, and she's grown into such a sweet, lovely young woman. She spends much of her time in the children's ward, telling them stories. The boys in particular ask for her every day, or so the nurses tell me.

"But then her younger brother, Robby, disappeared, a little less than two months ago. It's believed he fell into a canal and drowned, but his body was never recovered. Willa isn't convinced he's dead, and has become obsessed with finding him. She's become enamored with Spiritualism, and believes it can help her solve the puzzle."

"Spiritualism? Do you mean to say Miss Ashton attends séances—or that she is acting as a medium herself?" I asked, firmly redirecting my attention from the tray of truffles, which, thanks to Dylan and Evaline, had been pared down to a meager trio of chocolates.

"She is attending them—quite regularly, in fact. And, I suspect, is paying quite a bit of money to the mediums she uses. Willa insists her mother is speaking to her from beyond—and although that may very well be true," the princess added hastily, surely thinking of her own mother-in-law's attraction to spirit-talking with the Queen's dead husband, Albert, "I fear there is some other unpleasant purpose at work here. For I am concerned . . . well, I suspect either someone is attempting to fleece her fortune out from under her, or—worse—that someone is attempting to drive her mad."

ABOUT THE TYPE

This text is set in a variation of John Baskerville, a typeface created by the accomplished engraver and printer, who endlessly labored to refine the quality of his printing press by developing a faster drying ink and smoother paper. Yet, Baskerville's greatest innovation is the typeface that carries his name. It was one of the earliest fonts to transition away from the old Roman style popular during the eighteenth century. Baskerville is open and clear, with sharp serifs, contrasting thick and thin strokes, and round characters that sit upright, rather than tilting one way or the other. This typeface is widely popular even today.